REBEL
EXCHANGE

A WESTERN CIVIL WAR NOVEL

J. ROBERT JOHNSON

J Robert Johnson

Cover Design and Graphics: Jen K. Johnson

My deepest appreciation
To my wife, Lynda,
who has given me encouragement and support
on this first adventure of publishing.

You have given me words when I needed them.
You have corrected my spelling and grammar.
You have read and edited multiple drafts.
To you I am forever grateful.

J Robert Johnson

REBEL EXCHANGE
Background

The American Civil War; The Western Campaign; The Battle of Glorietta; The San Elizario Spy Company (also known as the Santa Fe Gamblers or The Forty Thieves); Intrigue; Romance; Danger – All woven into the colors of the tapestry of the American Civil War in the West…and into **Rebel Exchange.**

Most people don't realize there were any battles fought west of the Mississippi. Yet, some scholars have compared the Battle of Glorietta to the Battle of Gettysburg – not because of the number of lives lost, but because it was a turning point in the Western Campaign.

The Confederacy had its eyes on the gold fields of Colorado and California, as well the Pacific ports. With the victory/defeat at Glorietta Pass, those hopes and dreams were dashed. As Sean would say, "It would seem that God gives us His protection, even though he withholds our victory."

There would be no more battles in the West.

J Robert Johnson

Chapter One

The howl of a coyote carried on the thin mountain air. The haunting call sent a shiver down Sean's spine. His mare lifted her head. Her left ear flicked back as if to make sure Sean had noticed the mournful sound. Sean stroked her neck to reassure her, but more to quiet his own nerves.

Autumn aspen leaves rustled like taffeta on the breeze drifting down from the Colorado Mountains. The afternoon sun warmed the air laced with the cold of the coming snows. A hawk screamed in its dive for unseen prey. Then all was silent save for the swishing from the hooves of two horses through the dry grass.

This was wild, unknown country to Sean. His only knowledge came from the stories told by Uncle Zeke as he had regaled his family on frequent visits; tales of hunting buffalo on the plains and trapping beaver in the rushing mountain streams. Sean was now in those same mountains following a path which led against the flow of the Arkansas River.

He shifted his gaze to take in the grandeur and immensity of the surrounding mountains. The rugged beauty only added to the apprehension of the unknown that lay ahead. He wondered if it was his fear of Indians or the thought of meeting enemy soldiers that worried him more.

"It's a grand sight, is it not?"

Sean was startled by his companion's remark. Patrick had spoken little since they had broken camp before sunrise. "Grand as well as intimidating," Sean replied.

1

"Not unlike our assignment, yes?"

His question needed no answer.

Their conversation was cut short. The trail narrowed, forcing them to ride single file. Boulders dwarfed the path on the left. The steep bank on the right dropped sharply to the water's edge.

Sean envied the ease with which his friend rode, at one with the horse-flesh beneath him. *That must come from riding a horse before you can walk.*

Yet Patrick McFerrin was more than a friend. He was far more a brother than any of the five half-brothers Sean had left behind in Missouri. Sean considered Patrick a comrade. "All for one and one for all," right out of Dumas' *Three Musketeers.* Sean smiled to himself. He had read and reread that book until the cover fell off.

The sun's rays shimmered on the running water. His thoughts drifted back to the days when he had fished and played along the banks of the Spring River behind Great Oaks. Some of those memories were good, but – Sean shifted his aching bottom in his saddle – most were filled with his mother trying to please her husband while taking care of his children.

Sean had forever been forced to fight for any scrap of kindness or attention from his father and survival from the wrath of his older half-brothers. There were times he wondered if he was any better off than the slaves that worked in his father's fields.

There had been no place for Sean on the plantation after his father died. Will, being the eldest son, had gotten the land and all that went with it. Begrudgingly, Sean realized his best recourse was to pursue a military career.

When Sean arrived at West Point, he shunned everyone. He fought with cadets and personnel alike – even his roommate, Patrick. His only friends were anger, distrust, and loneliness. After numerous probations, he was on the verge of expulsion.

Patrick's wit and humor and reason had finally broken through the stone-like bulwark Sean had thrown up around his feelings. For the first time in his life, Sean knew true friendship and brotherhood. Patrick and the corps became his family. More than once he and Patrick had defended the other's back, whether in a bar-room brawl or heated debate.

Sean had learned much at West Point – much about life as well as how to be a good soldier. Corporal Harris had summed it up well at the end of the last term. "Mr. McKay, now that you have learned to control your anger, you have the makings of a fine soldier. Now, focus that anger on your enemy."

But as the storm clouds of civil war billowed, who was the enemy? Cadets began to take sides, one against the other. Friend became foe. Sean was conflicted. He cared little for the South and all it stood for, yet it was from whence his roots came. The North might as well be a foreign nation. When Harry Starker, a fellow cadet and recruiter for Col. Madison, pulled him and Patrick aside and explained his proposal, it seemed the perfect solution. Yet it was the sojourn in Missouri that solidified his decision.

Sean was pulled from his reverie as Patrick paused at the convergence of a smaller stream that spilled into the larger Arkansas. Sean reined his big roan in beside him.

Patrick pointed in the direction they had been going. "If we continued, we would eventually reach the headwaters of the Arkansas." He then nodded to his left. "We will follow Clear Creek that passes through the heart of our ranch. From here on, we will be on *MC* grazing land."

Sean could hear the pride in his friend's voice. "We will soon arrive at your ranch?"

Patrick's tone changed. "Not my ranch. Rather my father's. But yes, we should reach the ranch house before the sun sets."

Sean could sense the tension in Patrick's reply. "Will there be trouble, do you think? Will your father be suspicious of our arrival?"

"No. They should be expecting us, and I gave no indication in my letter which side of this conflict we might be following, if any. Being the astute businessman that he is, I am sure Father will remain neutral. Yet down deep he would lean to the side of his father and his father before him, even though he detests the business of slavery."

"But you have apprehensions?"

Patrick sighed before he answered. "We did not part on the best of terms."

He seemed to search for the right words. "With all its beauty, this can be a harsh land. I was – am – a dreamer, an adventurer. I will be the first to admit it. You know me well enough to know I like a good ale, a good brawl, a good story and good friends to share them with. Out here, every day is as the day before, every year the same. Whether foolish or wise, I wanted more."

He pointed to a small herd of stray cows in the distance. "Father has worked all of his days to build a life here. He couldn't understand why I would not want to continue his legacy."

"And what of your sister?" Sean asked.

A smile spread across Patrick's face. "Ah, Abigail. I anticipate your meeting her. She is not like most women. One minute she will be breaking one of her wild mustangs. The next she will be breaking your heart. Father tried as best he could to raise her like a lady, but finally gave in and allowed her to be like one of us men. It will be quite interesting to see what a year back east on the family plantation in South Carolina has done to tame her."

They rode for a time in silence, each lost in his individual thoughts. Much had been discussed during their meeting with Col. Madison in Pueblo, but many decisions were yet to be made. Sean broached the subject, "What is your opinion of Madison's proposal?"

Patrick settled back in his saddle. He looked over at Sean and shrugged. "I like a good adventure. Becoming a spy seems to rank with the best of them."

"But Patrick, you're not from the South," Sean protested. "You've lived your whole life out here in this great, wild, free, wide-open place. Why risk your life for the Southern cause?

Look around you. You could stay right here on your father's ranch until all this blows over – or head into the hills and lose yourself – or pan for gold and become wealthy."

Patrick indicated the mountains with a sweep of his hand. "Many a man has lost himself in those mountains, some by accident, some by design. For me, I have no desire for such isolation."

His tone became bitter. "As for the cause, you know I have no use for slavery. I think it is despicable for one man to lord it over another, whether laborers or slaves. Yet you've seen the deplorable conditions in the factories and ghettos of the North. You've witnessed the way the elite treat their servants, most of whom are Irish immigrants just as were your grandparents and mine. They are treated worse than the slaves on my uncle's plantation and live in worse conditions."

He gestured with his finger as if giving a lecture. "I agree with Professor Gilding in second year Economics class. Given time, the economy and public opinion would have ended the slavery issue. It happened in England and is happening all over the world. Yet the Northern bureaucrats and politicians and industrial magnates want to force the issue for their own gains. The Federal government was never meant to control the states. Quite the opposite was the original intent."

He shook his head and shrugged his shoulders as he looked over at Sean. "Do I want to die for the Southern cause? No. But I saw what those Kansas Jayhawkers did to your family and your home. I will gladly take up arms for my friend. Besides, we're talking about an adventure here. I can't let you have all the fun."

Their laughter was cut short. Patrick raised his hand in warning.

"What is it?" Sean whispered.

"I'm not sure. I simply sense something is out of place."

"Indians?"

"Possibly. Just keep riding. But have your rifle ready."

Chapter 2

Abigail paced between the towering trees. The heat of the day was past. The sun had started its plunge toward the Collegiate Mountain peaks. Still, she could not contain her anxieties which resulted in quite un-ladylike perspiration.

The rumors of Comanche unrest had been confirmed by a courier from Fort Bent. The conflict that had seemed so far away back east had escalated, reaching even here in the Colorado territory. Just the past week, a merchant friend in Fairplay sent word to her father that cows with the *MC* brand had been slaughtered to feed Union troops. Abigail took her revolver from its holster. She spun the chamber to check the bullets, as much from disgust as necessity. *MC* cattle, even strays down near the Arkansas, were for sale, not for the taking.

But it was for Patrick she was mostly concerned. Her brother was two days late. Visions of him lying beside the trail after his horse had thrown him – or worse, a hostile Indian arrow or enemy soldier's musket ball tearing through his body – had her completely distraught.

His letter had been cryptic and short.

> *Dearest Sister,*
> *Coming home from the Point.*

See no way to avoid engagement in this dispute.
Plan to get my assignment when I get to Colorado.
Will be home before the fall festival.
Hope Pa has forgiven me.
Your loving brother,
Patrick.

She had sent back a reply that the festival was to take place, in spite of the escalating conflict. In addition, Mr. Larimer and Governor Gilpin would be present at the festival, and would be attending a dinner party this evening. She had also assured him that Father was as anxious to see him as was she. His only reply was his expected arrival date.

She flicked a piece of bark from a tree with no purpose except as a diversion from her thoughts. This grove of aspens had always been a haven for Abigail; a sanctuary in which she could contemplate her world; a snuggery in which to read *Jane Eyre* or *Pride and Prejudice* or *Harper's New Monthly Magazine* when she could smuggle a copy from her father's office; a refuge where she could contemplate whatever dilemma might be facing her. But today it gave no respite from the heat or her concerns.

Movement across the meadow caught her attention. She chuckled at the sight of the two Indians on the opposite bluff who apparently had a fox or rabbit or chipmunk cornered. She spoke to the blue roan beside her. "They can act more like children than children." She scratched behind the horse's ear and offered her a bite of apple. Abigail added with pride and admiration, "But they would give their lives to protect me, that I know." The horse nodded as if in affirmation.

Running Deer and Little Fox were very near her own age, sons of a Ute chieftain. Since she was fourteen, her father had paid them to accompany her when she wandered alone from the ranch, as she did often to his disapproval. He had raised her to be independent. Now she wondered if he regretted that decision.

Abigail knocked the dust from her woolen pants and pulled each finger free from her leather riding gloves. She shielded her eyes with her hat, her gaze following the outline of Clear Creek as it meandered through the meadow below, spilling its waters into the Arkansas and eventually joining the great Mississippi, pushing its way to New Orleans and the Gulf of Mexico. Lissette so often had painted such verbal images of that vibrant city of her childhood.

A growl from the depths of her stomach reminded Abigail she had not eaten the lunch Lisette had packed for her. She retrieved the fried chicken and hard-boiled eggs from her saddlebag. The spices of the chicken were a delight to her tongue. Lisette insisted on her Louisiana Cajun spices, especially for her fried chicken.

Lisette was much more than a Creole housekeeper. She was the only mother Abigail and Patrick had ever known. A tinge of guilt crept into Abigail's thoughts of Lissette. She had left the older woman to finish the preparations for this evening's dinner. But Abigail needed a bit of time alone, away from the bustle back at the ranch. Besides, she and Lisette both knew she was more than useless in the kitchen.

Abigail wiped her hands on Beauty's saddle blanket and took a long drink from the canteen as her mind wandered over the course of the last two years. She sighed as her fingers caressed her sun and wind tanned cheek.

Her abilities to rope and ride and shoot as well as any man on the ranch had been a source of pride. She had given little thought or concern about the fact that she was a *girl*. However, even the trips with Father to Fort Bent and as of late to Denver City had not prepared her for the jolt to her cultural senses as a "lady" in her recent visit to South Carolina. The family plantation was a world away from Colorado.

Her reverie was interrupted by the glimpse of two riders in blue uniforms emerging from the shadows of the trees. It seemed strange that only two union soldiers would be scouting for stray *MC* cows to confiscate for the cause. Something did not feel right, but Abigail could not quite reason what it was.

She had hoped to see Patrick. But these men were in blue. Besides, Patrick had not mentioned anyone else traveling with him.

The riders faded out of sight beyond a pile of boulders. At the same time, two figures materialized from the aspens on the opposite ridge.

Abigail whispered to the mare. She quietly mounted, pulling her rifle from its holster. It was time to see who had invaded her land.

Chapter 3

The click of the rifle hammer brought the two blue-clad riders to an abrupt halt. Abigail managed a low husky tone with a twinge of a southern drawl to break the ominous silence. "Riding alone up here in Colorado Indian country might not be the smartest of decisions."

The two men slowly raised their hands away from their side-arms. The look of concern in the eyes of the larger man changed to one of astonishment as a broad grin spread across his partner's face. "Patrick, what the…?"

Patrick winked at his friend and turned to face their opponent. "Sean, allow me to introduce Miss Abigail McFerrin, my baby sister. And sis, the man you have in your gun sights is my good friend, Sean McKay of the Missouri McKays."

Abigail lowered the rifle as she brought the hammer back to its rest. She let out a breath of relief and smiled. "Paddy. I hoped it was you. But you are two days late. And we can't be too careful in these troubled times." She shook her head and smiled. "Oh, but it's good to see you."

In unison Abigail and Patrick jumped from their horses. She hugged his neck as he spun her around, both laughing like children.

He set her down and stepped back. "Let me have a look at

you." With a theatrical flourish, he put his hand to his chest. "Lord a-mercy. My little Abby has become a woman." Then with a tilt of his head he added with a drawl, "And a mighty fine woman."

"You watch your tongue," she retorted as she cocked her head, feigning insult. "I'll not have you speak of me like one of your military…women." She fanned herself with a gloved hand. "And a year under the tutelage of Auntie Maud and cousin Rebecca and cousin Virginia back in South Carolina taught me the finer things of being a southern lady."

He laughed, "Ah, Riverglade Plantation. A mighty pretty place, if I remember. And I'm sure you taught them a thing or two as well."

She raised her brows in coy agreement.

Slowly she circled him, inspecting him as she would a fine horse. Again facing him, she looked from head to toe and back. With a wave of her hand, she nodded. "And my compliments to your trainers, or whatever they're called. Four years at West Point has definitely made a man of a boy." Her tone softened. "Oh, Paddy, I've missed you so much."

"And I you."

The stranger's horse pawed the ground, which brought Abigail back to the moment. "How rude. We have completely ignored your guest."

He had dismounted and was stroking the mane of his steed. Abigail was not displeased with the sight before her. He looked to be about Patrick's age, but she judged him to be an inch or two over her brother's six foot. His black hair hung in waves from under his hat which was tilted at a slight angle. *Hmm, broad in the shoulders, narrow at the hips…with long, strong legs like a good stallion.*

But it was his eyes, that dark piercing gaze that held her attention. His eyes opened a bit wider with his broad smile. Was that a trick of the afternoon sun, or did those mesmerizing eyes just twinkle?

He doffed his hat and bowed. "Ma'am, it truly is a

pleasure to meet you. Patrick has talked of little else these past days."

She curtsied, self-consciously grasping the edges of her leather chaps. "I'm afraid you have the advantage." She glanced at her brother and then back to his comrade. Those intense, brooding eyes were fixated beyond and behind her.

She smiled as she turned. "Again forgive my insensitivity." She indicated the two young Indian braves who had waited patiently throughout the unfolding scene. "These are my friends and guardians, Running Deer and Little Fox."

Little Fox curled his lip as he looked with contempt at the tall visitor. "Welcome to *our* country."

Running Deer looked with disapproval at his companion. "Apology for my brother. We are not fond of soldiers, but a friend of Miss Abigail, Master Patrick, and James McFerrin are friends of Ute's."

Patrick went to each of the braves and clasped their arms in friendship. "I thank you for watching over my sister and my family." He added, "And your English is much improved."

Running Deer nodded. "Miss Abigail is good teacher. She has taught us not only the English, but also to read and write." He proudly recited, "In beginning, God created the man and the woman, and He say it is very good."

Little Fox added, "Quoth the raven, 'Nevermore'."

Patrick's laughter echoed off the canyon walls. "Ah, the Bible according to Edgar Allen Poe. Only my beloved sister would mix the two."

Abigail shrugged. "One must use the literature one has. Besides, I like Poe. Aunty Maude gave me a whole collection of his works to bring back with me. But enough of this prattle. It'll be dark soon and the two of you need to wash the travel dust off before supper. We have guests."

***

Abigail swung into the saddle and kicked her mount into a gallop as she shouted over her shoulder, "Catch up if you can.

Paddy, I trust you remember the way."

Sean leapt into the saddle in anticipation, but Patrick just shook his head. "You don't have a chance. No matter how hard you ride, you'll not see anything but the back end of that horse. Abby's the best rider in the territory, and I'm sure she's bred that pony to be the fastest."

Running Deer shook his head. "He will learn hard way."

Patrick smiled and nodded. "Yes, he will have to learn, but the lesson should be an interesting one."

"We'll see about that." Sean spurred his horse to a gallop leaning into her neck. He gave the steed full rein, but quickly realized the truth in Patrick's words.

Sean admired her ease in the saddle, to say nothing of her slender physique and red curls blowing in the wind. He had to admit, she intrigued him. He had never seen a girl with such athletic abilities. Heavens, he had never seen a girl in men's pants. The image pleased more than his eyes.

Abigail pulled her black filly to a sudden stop at the main gate. Sean wheeled his horse beside her. With a flourish, he tipped his hat in acknowledgement. "That truly is a fine horse." He hesitated and smiled. "And an even better rider. My compliments to the lady."

She patted the horse's neck. "Beauty has been bred to run, and run she does."

"A beauty astride a Beauty. How could one ask for more?"

Patrick and the two braves joined them. "Should I question who won?"

Before Sean could answer, Abigail replied. "It was hardly a fair race as I did have a bit of a head start. But Mr. McKay made a handsome showing for himself." She caught her breath as she realized her play on words.

To distract from the awkwardness of the moment, Sean pointed to the *MC* above the gate. "What is the purpose for the initials?"

Patrick straightened. "My friend, you are about to enter

the McFerrin ranch, better known as the *MC*." He went on to explain. "Each ranch in the valley brands their livestock. Ours is *MC*. It helps us keep track of our herds on the open range."

They stopped to take in the scene stretched out in the valley below them as the sun hovered over the snowcapped peaks of the Collegiate Mountains. Sean was awed by the beauty of the panorama. The setting sun reflected off the autumn aspen, which appeared as shimmering gold in contrast to the dark green of the Spruce and Pine on the upper ridges. The ranch house and out buildings nestled in a grove of pines on a rise overlooking Cedar Creek.

Patrick exclaimed with a catch in his voice. "Sis, I wouldn't know the place if I hadn't seen the *MC* above the gate back there." He indicated the buildings in the distance. "All of this was nothing but sketches on paper when I left for the Point."

As they walked their horses down the lane, Abigail described the buildings. "The barn is three times the size of the old one, with a loft for hay and stalls for a dozen horses. At the back, we've added a blacksmith shop and tack room."

She continued with enthusiasm, "But Paddy, you won't believe the house. There's a veranda on all four sides with the kitchen and smoke house attached on the back by an enclosed walkway. The parlor and dining room are across the front. Behind them are father's office and bedroom and private rooms for Lisette and Thomas. Each of the front and back dormers on the second floor are bedrooms with a hall down the middle. There's even glass in the windows. It came by freight down from Saint Louis by way of Denver about a month ago. Miguel and Jose have been working steadily to have them all installed for this weekend."

Patrick shook his head. "'Tis a bit different than the log cabin we grew up in."

Abigail laughed. "Just a bit." As an afterthought, she added, "Father has given William the old cabin for him and his new wife. Lisette has talked William into paying for a wife from New Orleans. A Creole like her. She's supposed to come out next spring, providing this silly war doesn't interfere."

Sean's curiosity was piqued. "William? Paddy, I don't remember you mentioning him. He chuckled. "And a mail-order wife? I've heard tell of such a thing, but I didn't know it really happened."

Patrick hesitated before he explained. "Lisette is Father's housekeeper. William is her son, tough as leather and strong as a bear. He's our age and we've always thought of him like a brother." Sean could not help but notice that his friend looked at Abigail as if a secret passed between them.

Patrick shrugged. "As for his wedding arrangements, I know some of the miners have done it. I think this is the first I've heard of a mulatto buying a wife. But if she's anything resembling the beauty of his mother, he shouldn't be disappointed."

They had reached the front of the house. Abigail dismounted and handed the reins to her brother. "Take Beauty on down to the barn. William should be down there to take care of the horses. Paddy, he'll be glad to see you. I'll ask Lisette to get your baths ready in the wash room off the kitchen."

Sean watched her every move. This should prove to be a very interesting visit.

***

Steam filled the small room from the two tubs. Sean wiped the soapy water from his eyes. Patrick came up for air after rinsing the soap out of his curly red hair. "I had almost forgotten how good a hot bath could…" He stopped mid-sentence as the door swung open and Abigail entered with a stack of towels and folded clothes. Both men dove below the water's soapy surface.

Patrick came up sputtering, "Abby! You should at least knock."

"Excusez-moi." She turned and knocked on the open door and continued without a pause. "Paddy, there's a clean shirt for you, and I've borrowed a shirt from William for Mr. McKay." She purposely kept her gaze diverted from the men as she continued. "Sorry, Paddy, but I fear Mr. McKay might rip your shirts, as he is a bit broader in the shoulders than you.

"Supper this evening is formal, so a tie is required." She paused before she asked, "By the way, why blue and not grey?"

Sean choked. He looked guardedly to Patrick with the hope he could give a suitable explanation. Patrick returned Sean's gaze with raised eyebrows. He took a deep breath and let it out slowly. "It, uh, poses less of a problem to travel in the Colorado territory in blue."

Abigail toyed with her left earring for a moment, then shrugged. "That would seem to make sense, I suppose." She placed the clothes on the bench by the door. "Supper is served promptly at 7:00. Don't be late." Her exit was as dramatic as her entrance had been, yet the door was left ajar.

Sean glanced at Patrick and shook his head. "I truly have never met a woman quite like your sister."

"Is that good or bad?"

"Why, it's good, I think. I just wish she didn't have such disdain for me and was less formal. It's always 'Mr. McKay' rather than Sean."

Patrick laughed. "Friend, if my little Abby didn't like you, she'd just ignore you like she would a stray cat. The fact that she came in here hoping she'd catch a glimpse of you without your shirt is a good indication she's at least curious."

Sean sputtered and felt the blood rush to his face. "I hope that's all she caught a glimpse of. Now how am I going to face her at supper?"

"Just be your usual charming self. She'll either be charming right back, or shoot you between the legs. That will be a good indication whether she likes you or not."

Patrick's comment did nothing to bolster Sean's confidence.

Chapter 4

Lisette guided Abigail into the late afternoon light streaming through the dormer window. Carefully she threaded the last of the laces and gave them a tug.

"So help me, Lisette, if you pull on those corset cords one more time, I'll scream."

"Miss Abigail, you're the one who wanted this contraption on, so you just hush."

"Oh, very well. Give it one more tug. I just hope I don't faint at supper from lack of breath."

Abigail pulled the dress on over her head, being careful not to muss her hair. She moved to the full mirror as Lisette finished the last of the buttons. Her reflection did not disappoint her.

"Mon Dieu, Miss Abigail, you are absolutely stunning. Your father will be most proud."

Abigail turned from side to side to get the full effect of the new garment. She was grateful that the new dresses had come with the shipment of window glass. She would have hated to wear one of her old dresses for tonight's supper as well as the weekend festivities.

She liked the style of the dress. The dark green velvet was a perfect complement to her auburn curls, but the low neckline made her a bit uncomfortable. She posed once more. "Lisette, is this too revealing? I don't want to look like a Cheyenne hussy."

"Missy, Mister Sean will be duly impressed."

Abigail whirled, with her hands on her hips. "I care not a whit what Mr. McKay thinks. I was thinking of my father and the governor."

Lisette laughed and shook her head. "Girl, you haven't taken your eyes off-a that boy since y'all rode in. And Miguel was quite capable of taking my William's clothes into the wash room. But if it's any consolation, Master James and the governor will be pleased as well."

She took a necklace from the velvet-lined box on the dresser. "Now let me put your mama's emerald pendant around that lovely neck. Then I best go check on supper. Alfred has two new girl's helping him in the kitchen. With the governor and Mr. Larimer both here at the same time, the last thing we need is for the venison to be undercooked. Besides, he never uses enough seasoning to suit me."

Abigail once more adjusted her neckline and practiced a curtsy in the mirror, then shook her head in dismay. The reflection before her was of a pretty young lady. But inside, she felt neither pretty nor like a lady. She could dress like a southern belle and even act the part if need be. But she was most comfortable with her horses and riding with her father's hired men.

She sat for a moment on the window seat, watching the last of the sunset fade from purple to gray behind the mountain ridge. However, in lieu of the towering pines, images of South Carolina oaks gracefully draped in moss crossed her mind.

Riverglade Plantation and Aunt Maude had been just as Father had described…both large and impressive. Her aunt seemed to flow down the front porch steps, all satin and lace over crinoline and hoops.

Aunt Maude had gathered Abigail into her fold like a mother hen would her chicks. In her thick southern drawl, she would cajole and guide, compliment and reprimand. Abigail had quickly been introduced to the "finer" things in life, as well as the rules that went with them – at least rules as Abigail remembered them.

"Ladies never let the sun shine on their face. That might mar their china-white complexion."

"Ladies days should be spent embroidering silly designs on handkerchiefs and crocheting doilies while they catch up on the latest gossip."

"Ladies should never presume to think for themselves. They, after all, are simply the adornment on the arm of a man."

"A lady's purpose in life is to marry well, keep her husband happy and satisfied, manage the household, gossip, plan parties and produce heirs."

Abigail had learned quickly how to play the game. Her wit and humor, her confidence and daring, along with her grace and poise soon made her the center of attention at parties. Her cousins loved it, the boys were intrigued and the other girls hated her.

Yet in spite of her outward appearance of confidence, Abigail felt lost in a world completely foreign to her. As much as she wanted to be back with her horses, she realized she was quickly becoming a woman. That thought and the responsibilities that went with it petrified her. She had no idea how to fit into either world. She had been only too happy when her visit was cut short by the shelling of Fort Sumter and the possibility of a civil conflict.

As Abigail gazed, the shadows dulled the view of the mountains. Laughter from the men below brought her back to reality. She stood once more before the mirror. She straightened her back and lifted her head. In spite of her insecurities, tonight she was the mistress of the house, her father's confidante, and this evening's hostess. She had been that oft times before. Tonight she could and would be that and more.

Adjusting the necklace, she considered the dynamics of the evening's guests. The political conflict between her father's friend and business partner Mr. Larimer and Governor Gilpin was more than a rumor. Along with that, their Union support was a strong contrast to her father's neutrality. In addition, she was not sure how the addition of Patrick and Sean would affect the discussions.

She smiled as she recalled the conversation between Patrick and Sean in the wash room. She felt not the least bit guilty that she had listened through the cracked door. This would be one man she would definitely not shoot or ignore.

Mr. McKay aroused her interest. She admired his ease in the saddle as well as his overall good looks, but there was something about him that troubled her. Maybe it was the way his dark brown eyes seemed to pierce through her. She certainly was intrigued. Yet her intuition reminded her to be wary. Previous experience had proven that men were not always as they seemed.

Patrick's comment, "It poses less of a problem to travel in the Colorado territory in blue" came to mind. Her curiosity begged for an explanation.

Her confidence had returned. This truly promised to be an interesting evening.

Chapter 5

Sean struck a match to ignite the kerosene lantern, bringing the shadows to life. The room smelled of sawdust and pine tar, horse flesh and cow dung, and the lingering odor of stale sweat and hard-working male bodies.

Sean surveyed the bunkhouse, empty now as the men were over at the cook shack. This building was not that much different than the barracks at West Point, and these men were not that different from the friends he had left behind. Their laughter drifted from across the courtyard. Maybe not as disciplined as West Point graduates, but just men. Cowboys. The thing of legends. Sean had read about them in dime novels. Patrick had talked about them. They were just men, putting in a day's work.

Sean tried to make a comparison between ranch life here in Colorado and his family's plantation in Missouri. He had expected mud huts or teepees, wild mountain men with long shaggy beards, and wild savages lurking behind trees. Instead, he was finding well-built buildings, rowdy but well-mannered ranch hands and friendly Indians. He shook his head in wonderment. That, plus a striking young lady with curly auburn hair; striking not only in her beauty, but in the fact that she dressed and rode like a man.

He turned up the lantern and wiped the dust from the small mirror hanging on the wall beside the door. For the fourth time he adjusted the tie at his collar, wondering why his hands were shaking and a knot had formed in the pit of his stomach.

The door swung open, allowing the cool night breeze to freshen the stuffy air. William's broad frame filled the open doorway. His gaze traveled Sean's length and breadth before he spoke. "The shirt seems to fit nicely, sir."

Sean nodded. "The loan of a clean shirt is much appreciated. The stench of the one I have worn for the last weeks of travel would hardly be appropriate for a dinner party."

A slight smirk crossed William's face. "You may keep the shirt. My shoulders outgrew it a year ago."

Sean once again adjusted the tie. *This man might be several years my junior, but I would want him fighting with me rather than against me.*

William leaned on the doorpost. "You and Patrick are wearing the uniform of a soldier. Would I surmise you have not brought him home to stay? And why the blue and not the grey?"

Sean slipped on his jacket and buttoned it before answering, not sure what the young man might know, or what he might think he knows. "We have trained to be soldiers. Duty calls."

Sean tried to choose his next words carefully. He wished that Patrick had given him a bit more information regarding the man before him and his place at the *MC.* "Patrick loves his father and this ranch and this land. Yet, he by nature longs for adventure that he does not seem to find as a rancher. Besides, he has spoken well of you and the valuable aid you give to his father."

William visibly relaxed, but continued to press the issue. "That's good to hear. Yet, what of the uniform? Mister James wishes to remain neutral in this conflict."

Sean took his time brushing the dust from the sleeve of his coat, trying to think of a good answer. He was much relieved when Patrick appeared behind William.

"Ah, William, I appreciate your taking the time to entertain my friend." He gestured to Sean, "And our presence is requested. We best not be late for supper. I assure you, one does not want to keep Lisette waiting."

William chuckled as he stepped out of the doorway. "Ce'st la ve'rite'. That is quite true."

Patrick led Sean across the compound. "How was your visit with William?"

Sean shrugged. "If being cornered by a grizzly could be considered a visit, I survived."

Patrick laughed. "William can be a bit intimidating, but he has had to be. Father has given him more and more responsibilities. He is now foreman, second only to my father. The men don't question him. If they do, they answer to his fists."

Sean considered the past few moments. "He is also quite.." Sean searched for the right word, "...literate."

"You mean, for a mulatto?" Patrick's answer was tinged in sarcasm.

"I meant no disrespect," stuttered Sean.

Patrick sighed. "William has had the same training and education as Abby and me. He speaks fluid French and can quote Shakespeare and Tennyson. Don't underestimate his abilities in word or deed."

"My apologies. I can tell you are close."

Patrick nodded. "He is like a brother to my sister and me, and Father has treated him as such."

"And your meeting with your father went well?"

Patrick pulled Sean into the shadows of the porch and lowered his voice. "I shared with him our position and our over-all purpose for being here – besides my wanting to be here for the fall festival. He was not overly pleased. He wishes to remain neutral. Everything with Father is a financial decision."

He looked around to ensure no one was listening before he continued. "Father certainly understands your position; not so much mine. However, he will do what he can to aid our endeavor. After all, our family is steeped in Southern traditions. And, quite frankly, he has no love or respect for Governor Gilpin."

"Tell me about our marks."

"Mr. Larimer is a long-time friend of Father. They fought together in the war with Mexico, and Father has invested in Larimer's endeavors at Denver City. I have not met Governor Gilpin, but from what I understand, he likes to hear himself talk."

"That could be to our advantage."

"'Tis true. Now we must join the men."

Sean followed Patrick through the main door. The three older men were gathered in front of the large, stone fireplace. A crackling fire warmed the room. The smell of wood smoke, pine and mint permeated the air.

The imposing head of a twelve-point buck protruded over the fireplace as if holding court. A bear-skin rug in front of the hearth and a leather sofa and two leather chairs gave the room a masculine, yet comfortable feel.

In contrast, oil lamps on the walls and a chandelier over the formal dining table brightened the adjoining room. A lace cloth graced the table. The glowing lights danced in the reflection off the settings of china, silver flatware and crystal goblets. Sean marveled at the refined civility in this wild country.

Patrick introduced Sean to his father, who then introduced Governor Gilpin and Mr. Larimer. However, their conversation ceased as all eyes turned to the curved staircase which led to the upper floor.

Sean leaned against the arm of one of the chairs for support. His heart skipped a beat, then his pulse quickened. Abigail, the girl who had earlier in the day dressed like a man; Abigail, the girl who had beaten him in a horse race; Abigail, the girl who had blatantly entered the washroom with the shirt that he was now wearing, began the descent with the appearance of a princess out of a child's fairytale.

Chapter 6

Abigail paused at the top step. Five heads raised. Five pair of eyes gazed up at her. Her confidence waned. Her fingers trembled on the smooth sanded banister rail. Images of her stumbling down the steps flitted thought her mind.

Aunt Maude's instructions came to mind. *A lady exudes an air of confidence, even if there is a feeling of mush in the pit of your stomach. Hold your head high. And never, never let them know you are afraid!*

Abigail locked her gaze on her brother. He winked and nodded. A smile curled at the corners of his mouth. That was the encouragement that she needed.

She took one step. How she wished she could pull up the front of her neckline, but it was too late now. Why she had worn this low-cut dress instead of one with a high collar she wasn't sure.

Another step. The stays of her corset dug into her ribs. A brief wave of dizziness swept through her consciousness, then was gone. She smiled at her brother, carefully ignoring the man to his right.

Another. Why this stranger was affecting her in this way was a puzzlement. There was something about him that intrigued her, and *that* was troubling. It was those eyes, she decided. Those piercing brown eyes.

The steps came easier. This was not her first party and not the first time she had aided her father as his hostess. Again, Aunt Maude's words flashed across her consciousness. *The responsibility of the hostess is to ensure that all her guests feel welcome and comfortable, no matter how uncomfortable the situation might be.*

Her father broke the silence with his deep, booming voice. "Gentlemen, may I introduce my daughter, Abigail."

He strode to the base of the steps and took her hand as he whispered, "You look as fetching as a doe in spring. That dress on you is worth every penny it cost to get it here from Saint Louie."

He led her first to the one unfamiliar person in the room. "My dear, I would like you to meet Mr. William Gilpin, the first governor of the newly established territory of Colorado."

Abigail offered her hand. "Governor Gilpin, I have heard many stories about you from Uncle Henry. He talked often of the Fremont expedition with you and Mr. Kit Carson. It was into the Oregon territory, was it not?"

Governor Gilpin took her hand and nodded as she continued. "I believe it was that experience which convinced him and father to come out to this beautiful, wild, rugged land." She withdrew her hand, thinking he looked as puffed up as a disturbed toad. "I trust your new position has been a favorable one?"

The governor nodded. "The position has been challenging," he glared at Larimer, "but rewarding. I am of the opinion that we should settle this land as quickly as is possible. As I have said on many occasions, and firmly believe, the destiny of the American people is to subdue this great continent."

He bowed slightly. "But I bore such a lovely lady with my political rhetoric. It is a pleasure to be in your home."

Abigail smiled politely but her answer was laced with ice, "I would be interested in a discussion regarding your ideas of 'subduing' the continent." She softened her tone after a harsh look from her father. "But possibly at a later time."

She turned and extended her hand to Larimer. "Mr. Larimer, it is good to see you once again. I hope your family is well. And I trust our, pardon me, your little Denver City is thriving?"

"Ah, my dear Miss Abigail, you truly have developed" – he stuttered, raising his gaze back up from her exposed neck – uh, matured, into a lovely young lady. My family is well. Thank you for asking. They have moved back to Leavenworth while my eldest son has remained in Denver to oversee the Denver City Land Company. I am pleased to report that the city," he nodded to James, "as well as your father's investments, are growing. It is unfortunate that growth has slowed due to this civil conflict in which we are engaged."

Before he could continue, the mantle clock struck seven. Abigail glanced over at Lisette who had been patiently waiting at the doorway to the kitchen hallway. Lisette nodded and Abigail announced, "Gentlemen, I believe supper is ready to be served."

Her father led the way to the head of the table, with Larimer on his right and Gilpin on his left. Patrick took Abigail's arm. "Sis, you look absolutely ravishing."

She whispered, "I wish I felt the same. I'm as nervous as a cat cornered by a pack of dogs."

He leaned into her. "I assure you, Mr. McKay is just as impressed." She glared back at him as Sean pulled out her chair for her. She nodded her appreciation, sitting so that the men around the table could do the same, with Sean on her right and Patrick on her left.

After her father said a blessing on all those present and the food, Abigail, as hostess, went over the menu. "Lisette and Alfred have prepared what I hope will be an appropriate meal for such an auspicious gathering." Smiling, she nodded to each of them. "We will begin with cream of pumpkin soup, followed by spinach salad with the last of our tomatoes gathered before last week's frost. The main course will be venison," and she nodded to Lisette, "which William shot up at Clear Lake. It is served in mushroom gravy with potatoes and carrots. Dessert is Alfred's special dried apple pie with coffee which just arrived from Fort Bent this morning. Gentlemen, please enjoy."

She glanced over at her brother. "At least with this silly conflict, supplies like coffee are in regular supply via the Union supply trains."

"It's hardly a 'silly conflict'," sputtered Gilpin. "If it wasn't for our Union boys out here, the Injuns and those Confederate Texans would be taking over our fine territory. Those mule trains keep Fort Union and our westernmost regions well supplied with necessary provisions. By the way, where is it you boys said you were headed?"

Abigail could see Sean's muscles visibly tighten. Patrick's fingers hesitated on his glass, then took a sip of wine before he answered. "Fort Union is our final destination. My friend and I felt it only fitting to use our attained knowledge and training to protect our cause here in the West."

"Gentlemen," Abigail said, raising her fingers in mock protest. "I certainly had no intention of causing a disagreement. I am quite sure we would all like to see a speedy and peaceful end to this unfortunate conflict. Please, let's enjoy this fine meal and friendly company."

Her father nodded his appreciation. Carefully he steered the conversation to the coming winter weather. Abigail whispered to her brother, "Quick of thought and eloquent of speech. Lisette always said you should be a preacher."

He smiled behind his glass, "Or a con man."

As the new girls began serving the soup under Lisette's watchful eye, Abigail turned her attention to the handsome young man on her right. "Mr. McKay, I see William's shirt seems to be a good fit."

Sean smiled, revealing slight dimples at the corners of his mouth. "It is a very good fit." He added, "And William was quick to assure me that I could keep it, since his shoulders had outgrown it some time ago."

Patrick chuckled. "He has certainly added the muscle. We wrestled before I left for West Point. I would say, that will be the last time I will take him down."

Abigail nodded. "There's not a man, young or old, that

has challenged him in the last two years that did not find themselves in the dust when all was said and done."

She glanced around the table to ensure all was going as planned. Her father was holding court between Larimer and Gilpin as they discussed politics and Lincoln's leadership or lack there-of. Patrick pretended to listen, but she could tell his mind was elsewhere.

She turned her attention back to her guest. Sean indicated the room and the table. "If I didn't know better, I'd think I was back home at Great Oaks. This is the kind of supper Mamma would have prepared when the cousins came to Missouri from Kentucky. She would always do what she could to impress."

"Well, Mr. McKay, this may be rugged country, but we can be civilized. After all, it isn't every day that we entertain the territorial governor and the founder of Denver City, as well as my wayward brother and his friend." She took a sip of wine. "Tell me more about your family back in Missouri and your Great Oaks."

He finished his last bite of salad before he replied. "Great Oaks was our plantation in the southwestern corner of the now state of Missouri in the foothills of the Ozark Mountains."

Abigail perked up. "There are mountains in Missouri? I was not aware."

Sean laughed. "Compared to your mountains, they are just big hills, but we like to call them mountains, anyway. My father's father settled there in the early part of the century from Georgia where he raised cotton and tobacco. Father inherited the land while he was married to his first wife." He sighed before he continued. "Shortly after her death, he married my mother, the daughter of Felix Alexander of the Louisville Alexander's. From the stories Mamma told, that was one fine wedding."

He lowered his voice to a whisper as he glanced at the other end of the table. "It's said that her dowry included a dozen slaves that were brought back to Missouri."

Abigail raised an eyebrow as she tore at the meat with her

knife.

Puzzled, Sean asked, "Your father has slaves, does he not?"

Abigail glanced at her brother, who was now engrossed in their conversation. He raised his wine glass as he gave her a "now how are you going to answer that question" look.

She took a sip of wine as she watched Lisette prepare the desserts for serving. Abigail had had no intention of sharing with this stranger any of her own family stories, but there was something about his manner that kept attempting to break through her intended barrier.

After another glance at Lisette, she decided to answer his question. "When Mother and Father decided to come west with their young son," she nodded to Patrick, "they knew little of what to expect, but it was doubtful that a large group of slaves would be of advantage. Lisette had been given to mother as a wedding present from a family friend. Father had purchased Thomas from the slave auction in Atlanta to keep him from being beaten to death. They were both freed shortly after we settled here."

"Then William is Lisette and Thomas' son?"

Abigail again looked to Patrick for an answer, but they were interrupted by her father's question from the other end of the table as the girls cleared the table and served dessert.

"Abigail, would you have time in the morning to show these gentlemen some of our available horseflesh? They are interested in purchasing some of our horses for their Colorado volunteers who have been training south of Denver." He glanced at Patrick and lifted an eyebrow. "They would like a dozen or so to take back with them. We can make arrangements for the remainder to be delivered after the snow melts off the pass."

She pondered the question and then nodded. "Lisette and Thomas have everything under control for tomorrow's party. The band of horses is wintering up in Bryce canyon. If we leave directly after breakfast, we should be back by midday when the rodeo begins."

Her father turned to his companions to explain. "My daughter may be the epitome of a lady this evening, but she is by far the best horseman in these here parts. If she says it's a good horse, it's a good horse."

He hesitated as he winked fondly at his daughter. "Oh, and don't try to bargain the price down. They'll be worth every dollar she asks, and she won't take a penny less."

The men nodded and he continued. "It's settled then. We'll ride out of here at daybreak. Now gentlemen, let's move to more comfortable seating for brandy and a cigar."

Patrick spoke up. "Father, if we might be excused, I'd like to check on the horses. I think mine may have picked up a stone in his front hoof."

His father nodded and led his companions back to the fireplace where Thomas had added some logs.

Abigail stood and leaned in to her brother. "Get a bottle of brandy and some glasses. I'll get a shawl and meet you two out at the stable."

Seeing the look of discomfort in her brother's eyes, she added. "Don't be bothered. I won't interrupt your plans, but I would hate for your friend to be left by himself his first night at the *MC*."

Trying to seem innocent, Patrick replied, "Sister, whatever do you mean?"

They both laughed. "You know full well what I mean. You just best hope that Florence's father or brothers don't get wind that the two of you are meeting tonight, or there'll be hell to pay. I don't want any fighting at the festival tomorrow. Now go, and I'll see you down at the stable."

Abigail said her adieus to Larimer and the governor and kissed her father good-night. She went through the kitchen hallway, draped a shawl over her bare shoulders and went out the backdoor. The night air made her shiver in spite of the warmth of the shawl. The snows weren't far off. It could prove to be an early, cold winter. She was glad the cattle were down off the high plains and safely in the winter pastures.

And she was anxious to find out more regarding the true reasons for her brother and his friend's appearance on this particular weekend.

Chapter 7

Sean leaned against a porch post, letting out a sigh of relief. Finally he could relax. He felt as though he had held his breath for the last hour. The anxiety of sitting across from Gilpin and Larimer and next to the prettiest girl he had ever seen had kept his nerves tied in knots. The night air chilled the sweat that still dampened his shirt.

He wasn't sure he was cut out for this spy business. He had no doubt that he could march and shoot and fight with the best of men, but he became tongue-tied when he was forced to talk, especially to women. If only he could be as eloquent as his friend.

Patrick came through the door with a decanter and two glasses. He slapped Sean on the back and pulled him down the steps toward the barn. He was in a gay mood. "That went well, don't you think?"

"I felt like a stuttering fool," Sean replied with a shake of his head.

Patrick snickered, "I don't mean the conversation between you and my sister. Larimer and Gilpin. We should be able to get the information we need by the end of the festival tomorrow and be on our way."

William had already saddled Patrick's horse. Patrick set

the decanter and glasses on a bench. He thanked William and swung into the saddle as Abigail strode through the door of the barn. She went over to her brother. "Patrick, do be careful. Old man Anderson would as soon put a bullet in you and ask questions later."

"Sis, don't worry. We'll be careful." He leaned down and kissed her on top the head and put the spurs to his bay.

Sean shook his head as they watched Patrick ride into the night. "I tried to talk him into my riding with him, but he said I'd just be in the way. Do you think he's really in danger?"

"It's not the wisest move he's ever made, but he should be alright. Mr. Anderson's pretty protective of his only daughter, but he has always liked Patrick. It's her brothers that would give him a thrashing if they find out. They can be a mean bunch when they're riled."

William cleared his throat. He glared at Sean as he spoke to Abigail, "Will you be Ok?"

She smiled. "I will be fine. Thank you, William. Go get some sleep. We will need to be up early to take the men up to the horses. Plus, we have a full afternoon and evening tomorrow." He gave Sean another look which Sean could only assume was a "watch your step" look, then went into the night.

Abigail took Sean's arm, leading him down between the paddocks. "William can be a bit over protective, but he means well."

Quite, thought Sean, but he said nothing. He watched her with admiration as she spoke softly to each horse like an old friend.

She was a puzzlement to him. His half-sisters had been his only avenue to the ways of women, and they had both been much older. Only the one encounter with Mellissa from a neighboring plantation when he was fourteen was the exception. That had turned out badly when her father caught them kissing by the big oak in the curve of the river.

Patrick was the one who wooed the girls. Sean usually stood watching from the shadows. But this girl was different.

He felt comfortable with her in such a short time. Nervous still, yet strangely at ease.

***

Abigail smiled when she spied the decanter of brandy and two glasses on the bench at the end of the run in the pale light of the kerosene lantern. "It would seem that my brother was thinking of us after all. Mr. McKay, would you care to pour?"

She watched him as he poured a bit in each glass. He was quite handsome, and the uniform fit a bit snug, which only tended to emphasize his biceps and broad chest. She felt herself blush. It was as if she was describing a beau to one of her cousins after an evening of dance back in Charleston.

Yet in spite of his good looks, he seemed shy. Not like the cads back east. And a gentleman. Not like the men here. And certainly not like Edward.

She stared into the undulating shadows of the lantern. Edward whom she had known as long as she could remember. Edward, whom she had thought of like another brother. But he had made it known that he thought otherwise. She shuttered at her recollections of that day when he had tried to force himself on her.

Sean broke into her thoughts as he handed her a glass. "You're shaking. The night is much too cool for such a..." he hesitated, "...uh, lovely gown. Let me take you back to the house."

She smiled inwardly. He truly was a gentleman, in a rough sort of way. "I will be fine, but it is a bit cool." She handed him a blanket from a peg behind them. He joined her on a bench draping it over both their shoulders. As his arm lingered for a moment, a feeling pulsed through her that wasn't from the night air. The warmth of his body, the blanket and the brandy made her a bit light headed.

She finally broke the silence. "You were telling me about Great Oaks. Why did you leave?"

He relaxed as he took a sip of brandy. "I was the last of

six boys and two girls. When pa died, my oldest half-brother inherited the plantation. There wasn't much of a place for me there – not that there ever was," He added, more to himself than to Abigail. "So I went to West Point. That's where I roomed with Patrick."

He hesitated. Abigail felt his body tense as he continued. "After graduation, I invited Patrick to join me for a visit back to my home in Missouri. Little did I know what awaited us there. This conflict between the Federal government and some of the southern states had just begun, but Missouri was supposed to be neutral.

"We arrived two weeks after a group of Union sympathizers from across the Kansas border raided Great Oaks. They had killed two of my half-brothers, burned the main house and several of the out buildings, and 'freed' our slaves, even though they didn't want to go. Great Oaks was in ruins. My remaining half-brothers took Mamma back to Atlanta to be with family. I hear they joined the Georgia volunteers."

He took a sip of brandy. "After that, our course was set. Patrick urged me to come west with him."

Abigail put her hand on his. "I'm so sorry for your loss. I don't know what I would do if I lost Patrick – or the ranch."

As she drained her glass, a question came to mind. Turning to look him in the eye, she asked, "Then what of the Union uniforms? They really are just a disguise, aren't they?"

He pulled away and she could tell he was searching for the right words. He took a deep breath and said, "I need another glass of brandy."

She laughed and poured each of them another glass.

He turned to face her. "Patrick will beat me for telling you. He didn't want you or your father involved."

"Mr. McKay, if you haven't already noticed, I'm not your normal female. I was motherless the day after I was born in the middle of a snowstorm. I was raised in this beautiful, rugged, wild country amongst Indians and outlaws, ranchers and cowboys. My father has taught me to be a woman in a man's world. Nothing you're about to tell me will shock me nor frighten me."

Sean smiled. "You're sure not like most women, I'll give you that, not that I'm complaining."

He stood and began to pace. "Patrick and I went south into Texas with the intention of joining up with Brigadier General Henry Sibley. Sibley's putting together an army of Confederate volunteers with the intent to invade Colorado and take over the gold mines for the Southern cause."

Abigail brought her hand to her chest as she tried to mask her surprise.

Sean took a deep breath and continued, "But Sibley needed to know the strength of the Union forces here in the west and especially Governor Gilpin's volunteer forces."

He worked the dust with the toe of his boot. "Colonel George Madison had been commissioned to form a Confederate spy ring in northern New Mexico and southern Colorado. Patrick and I joined his regiment."

He sat again beside her. "When you wrote Patrick that the governor was planning to be here for the fall festival, Madison sent us up here to see what we could find out. Therefore, the need for the blue uniforms, as difficult as it is to wear them."

Abigail's mind was spinning from all of this new information. She loved an adventure, but this was one right out of Arabian Nights. "So you and my brother are spies? Spies get hanged or shot or some other nasty way to die, do they not?"

"I suppose they do…if they get caught."

Abigail pulled her shawl tight around her as a shiver pulsed through her body. She rubbed her temples with her fingertips, wishing now that she had forgone that last glass of brandy. She needed all her wits about her, with this last bit of news.

Sean stared at the ground as he whispered, "My apologies, Miss McFerrin. I should not have shared our intentions with you. I am so sorry to have upset you."

"Ah, Mr. McKay, upset I'm not, just surprised and a bit

concerned."

She searched for the correct words to express her thoughts. She touched his arm and he looked up. Gazing into those gorgeous brown eyes gave her strength.

"Mr. McKay, I do sympathize for your loss. I can only imagine what you are feeling." She pulled her gaze from him, staring into the light of the stuttering lantern. She clenched her fists as she continued. "However, I have visited the southern home of my family. What I saw wrenched my heart. I had heard stories of the plight of the colored people of the south and the treatment of the slaves there, but it was far worse than anything I could have imagined."

He pulled away, protesting. "But we did not treat our slaves badly. My father would never allow the use of the whip or any other such treatment."

She shook her head. "But they were not free to come and go as you and I are free. They were still slaves."

"Yes, they were still slaves," he said sadly. "That is one of the reasons I could not stay at Great Oaks." There was a catch in his voice. "But that does not give the government in Washington the right to take away our way of life because they do not agree with it." Through gritted teeth he continued, "It does not give them the right to kill my brothers and burn our home in the middle of the night."

Abigail replied softly, "No. I agree it does not."

She ran her finger around the rim of her glass and drank the last of the liquid. "Sadly, men's hearts are cruel, whether in the north or the south, the east or the west. Our federal government would denounce the awfulness of slavery, yet would treat the Indian even worse."

Try as she would, she could not keep her anger in check. "The Sioux and the Ute, the Arapaho and the Comanche are human too. Yet we continually take more of their land. And in return, all our government gives them are broken promises and treaties while slaughtering their very existence for sport."

Sean gave her a side-long glance.

She relaxed. "My apologies, sir. You see, for so long we have been rather isolated from the rest of the world. However, between the discovery of gold 'in them thar hills' and this silly war we can no longer go unnoticed. It seems we must all make a decision on which side we stand."

She took a deep breath and let it out slowly. "Besides, I trust Patrick's judgment. If he is willing to fight and die for a cause, who am I to disagree?"

She stood and adjusted the sputtering lantern. Then, turning back to him she said coyly, "Mr. McKay, you do realize I will be with both Mr. Larimer and the governor in the morning. Is it not possible that an innocent young lady might actually overhear more than a couple of men of questionable reputation? With your permission, might I aid you in your endeavor?" As an after-thought she added, "However, it will be up to you to explain this to Patrick."

"Are you sure you want to get involved? As you have already stated, if we are discovered, we could be shot for treason."

"Mr. McKay," she whispered. "I'm sure I would like to help you."

He stood and gently held her hands in his. She looked into those dark eyes that seemed to glow with fire and passion. A warmth of desire coursed through her body, but she knew this was not the time nor the place for such feelings.

Slowly and gently she pushed him away. "Mr. McKay, as attractive as I find you, and as exciting as our new partnership may be, some things must wait for a later time."

He sighed. "I understand. But please call me Sean."

She smiled. "Very well, Sean. But you may not call me Abby. We have yet to become that familiar. Abigail will have to suffice. Now, tell me what information you desire from Governor Gilpin."

***

Sean lay staring at the dark ceiling. She had called him

Sean. He had held her hand. How he wished she had allowed him to kiss her – yet she was right to pull away. How could he expect her to allow such. They had only just met. And who knew what might lie ahead in the coming days. He did not need the regrets of a brief encounter to follow him into the unknown battles ahead. And yet…

He sat up on the side of the bunk. And what had he gotten her into? He bit his lip. Why had he told her of their plans? And why had he not stopped her from becoming involved? And how was he going to explain all this to Patrick?

He pulled on his boots and reached for his coat. Maybe he could sort out his thoughts and feelings and come up with a plan in the cold night air. He certainly wasn't going to get any sleep with her on his mind.

Chapter 8

The crisp morning air stung her nostrils making it difficult to breathe. A heavy frost clung to the pine branches and the corral fence. Fall could be such a wonderful season of the year if it wasn't the precursor of the winter to come. Abigail was glad to be back in her riding pants, linsey-woolsey shirt and lambskin lined jacket. The deer hide gloves that William had given her as an early Birthday present felt especially nice against the cold reins. The new chaps from her father were an added protection from the chill of the saddle.

The sun had not yet revealed itself over the eastern ridge as the riders left the stable and headed north and west. Abigail and William were in the lead with her father, Larimer and the governor close behind. Gilpin droned on about the need of Lincoln to get this civil unrest under control. Abigail wondered if he ever stopped talking. She smiled to herself as she envisioned him talking in his sleep. Four ranch hands brought up the rear.

She could not keep the thoughts of the previous evening out of her mind. Since returning from South Carolina, she had kept any thought of men or courting from her mind. She had especially done her best to evade any contact with Edward, although he had made several attempts. Now she was in turmoil, both with her sudden feeling for this friend of her brother and the real reason for their visit.

She overheard the governor ask her father, "What're those injuns doing coming along on this little excursion?"

Her father chuckled and replied, "Abigail doesn't go far that those two are not close at hand. They have taken quite a liking to her. Of course, what I pay them doesn't hurt any, either."

He added with a sigh, "We are becoming less wild and more civilized, especially now that we are officially a territory, but we still have a way to go." As an afterthought he added, "And I will ensure that their father, the chief, escorts you to the pass with your horses. I'd hate for something to happen to the new governor on my watch and then have it blamed on the Ute's."

Gilpin harrumphed and fell silent for a time. *A nice respite,* thought Abigail as the sun peaked over the ridge, beginning to burn away the fog and taking the bite from the air.

William rode on ahead to check out the entrance of the canyon. She admired the ease her half-brother rode in the saddle, as if he and his horse were one.

Her half-brother. Growing up, that fact was not an issue. If anyone in the valley had had a question about his lineage, they did not ask. Now things were different. People were choosing sides in this conflict. The role of a black man, freedman or even a mulatto was in question. She certainly was not ready to attempt to explain her family situation to a stranger, even if he was her brother's best friend.

Although William was a full year younger than she, most people would assume by his demeanor that he was several years older. He had the fine features of the French side of his mother's heritage which made him quite comely, with almost pretty eyes. Naturally he would beat any man half to death if they should utter such words. He was not quite six foot, yet had the girth and strength of their father. He was strong as an ox and quick as a fox.

Larimer commented, "You treat your slaves well.' He nodded at William. "It does seem greatly unusual, however, for a slave to be the foreman over your cowboys."

Her father took a long drink from his whiskey flask, as much in disregard of Larimer's temperance as to quench his thirst. "I have no slaves," he said coolly. "Thomas and Lisette have been free from the time we first settled here. And William," he hesitated and his voice softened, "and William is a fine young man and a born leader."

Larimer sputtered. "My apologies, my friend. I meant no offense."

"None taken," was his reply, but they rode for a time in silence.

Abigail broke the tension to explain the procedure regarding the horses. "In the fall, we round up all the horses and mules that we have not sold to immigrants heading west, the army, the pony express or herded to San Francisco, Santa Fe or Kansas City to be shipped around the world. We winter them here in Bryce canyon, where they are protected from the heavy snows and they can be fed as needed."

Ahead, William was talking with two other cowboys as Abigail further explained. "Each spring we round up the mares and breed them for size, strength and speed." She ignored the men's shock that she would use such language. Her father smiled and winked.

She continued, "We always keep two or three studs – good strong stallions, as well as two American Mammoth Jack-stock that are descendants from General Washington's Mule Jack studs."

She nodded to her father, then looked directly at Gilpin. "The strongest and slowest are *bred* for mule trains and pack animals, others for their reliability, agility, and endurance. The best horses are like Beauty," she said as she brushed the mane of her horse, "that are meant to run like the wind. I would put Beauty up against any horse in the territory in a quarter mile race." She added as an after-thought, "I would not, however, want to ride her over the pass in the dead of winter. Give me a good mule for that."

She added proudly, "Horses from the *MC* have been shipped to England and France and ridden by the King of Prussia. I'm sure we can find some to your liking."

William turned and led the group through the narrow opening of a canyon which was actually a river bed where now only a small stream ran. Yet during the spring thaw or a summer thunderstorm it could quickly turn into a raging river.

Once through the opening, the box canyon opened into a large meadow with a hundred or more horses grazing on the fall grass. Smoke curled upward from the rock chimney of a bunkhouse that protruded from the canyon wall; shelter for ranch hands who took weekly turns watching over the herd from fall until the spring thaw.

Abigail spent the next two hours pointing out different horses to their guests. Finally, William and the other cowboys had separated out two dozen horses and a dozen mules to Gilpin and Larimer's liking. The equines were tied together for the trip back to the ranch.

With her and Sean's conversation fresh in her mind, Abigail suggested that they rest at the bunkhouse over a pot of coffee. As she poured the hot black drink into borrowed tin cups, she steered the conversation to her liking.

"Governor, you have chosen some of the best of the herd. You have a good eye for horseflesh."

He puffed out his chest a bit. "I have had need for that good eye. Why, when I was with Fremont in Oregon…"

Abigail interrupted him rather than be forced to listen to him regale them with another of his long and arduous stories. "Why yes. Uncle Henry has told us much of that excursion. You are aware he will be at the party today. You must get together to compare stories."

She asked pointedly, "And will you be paying for the horses with your personal funds?"

"No need," he answered. "President Lincoln has approved

any necessary funds that I might need to protect our territory."

"Do you really think this silly misunderstanding between the northern and southern states will actually be felt all the way out here?"

Larimer spit a wad of tobacco that raised a puff of dust from the dry soil. "It seems a bunch of Texas Confederates mean to do just that – bring that conflict right to our doorstep."

Her father interrupted the conversation. "Texas Confederates?" He asked. "There are Texans in Colorado?"

Gilpin shook his head. "Not yet. But the rumor has it that Col. Sibley is putting together his own little army of Texans with eyes on the New Mexican and Colorado territories."

"Sibley? You don't mean Henry Hopkins Sibley that we fought with in the Mexican War?"

"One and the same."

James stroked his beard. "As I remember, Col. Sibley was a brilliant man and inventor, but not much of a military leader."

Larimer chimed in. "That may be, but I hear Jeff Davis has made him a Brigadier General, in spite of his over indulgence with the liquid spirits."

James persisted. "But why Colorado?"

Gilpin took a long drink of coffee. "Why are wars declared and battles fought?" He answered his own question. "For land. And in the case of Colorado, for the gold and silver there-in."

Larimer added, "And the control of trade and goods from East to West."

With her heart racing, Abigail refilled Governor Gilpin's cup. "Do tell me of your young recruits and your training camp."

He raised his head and gestured grandly with his cup. "I have been able to enlist a fine group of young men, willing and able to defend our Union and protect this new territory against Indians, those pesky Texas Confederates, and any and all who might challenge us."

Larimer interrupted with a loud harrumph. "Fine young

men indeed. A wild bunch of hooligans would be more like it. They've done little but harass the shop keepers and saloon patrons of Denver City. Your 'little lambs' are more like hungry wolves."

Abigail could not keep from laughing. "Little lambs?"

Gilpin glowered at Larimer. "That seems to be the name my jealous opponents have given my troops."

Abigail found all this information interesting, but not exactly what she needed. As she began to clean the cups and coffee pot, she directed a question back to Gilpin, "And how many lambs do you have in your fold?"

Proudly he stated, "I have almost 900 fine young men in camp presently, and hope to have a few more by spring." Turning to Larimer, he added. "They may be a bit wild, but they will fight bravely for the cause."

"Wild indeed" retorted Larimer. "Come spring I plan to put together my own regiment of volunteers – disciplined men who will take orders and actually do more good than harm."

Her father stood and came between the two. "Gentlemen, let's not argue on such a day as this. After all, you have purchased some fine horses, I will receive fair payment, and we are about to celebrate our fall festival."

Abigail smiled to herself. *And I have acquired valuable information.*

As they were preparing to leave, Larimer commented, "James, I was pleased to see your son and his friend in blue uniforms as they rode in last evening. What regiment have they joined?"

Her father glanced at Abigail as he replied. "Yes. They just recently graduated from West Point."

Abigail interrupted. "I believe Patrick mentioned something about wanting to get to Fort Union down on the Santa Fe Trail before the pass is closed for the winter."

Larimer nodded. "That would be good. Part of Canby's regiment, I would presume. Fort Union is an important supply depot for all the other Union forts to the west. It sits just above

Glorietta Pass, which is the only east to west pass through that mountain range."

Abigail commented, "Fascinating. We've never been that far south, have we Father?'

Without waiting for a reply, she turned to Governor Gilpin. "Sir, would you mind if I rode back to the ranch with you? I'd love to hear more about your 'little lambs."

Abigail smiled to herself. *This spy business is not as difficult as I thought it might be.*

***

Sean rubbed oil into the leather of his saddle. It had been far too long since he had the time to take proper care of his equipment. Besides, it gave his hands something to do as he tried to formulate his explanation to Patrick regarding his actions of the previous evening.

Patrick sauntered into the tack room carrying a plate of biscuits and sausage gravy and a tin cup of coffee. "Did you get breakfast?"

Sean nodded. "Yes, about two hours past. You do realize it's half way to noon." As an after-thought, he asked, "What time did you get back, anyway? I never did hear you come in."

Patrick looked sheepishly at the ground. "We fell asleep up at the line cabin. I barely got her back home before her folks woke up. I just got back a bit ago."

Sean shook his head in disgust. "You do know you're gonna get your behind full of buckshot one of these days. A present from some daughter's father."

"Better that than a musket ball from some Union soldier. Which brings us to the task at hand." Patrick looked around to make sure no one else was listening. "Florence let it slip that Edward and his two brothers are planning to join one of the Union regiments in Denver City after Christmas. Just like the rest of the country, this valley is splitting up and taking sides. This year's festival will probably be the last, at least until this mess is over."

He scraped the last of the biscuits through the remaining gravy, then licked his fork clean. "Lissette sure knows how to make good biscuits." He drained the cup of the last bit of coffee. "Anyway, we best be out of here before daylight tomorrow, with whatever information we can gather. Else we might truly find ourselves looking down the barrel of that shotgun."

He chewed absentmindedly on his thumbnail. "Somehow, we've got to get close enough to Gilpin and Larimer to get the information we need."

Sean placed the can of oil on the shelf, then wiped his hands on a rag. "Uh, I may have taken care of that."

Patrick looked up in surprise. "How so?"

Sean shrugged his shoulders, looking at his friend sheepishly. "Well, your sister and I were talking here in the barn last night after you left."

"Ah yes." Patrick laughed. "You didn't get all tongue-tied and say something stupid, did you?" Then his attitude shifted. "Wait. You didn't do anything inappropriate with my sister, did you?" He hesitated, then smiled. "She didn't try to shoot you, did she?"

Sean put his fingers to his brow and rolled his eyes. "No, no and no. Well, maybe." He put his hands up as Patrick made a fist. "No, nothing like that."

He briefly explained their conversation, leaving out the part where he held her hands. He concluded, "I'm sorry I got her involved. I had no intention, but she offered out of the blue. At the time, it seemed like a good idea."

Patrick relaxed. "Actually, it is a very good idea. Abigail can be quite persuasive when she puts her mind to it. I am a bit surprised at her offer, however, knowing her aversion to the whole slavery issue. Yet, she is just as adamant about the treatment of the Indians by the Federal government.

"But I feel I may have put her in danger," Sean insisted. "We must do what is needed to protect her."

Patrick nodded. "True. Once we have the information we

need, we must be on our way." As an afterthought, he added, "And then she must not pursue the matter further." He looked at his friend with an uplifted brow. "Nor you, either."

Sean nodded his agreement, but his heart felt otherwise.

CHAPTER 9

The sun had just reached its zenith as Abigail joined Patrick and Sean on the top rail of the corral fence. They waved and nodded to guests who continued to arrive from all directions. Buckboards, buggies, and horses of many types and sizes jockeyed for places under the trees. Ranchers greeted ranchers. The women swapped recipes. Cowboys huddled in groups, bragging about their horses and wagering on the coming events.

Patrick polished an apple on his sleeve, then cut a third for each of them with his Bowie knife. "I was just explaining to Sean what to expect." He waved the point of the blade in her direction. "You see, Abby thinks all of this is for her birthday. Actually, it's our annual fall festival after the cattle are brought down from the high country. This year, it just happens to fall close to her eighteenth birthday."

Abigail pretended to pout. "What? It's not all about me? Why, I'm devastated."

Patrick shook his head, rolled his eyes and continued. "There'll be calf roping,   and we'll see if anyone can stay on whatever horse William has chosen this year for the wild horse riding. But, of course, it all starts with a horse race."

Sean nodded toward Abigail. "Would I be wrong to

assume that Miss Abigail will be riding Beauty in that race?"

"You would not be wrong. From what I've heard, she's won it the last two years," her brother said proudly.

She replied. "That I have. But I've heard tell Tommy Rafferty from over at the Circle T has a mighty fast sorrel he's planning to ride today. It could prove to be a good race. Be careful how you place your bets. Now, if you'll excuse me, I have to get Beauty saddled and ready."

She jumped down from the fence then turned back. Under her breath she said, "If anyone should ask, the two of you are headed for Fort Union, where you plan to spend the winter."

***

Beauty was skittish, as if she could sense Abigail's own tension as they trotted out to the starting line. Tommy Rafferty was already there. She liked Tommy. The Raffertys had come out from Missouri about ten years ago and started a small ranch over east at the foothills. Tommy was the last of seven brothers and was always referred to as the runt of the litter because of his size. But she knew he could ride like the best of them.

She waved, but was cut off by a big black gelding. "Well, if it ain't the runt and the little birthday girl. I hope y'all are ready to git whupped, cause that's jus whut's gonna happen."

"Mornin' Grady," Abigail replied. "I'm surprised that poor nag isn't sway-backed from carrying all that weight. I wasn't aware this was a competition between race horses and drafts."

Grady spit a wad of tobacco which splatted in the dust. "We'll see whose ridin' the horse or the draft." Turning to Tommy he snarled, "And you best watch yerself. Yer ridin' with the big boys today."

Abigail sidled over to Tommy who was visibly shaken. "Don't pay him no never-mind. Of all the drunk cowboys that show up for the festival, he's always the worst. I've never understood why the Longs at the Bar S put up with him."

"It's alright. I'm used ta gettin' picked on with six

bothers. I jus' hope me and Sadie can beat him."

William whistled for the riders to gather around. Each of the riders representing the seven area ranches picked a number from his hat for pole positions. Tommy drew the number two position, with Grady next to him in third. Abigail drew the fifth.

Leaning down she whispered in Beauty's ear. "Alright, girl. We've got some making up to do. We truly will have to run like the wind."

Abigail settled herself in the saddle as her father gave the rules for the race.

"The idea is to race to the three cottonwoods down by the creek. You must go 'round them on the left. If you ride on the right of them or through them, you're disqualified. You then ride from there to the main gate and down the quarter mile lane to the house. The finish line is the line between the outer corners of the two corral fences. Mrs. Lane and Auntie Katherine will be on each side as judges. What they say goes with no argument. Is all that understood?"

All seven riders nodded agreement and edged their horses to the starting line.

Sweat trickled down Abigail's spine and she wiped the perspiration from her forehead with the back of her gloved hand. She didn't know why she was nervous until she glanced over at Patrick and Sean sitting on the top rail of the corral fence.

"Darn," she mumbled to herself. "I've never let a man get next to me before. But he's so dad-gummed handsome."

Her gloves reminded her of his gentle touch the night before. That strange tingle went through her body and she had to wipe her brow again. How different was that touch compared to Edward's rough hands.

"Ready?"

She shook her head to clear those images from her mind, forcing her mind to concentrate on the race to come.

Grady spat a wad of tobacco at the ground, making Tommy's horse shy away. Joe O'Mallory's horse between

Abigail and Tommy got spooked and reared up, forcing everyone out of line. The riders walked their horses and edged back up to the starting line.

"Ready!"

The shot echoed off the canyon wall. Grady and Tommy jumped to the lead. Joe's horse again bucked at the sound of the gun. Beauty side-stepped to avoid getting hit.

Abigail dug her heels into Beauty's flanks. Even with the late start, she was in a close third by the time they neared the cottonwoods.

Tommy laid into the sorrel's neck, giving her full rein. Grady was close behind, swearing and whipping the big gelding. Abigail could feel the heat from the horses in front of her. She ducked as a clod of dirt was hurled skyward from the horses' pounding hooves.

As they reached the first cottonwood, Grady pulled back slightly. Abigail gasped as he charged at Tommy, knocking him sideways and down the creek bank. Abigail screamed as she rounded the trees, looking back over her shoulder to see if Tommy was alright. He scampered up the bank and waved her on. She couldn't tell what he was yelling, but she had a pretty good idea.

Kicking Beauty's flanks, she caught up with Grady at the main gate. Halfway down the lane they were neck and neck. Grady was whipping his horse for all he was worth. As she edged in front of him, he raised his whip and swung. The wind from the tip of the whip brushed her cheek. The crowd gasped in disbelief. With a lunge, Beauty crossed the finish line a full head in front of him.

As Abigail slowed Beauty to a trot, she saw the guns drawn all along the corral fence. Grady didn't hesitate, but headed for the ridge at a full gallop.

She turned and galloped to the cottonwoods, where Tommy was dusting himself off. A couple of riders had gone to catch his pony. She reached down to help him swing up behind her.

"Tommy, I'm so sorry. Had Grady not done what he did, you would have won hands down."

"I jus' hope I have a shotgun handy the next time I see 'm. I'll fill his behind full of buckshot without thinkin' twice."

They passed between the cheering crowd. Tommy swung down into the concerned and admiring attentions of a group of young girls. Abigail assured Patrick and Sean who had rushed to her side that she was alright.

Mr. Long also came to check on her. He shook his head. "That fella can be a right good cowboy when he's sober. But ya let him get a little whiskey in him, and he just turns mean. You can be sure he'll be gone by this time tomorrow, if'n he sticks around that long."

Abigail walked Beauty back to the stables. She took the saddle off and brushed her down before rejoining the boys. The kids twelve and under were showing off their roping and riding skills to the cheers of the crowd.

"Sis, you sure you're OK?" Patrick asked as they helped her up on the fence between them.

"Yes, I'm just a little shaken up, but I'll be fine."

Sean's arm lingered at her waist. She again felt that sensation course through her body.

After the youngsters had finished, Patrick swung his long legs over the fence. "Abby, can you stay here with Sean? You can explain to him what-all is going on. I promised William I'd help him with the bulls. Then I've got to get ready for the wild horse riding."

Sean gave Abigail a questioning look.

"I'm assuming Patrick didn't give you much background as to what's about to happen," she asked.

Sean shook his head.

"Well, as with the horse race, the seven ranches are represented in the last two events. Next up is the bull riding. The big finale is the wild horse riding. For the bull riding event, each rancher drives over his meanest, orneriest bull. One dumb cowboy from each ranch pulls a number out of a hat which matches him up with a particular bull."

"Who's riding for the *MC*? Not Patrick, I hope," Sean asked.

"No. It'll be William. He usually does pretty good, depending on the bull, but it looks like he wound up with the Rafferty's Texas longhorn. They've nicknamed him Lucifer, and rightly so. That bull is the nastiest of the lot."

She gestured to the pen across the corral. William, Patrick and two other cowboys struggled to restrain a bull with horns wider than a man's reach. The animal pawed the earth. Dirt and dung flew into the air mixed with snot from flared nostrils. The air reverberated with angry snorts and deafening bellows from six additional behemoths awaiting their turn in the chute.

Abigail grimaced. "To me, it's a dumb, dangerous sport." She glanced over at Sean. His eyes gleamed with excitement and anticipation. She added with disdain, "The men love it."

A stocky young Mexican eased himself onto the writhing creature. Nothing separated him from the quivering animal's hide save for his chaps and wool pants. He worked his gloved hand through a rope tied snugly around the bull's chest. Taking a deep breath, he nodded to William.

The gate swung open. Bull and rider burst from the chute like a mass shot from a cannon. The bull bucked, sending clods of dirt high into the air. He shook his massive horned head from side to side as snorts and bellows echoed through the valley. He twisted and turned as if the rider was a mosquito on his back. With a sudden jolt, he buried his head between his front legs, his hind quarters arched skyward. The young Mexican flew through the air, rolling to a stop at the edge of the corral fence. Eager hands pulled him over the fence as the bull pawed the earth in defiance, before cowboys on horseback herded him through an open gate into an adjoining lot.

The next two riders were tossed off in a matter of seconds and the fourth came close to being gored as he fell. Sean leaned over and whispered, "This really is dumb. At least in a fist fight, you have some chance of knocking the other guy out. With this, all the advantage is with the bull."

Abigail nodded. "That is true. But I suppose, out here in the middle of nowhere, you must get your fun wherever you can."

Their eyes met. They both laughed and she added. "So, what did you do for fun back in Missouri?"

He shook his head. "Nothing that would compare to this."

Their attention was drawn back to the corral. William was the fifth rider. Instinctively Abigail put her hand on Sean's leg. Before she could take it back, his big hand had covered hers and held it in place.

William eased onto the back of the huge beast and wrapped his hand under the rope tied around the bull's middle. Abigail squeezed Sean's leg and he responded in kind.

William nodded. The cowboys swung the gate open. For a few seconds there was no movement. Then bull and rider exploded out of the chute. William's hat went flying. He grunted through clenched teeth. His muscles bulged.

Half way around the corral, the bovine bellowed and kicked. He completely left the ground. Bull and rider hung in the air like dancers on a stage. When they crashed to earth, the bull stumbled. Abigail gasped, for it seemed that William would be trapped beneath the huge body. At the last instant, William jumped. He rolled to one side, then back on his feet as he ran for the fence. He jumped, clearing the top just as the bull slammed into the rails below.

Abigail went limp against Sean's shoulder, and he slipped his arm around her waist to steady her. Self-consciously, she pulled away as William jumped up on the fence and waved to the cheering crowd.

The next rider barely got out of the chute before he was thrown. The last rider was able to outlast the rest by a matter of seconds. He was rewarded a new pair of chaps for his efforts.

After the bulls were herded out to the back pasture, a black stallion was led into the corral between two horses. He was wild-eyed and frothing at the mouth.

Abigail whispered to herself as much as to Sean. "Oh, ain't he a beauty? Whoever can tame that one has got himself one fine horse."

James came to the center of the corral and addressed the crowd. "This here is one fine piece of wild Spanish horseflesh captured up in the high country this summer. We call him Black Sabbath. He's a wild one and never been ridden. Why, just gettin' a saddle on him is no small feat to say nothin' of tryin' to ride him."

The crowd laughed and nodded in agreement.

"Now we got seven cowboys who think they can do just that. If one of 'em does, Black Sabbath is his. Good luck, boys."

Abigail explained further to Sean. "As a rider, it's hard to know whether it's better to go first or last. If you're first and you stay on, you get the horse and the other six are out of luck. At the same time, if you're last everyone else has gotten bucked off. You can hope the horse is tired and you have a better chance of staying on."

She grasped the rail on each side of her and shook her head. "He's a beauty, but he's a wild one. I've seen a half dozen men try to ride him. It'll take one heck of a rider to stay on his back."

Patrick jumped off the fence across the way and headed for the center of the corral. Abigail added, "Well it looks like Patrick is up first."

Patrick settled gently into the saddle. Sabbath's eyes were wild as he strained against the ropes. Finally, Patrick nodded. The cowboys dropped the ropes and let him go.

The horse left the ground as if propelled from a spring. No sooner had he hit the ground than his back legs kicked high. Patrick hung on for two more bucks and then went flying.

As the cowboys roped the steed and quieted him down for the next rider, Patrick limped over and climbed up next to Abigail. "I knew I was out of shape, but that horse ought to be named Lightning Bolt. At least that's what it feels like just went through my groin."

Abigail gasped. "Patrick! That's more information than I need to hear."

Sean laughed so hard he almost fell off the fence.

Five more riders tried to ride with no more success than Patrick.

The last rider was a tall, long-legged young man with blond wavy hair down to his shoulders and a faint blond mustache. His brooding steel-blue eyes locked on Abigail. Instead of going to the center of the corral, he first came over in front of Abigail and doffed his hat.

Abigail put a hand to her chest. Her heart was pounding. She felt light headed. Edward. She had done her best to avoid him since she had returned from the Carolinas, and now here he was making a spectacle of her in front of all their friends.

Edward nodded, then turned to mount Sabbath.

Sean asked, "What was the meaning of that?"

Patrick looked at his sister and then answered. "That's Edward Anderson."

Sean hesitated. "Anderson? As in Florence's brother?"

"One and the same. The Andersons came out from Independence with Ma and Pa. Edward and I are the same age. Florence is a year younger than Abby. Anyway, Mrs. Anderson helped raise me and Abby after Ma died, so all of us kids were like brothers and sisters. That is, until we got old enough to know better."

As Patrick was talking, images flashed through Abigail's mind of the summer evening two years ago. She had been at the Anderson's helping Edward with a young foal. She had let him kiss her, but then he wanted to go further. He had tried to force himself on her. She had kicked him in the knee and ran to the house. He later apologized, but since that time she had never felt comfortable alone with him; almost feared him.

"He's been sweet on Abby for a couple of years now," Patrick added.

Abigail elbowed him. "Just like you've been sweet on Florence." She glanced at Sean, then looked away. She added nonchalantly, "It's just that, since spending time back in Carolina, I realized there's more than one fish in the sea, as Aunty Maud would say."

Edward had eased into the saddle and was whispering to the agitated stallion.

Abigail added, both proudly and begrudgingly, "If there is anyone who can ride that horse today, it will be Edward. He is one fine horseman. I admire him for that."

Edward nodded to the men holding Sabbath down. He spoke softly, "Let him go." The men let go of the ropes. Sabbath made one quick circle of the corral, then planted his front hooves and kicked high with both back legs. Coming down hard, he then pawed the sky with his front.

At first, it looked as though Edward would end up like all the rest, but somehow he hung on. As the horse bucked, rider and beast became one. Slowly the horse tired and Edward gained control until he was riding the horse instead of the opposite. He made one last circle of the corral, stopping in front of Abigail. He again doffed his hat and bowed as the crowd cheered. Abigail nodded in response.

As he rode out of the gate, he declared, "I believe I just won a new horse," which brought another cheer.

Abigail watched him retreat. She admired his horsemanship. Yet she had come to realize she had no respect for him. She even feared him. She had seen a side of him, even now, that was haughty and cruel.

Patrick interrupted her thoughts. "I must say, as much as I hate to admit it, Edward is one fine horseman. If anyone deserves that horse, it's him."

He nodded toward the milling crowd. "As usual, will you be asking the girls into the house for a respite from the heat of the day, and to prepare for supper and the dance? Oh, and by the way, have you seen anything of Florence? I knew that she was going to be delayed, but I thought she would be here by now."

Abigail nodded. "Yes, I will be taking the girls inside. And, yes, I did get a message from Florence. She should be along shortly." She playfully patted his cheek. "Don't worry, brother, she will be here for the dance."

Patrick and Sean climbed down and helped her to the ground. Abigail nodded to Sean. "If you will excuse me, I must return to my hostess responsibilities." She turned to join a group of young ladies gathered under the trees.

Chapter 10

"So, what do you think of our rodeo?" asked Patrick.

Sean rested his chin on his arms on the rail of the fence. He looked over the now empty corral. "I think life out here is quite different than any of us back east could ever envision. I have read plenty of dime novels and so on, but until you have seen it for yourself, the mind cannot wrap itself around it all. The expansive beauty of the mountains, the rugged wildness of the environment, the strength and perseverance of the people. It's beyond anything I could have imagined." Sean looked over at his friend and grinned. "And you people are a bit crazy."

Patrick laughed. "We do push things to a bit of an extreme. But this can be a hard, lonely life. When we get the opportunity to get together, we make the most of it."

Sean looked up at the mountain peaks, then back to his friend. "And what of Abigail and Edward? Are they," he hesitated, then continued, "seeing each other?"

Patrick turned and leaned against the fence. He looked up at the house. A worried frown crossed his usually smiling face. With a sigh, he answered, "We all grew up together. Our families were the first families to settle here in the valley." He shrugged. "Florence and I have been sweet on each other from the time I realized the difference between a bull and cow."

Sean chuckled. "Yes, but…"

Patrick hung his head. "But, once I got back east, I realized there were lots of girls out there." He gave Sean a side-long glance. "And I wanted to get to know them."

"So you're leading her on."

Patrick looked at him sheepishly. "I don't mean to. I really meant to tell her how I feel. Then I saw her again." He bit his lip. "I'm really a cad, aren't I?"

Sean shook his head. "I won't argue with you, yea or nay. But what of Abigail and Edward?"

Patrick looked at the house, then off in the distance. "Abby is one of a kind. Even as her brother, I'll admit she's got beauty and brains to match. The boys around here never know whether to run from her or try to court her." He looked at Sean and smirked, "Present company included."

Sean slugged him in the arm. "Yeah, I might be interested." Exasperated, he exclaimed, "But what about Edward?"

Patrick rubbed his shoulder, but continued. "Well, since me and Florence were together, everybody just assumed Edward and Abby would be too. But before I left for the Point, I was beginning to see a cruel side to Edward, especially if he didn't get his way. It was my idea to send Abby back to Riverglade Plantation. I wanted her to see life beyond these mountains – and to see boys besides Edward."

"So, Edward considers me an adversary – an enemy?"

Patrick nodded. "You might say that. He can be ornery at best. He can be down-right mean when he's jealous. It's probably a good thing we won't be stayin' much past tonight's festivities."

Sean swallowed and looked away. He had been reluctant to come, wanting to get on with the fighting and his revenge. Now that they were here, he hated to leave. Yet he knew Patrick was right.

Patrick continued. "I love Abby. I want the best for her. If she loves Edward, so be it. But I will do everything in my power to keep her from getting saddled with him if she doesn't."

He looked over at Sean. There was a hardness in his gaze. "And, I've seen that look in your eye as well as hers. You're my friend, but I won't let you be a rapscallion like me. I will not let you lead her on – like I realize I have Florence. You are aware there's no place for either of them where we're going and what we are about to do?"

Sean answered nonchalantly, "I know. You needn't worry." However, in his mind, he wasn't so sure.

Patrick straightened up. "Now, we still have some matters that need attention. I'm going to talk with some of the men. I'd like to know the attitude of the valley concerning the war. I want to ensure Father and the ranch are safe." He glanced at Sean. "Will you be alright on your own for a time? Sorry, but they will be more apt to talk without a stranger with me."

Sean nodded. "I understand. I'll wash up and wait for you in front of the bunkhouse."

Sean watched Patrick walk away. He felt overwhelmed by all that had happened in such a short time. He walked a way down the lane, looking out over the valley. This was a wild place, yet peaceful. For a moment, he envisioned himself in a place like this – a place where he could belong – with Abigail on his arm. He shook his head. But that could not be. This war would see to that.

Turning, he saw William sitting alone on a rock out-cropping. He was gazing at the bulls grazing in the pasture below. Hesitantly, Sean approached him. "May I join you?"

William moved over to make room for him. They sat in silence for a time. Sean nodded toward the animals. "Big brutes. Yet they seem so docile when they're out there just munching grass, unlike a bit ago in the corral." When there was no response, he continued, "You did a good job staying on, at least from my limited knowledge."

Without looking at Sean, William replied, "Thanks. That bull of the Longs is a wild one. That's no excuse, though. I should have stayed on longer."

"I have to ask, why do you do it? A wild horse maybe. But a bull? Ya gotta be a bit crazy."

William chuckled, turning to him, actually acknowledging his presence for the first time. "It gives us something to do, and gives us a whole other field of competition." He shrugged and added rather sadly, "Plus only the strongest and dumbest of us do it. And for some of us, it is just another way of proving ourselves."

"And Patrick told me you are pursuing a mail order bride?"

Again, William smiled. "Yes. It would seem my mother is concerned about my wedded bliss, so she has become a match-maker. She has an uncle in New Orleans who has been given the task of finding me a suitable bride. It is rather unconventional, but prospects out here are sketchy at best. We shall see."

After another length of silence, Sean commented, "Your fath...., uh, James has given you much responsibility. You must be proud of that." He added, softly, "Something my father would never do."

William looked into the distance. "It is a blessing and a curse." He glanced side-long at Sean. "James has always treated me like a son. For that I am grateful. Yet, as a Mulatto with no legitimate father, it is always a struggle."

Sean replied, "I am sure I cannot really relate. However, I was the last of my five half-brothers. My mother was not theirs, and they were always ready to remind me of that fact."

"You had slaves, did you not?"

"Yes, my father had slaves."

"Yet you have on the uniform of the blue."

When Sean did not respond immediately, William answered the question for him. "It is a ruse, is it not?"

With a hesitation, Sean answered, "We are on a mission."

"When I learned Patrick was coming for the fall festival, I assumed it was more than a friendly visit," William replied. "He always loved an adventure." He broke off a stem of dry grass and began to chew on it. "But why the Southern cause?"

Sean briefly told of their visit in Missouri. He concluded, "So, I suppose it is my fault."

William spit out a piece of the stem. "It would seem there is no clear right or wrong, only an unfortunate set of circumstances." He tossed the remaining blade into the wind. "As with other parts of the country, we are divided here – friends and families divided. James will strive to stay neutral. It is best for the family and the ranch. I love him and Abigail, Patrick and this ranch, as well as my mother. I will fight for them all."

He continued. "As for you, sir, you have set your course. My admonition to you – take care of Patrick. He is a good man, but sometimes careless, especially when it comes to women. And," he hesitated, "You must not involve Abby. I have seen the look in her eyes as well as yours. Do not hurt her."

Sean could not help but hear those last words as a threat as much as a request. He answered, "I will do my best to protect Patrick." He added, "And, you can be assured, I would do nothing to hurt or endanger Miss Abigail"

William nodded as if to close the subject. He indicated the setting sun. "I must help with the preparations for the feast tonight. Good luck, sir, and may God watch over you."

Sean watched him go. Another warning. If there had ever been any doubt, it was no longer. He must not pursue Abigail. His head was telling him that. If only his heart would agree.

CHAPTER 11

Abigail invited the young ladies into the house to rest and relax from the heat of the afternoon. Lisette had made punch and cookies and pastries for them in the parlor. Abigail helped her carry trays as well for the older ladies out under the shade of the oaks.

Florence waved from across the way, hurrying from the direction of the stables. Abigail pulled her aside. "Where have you been? I've missed you all afternoon."

"Mother had one of her headaches this morning," she explained. "I had to stay behind to help her finish up her pies." She bit her lip. "I so wanted to see Patrick ride, but we only got here as Edward finished his." She shook her head and rolled her eyes. "Since he stayed on and won that horse, he'll be impossible to live with. He can be so arrogant."

Abigail laughed. "Said like a true sister." *But I agree whole-heartedly.*

Once Abigail had gotten the girls settled down, she filled a glass with punch for herself and one for Florence. They sat on a corner of the porch looking out over the quiet valley. Abigail questioned her friend. "Tell me about last night. I have not had a chance to talk with Patrick. Did you meet? How did you get away?"

Florence giggled. "I pretended to have a headache after supper, then snuck out my bedroom window. Patrick met me at the shepherd's cabin by the falls. I hardly made it back home this morning before it was time to leave."

"Did your father suspect anything?"

"Pa was too busy getting everything ready to come over here, but Ma was a little suspicious. I think that's the reason for our delay getting here." Without hesitation, she asked, "Who is that handsome fella you were sitting next to?"

"He's Patrick's friend from West Point. They rode in together yesterday afternoon." She took a sip of punch. "Did Patrick say how long they would be staying?"

Florence giggled. "We didn't spend much time talking." She continued with a more serious tone. "However, he was rather mysterious when I asked him that same question. He said something about only staying long enough to tend to some business. I'm just glad to see him for whatever time he has. Do you know where he's going from here?"

Abigail hated to lie to her best friend, but wasn't sure she could be trusted with the truth either. "I believe he said something about Fort Union down on the Santa Fe Trail." She sighed. "It is good to have him home for a spell."

"You were sittin' mighty close to that friend of Patrick's. Are ya'll gettin' on?"

"Oh Florence, I don't know what to think. I just met him yesterday. Yet last night, while we were talking, I let him hold my hand. Does that make me a hussy?"

Florence giggled. "If all you've done is hold his hand, I'd say maybe daring, but not a hussy." She added, "You do know Edward's gonna be as jealous as a bull."

Abigail thought of the bulls in the corral earlier in the afternoon. They could seem quite calm grazing in the pasture. Yet, when they were riled, they could become mean and ornery. She had seen the same with Edward. He could be kind, almost gentle one minute, only to lash out cruelly over some word or action the next.

Abigail answered, "I know, and I hate that. But..." She looked at Florence. "We've grown up together. Edward's like a brother. But I don't love him. I wish he could understand that."

"I know." Florence answered softly.

The mantle clock struck five o'clock. Abigail exclaimed, "It's late, and I haven't dressed for supper. Come up and help me change."

Abigail led the way up the stairs to her bedroom. She laid out her dress on the bed, then slipped out of her riding clothes.

Florence held up the dress. "I've always liked this dress. Your father had it brought up from Santa Fe, didn't he?"

Abigail worked it over her head with Florence's help. "Yes. It reminds me of the Spanish dancers we saw on that trip to Bent's Fort." She did a circle, then a curtsy. "What do you think?"

Florence giggled. "It's perfect."

The clanging of a bell interrupted their conversation. They descended the stairs. "Girls, are you ready. I believe supper is served," called Abigail. The young ladies streamed from the house.

From the front porch, Abigail and Florence looked out over the long rows of tables and benches that filled the front lawn. The glow of lighted torches positioned around the perimeter of the yard took the place of the setting sun. The aroma of smoked pork and fresh baked bread filled the air and tantalized the taste buds.

Patrick waved from across the lawn. They joined him and Sean.

"Ah, little sister, you look like a pretty senorita."

Abigail did a turn, letting her skirt flow around her. "Do you like it? Father brought it back from one of his trips to Santa Fe. They told him it came from Mexico City."

Sean bowed with a wave of his hand. "I am amazed. In less than a day, I've lost a horse race to a girl in men's pants, been dazzled by a southern belle at a dinner party, and seen a young lady win a horse race against a field of men. Now I am entranced by a Spanish senorita. The amazing thing is that all of those are the same beautiful young lady." He bowed again and kissed her hand.

Abigail replied, "And you sir, can be assured that flattery will get you everywhere." She mimicked fanning herself with her hand.

Patrick took Florence's arm. "And this is Miss Florence Anderson. Florence, I'd like you to meet my good friend, Sean McKay."

"Ah, Miss Anderson, you truly are as lovely as Patrick has so often said." He bowed and kissed her hand as well. "It is such a pleasure to meet you."

Florence giggled. "So is this how a true gentlemen acts?" Behind the back of her hand she half-whispered to Abigail, "I think I like it."

A voice growled from behind them. "Well, don't get used to it. Once the army puts an end to this uprising and slavery is abolished, our genteel *Southern* gentleman won't be so genteel – not when he has to actually work for a living."

Florence whipped around. "Edward, don't be rude. Mr. McKay is a guest. Besides, he's wearing the blue, not the grey"

Edward harrumphed, then nodded to Patrick. "Welcome home, Paddy. It's good ta see ya. Looks like West Point filled ya out some." He glanced at Abigail and then back at his sister. "He may be your guest, but he ain't mine."

The tension was broken by James announcement. "Ladies and gents. As always, it's our pleasure to welcome you here to the *MC* for the fall festivities. This is a tradition that goes all the way back to Uncle Henry's days in the fur tradin' business." He added, "And I want to congratulate Edward on a fine ride today." He nodded to Edward. "Son, you done good. And you got yourself a mighty fine horse, there."

A cheer echoed through the gathering.

"I'd also like to welcome two gentlemen who are our distinguished guests; my good friend from Denver City, Mr. William Larimer, and the honorable William Gilpin, the first governor of this great territory of Colorado." There was polite applause. "And now, before we partake of smoked pig and roast cow and all the great victuals ya'll have brought, I want to ask my son Patrick, who is back from West Point, to say a blessing on all this."

Patrick seemed a little embarrassed as he climbed up on the fence. His voice trembled as he began but strengthened as he continued.

"Lord, we thank you for this great clear day you've given us, to be together to race and rope and ride. We thank you, Lord, for good herds of cows brought safely down from the high pastures, good grapes in the vineyards and a good wheat crop, so's we can have roast cow, fresh bread and great wine."

A laugh rippled through the crowd.

"And Lord, I just give you thanks for letting me come back home for a bit, and I pray a quick end to this here conflict we've gotten ourselves into."

Several "Amens" could be heard.

"And now, Lord, we pray a blessing on all this food, and Amen and let's eat."

A chorus of "Amen" rippled from the crowd.

As Patrick rejoined them, Edward commented, "Paddy, you oughta be a preacher instead of a fighter."

Patrick shrugged. "Might be I'll do both." He hesitated. "But for now, let's eat, 'cause my stomach thinks my throat's been cut."

Edward sulked off as Abigail led Sean to the heavy-laden tables.

Sean exclaimed, "That's a whole pig with an apple in its mouth!"

She laughed. "That's mostly true. Actually, the carcass was buried and smoked for a couple of days and was brought out this afternoon." She continued, "The platters of beef were carved from the steer that has been roasting on the spit out in the back yard. Mrs. Long and Mrs. Anderson always bring the platters of fried chicken, and you must try Aunt Emma's sweet potato pie. Lisette and Albert have baked fresh bread and cornbread muffins and a mountain of mashed potatoes with rivers of gravy."

They continued down the tables. "There are bowls of peas and beans, squash and corn, candied carrots and pickled cucumbers and onions. And at the far end of the table are the ladies' favorite pie."

Sean simply shook his head in wonder. "This truly is a feast to behold."

***

After everyone had their fill and the tables were cleared away, several cowboys tuned up their fiddles and guitars. As they started a Spanish dance, Patrick led Florence onto the makeshift dance floor.

Edward came across the compound and held out his hand to Abigail, ignoring Sean. "This has always been our dance. Will you join me?"

Abigail glanced at Sean apologetically, then reluctantly accepted Edward's offer.

He held her close as the music started, then spun her away, catching both of her hands so they were facing each other. She stared into his steely blue eyes as he shook his head.

"Why have you avoided me since you got back from South Carolina? You know I've been beside myself wantin' to see you."

The steps of the dance saved her from having to answer immediately, giving her time to think. They whirled and stomped and clapped, trading partners for a time. Exhausted, she ended back in his arms as the guitars and fiddles pounded out the final chord and they finished with a stomp.

Florence ran over, pulling Patrick along. "That was so much fun. Don't you just love that dance? Remember the summer day when Isabella taught us those steps?"

Breathless, Patrick laughed. "How could we forget? Edward and I fell all over each other until we finally got the hang of it."

Edward nodded. "Yeah, and we had to beat up on the Long twins for makin' fun of us."

Florence giggled as she pulled Patrick to her. "That may be, but we were the hit of the fall festival that year, 'cause we knew all the steps. Isabella would be proud that we still remember."

Abigail smiled as she recalled that fall night so much like this one. All the adults were so impressed. It was that night, down by the spring, Edward had first kissed her. But that was before...

Edward pulled her to one side. "You didn't answer me. How come you been ignoring me? You know how much I care about you. Abby, I love you."

She looked up at him. "Edward, I love you." She hesitated. "But I love you like a brother."

Edward grabbed her by her shoulders. "But don't you realize. I don't want to love you like a brother. I want to love you like a man."

Abigail stared into his steely blue eyes. Through clenched teeth she hissed, "Mr. Anderson, it was your groping hands that got you in trouble before." She pushed him away. "Get them off me now, for it will be a freezing day in July before you will ever have my love."

He lowered his hands, but his eyes burned with anger. "As you will, sweet Abigail," he snarled with sarcasm. "Go back to your fine *Southern* gentleman masquerading in a Union uniform. May he wake up in hell with a Union bullet between his eyes."

He turned and stalked off toward the stable.

Abigail gasped. Her heart was pounding. She felt faint and grasped the fence rail to steady herself.

"Abigail. Are you alright? Did he hurt you?"

She turned and fell trembling into Sean's arms. After a moment, she composed herself enough to whisper. "No, he did not hurt me, except with his words. "

She looked around to see if others were watching. Ironically a cowboy was singing a ballad of a love gone wrong. "Mr. McKay. Sean. Would you please dance with me?"

He took her arm and gently led her to the circle. At first, she held him at arm's length, but as the story in song unfolded, she allowed his arms to enfold her with her head resting on his broad chest.

For the first time in a long time she felt safe; safe in his strong arms. She didn't have to put on airs. She didn't have to pretend to be strong. She wished the music would never stop.

They rejoined the others as the fiddles struck up a polka. Sheepishly, Patrick winked as he and Florence headed for the stable. "I'm taking Florence for a ride in the carriage. We'll be back before dawn."

Abigail sighed, then called after him. "Stay clear of her brothers, especially Edward. He's in a foul mood." Under her breath, she added, "Thanks to me."

Sean touched her arm. "Will you walk with me?"

She smiled and nodded.

She led him to the spring, each lost in their own thoughts. The light of the harvest moon shimmered like silver on the rippling pool. The evening was warm, but a cool breeze drifted up from the cold bubbling water.

An awkward silence hung between them. Abigail sat on a ledge at the edge of the pool, letting the water trickle through her fingers. Sean stared into the dark emptiness of the night.

He finally broke the tension. "I want to thank you for this past twenty-four hours. This is the first time I have been able to laugh since I discovered the burned-out shell of my home at Great Oaks."

He skipped a rock across the top of the water. "Before coming here with Patrick, I couldn't wait to get to fighting and avenge my brother's deaths. Now the war seems so far away. After today, I don't want to leave."

She replied softly, "And I don't want you or Patrick to leave. But you will leave. You must leave. You have a job to do, and a dangerous job that is."

Remembering Edward's comment, she shuddered. "Although the gathering today was cordial, there is tension and conflict beneath the surface because of this war. Of the seven families gathered today, three have strong southern ties and three are from the north. I am not sure how the Long's feel. I fear this war will divide our valley just as it has divided our families and our nation. Father will try to stay neutral." She chuckled, "After all, that is the best financial decision for him and the ranch." She looked away. With a sigh, she added, "But nothing will be the same."

The moon gave a soft glow to his face. His eyes reflected a sadness and lacked the sparkle they had held previously. She longed to reach out to him.

Instead, she broke the spell as she turned away. "Did you share with Patrick my participation in your scheme?"

He hesitated before he answered. "I shared our conversation with him during breakfast. He was not happy, but also not surprised, I think."

He skipped another stone across the pool. "Patrick is aware of Edward's suspicion of our presence. He is riding with Florence to tell her goodbye. His intention is for us to leave before day break."

Abigail stood. Her breath caught in her throat. She wanted to throw her arms around his neck and have his arms hold her tight. She wanted to feel his lips and hear him say that he would give up this fight and stay with her. Instead, she turned and coolly asked, "What are your plans when you leave here?"

Sean looked around to ensure no one else was near. In a whisper, he laid out their plan.

"We are to follow the Arkansas to Canon City, where we will meet up with Captain George Madison and his men. From there, we will go down to Mace's Hole, where a group of volunteers are in training. What men are ready will travel with us to join Sibley for Christmas in Fort Bliss or Mesilla. We will begin the campaign from there."

Abigail straightened her back. "Well, Mr. McKay, it would seem you have your orders and plans intact." She took a deep breath. "Patrick should return shortly. We must have things ready when he does."

Her heart ached. She fought back a tear. She tried to clear her mind so that she might concentrate on the necessary preparations. Her personal feelings and desires must not interfere with their plans. She knew in her heart that they could not, would not, see each other again.

When she turned to address him, she was no longer a young lady wishing for an embrace, but rather a woman in control of her household and the situation at hand. In a calm, business-like tone she explained, "Most of the guests will have bedded down for the night, before they return to their ranches in the morning. However, we must use caution that we not raise any suspicion. Once we get back to the house, you will need to get your personal belongings together, as well as Patrick's. I will have Lissette prepare some food as well as some supplies. William and I will get your horses saddled as well as a couple of pack mules." She added as an afterthought, "If anyone asks, we are taking a midnight ride."

Sean took her arm to stop her. His look met her gaze as he whispered, "I wish things were different."

She glanced away. She answered in a forced tone as cool as the spring's water, "But they aren't. Things are what they are." She pushed his arm away. "Now go. We haven't much time."

CHAPTER 12

Abigail and William were securing the last of the supplies on the pack mules when the sound of a carriage ground to a stop outside the stable. Lissette froze before dropping the last ham into the leather bag Sean was holding. They relaxed at the sound of Patrick's whistle.

They looked to Abigail for instructions. She whispered, "Lisette, quickly dim the lanterns." She nodded to Sean and William. "Bring the carriage into the runway."

Within minutes, the horse and carriage were inside the stable with the doors secured. Patrick stepped down and lifted Florence to the ground as William unhitched the horse and led him to a back stall.

Florence hurried over to Abigail. "Isn't it exciting, our boys on a secret mission?"

Abigail glowered at Patrick over her friend's shoulder. "Exciting indeed."

Patrick looked at Sean and then at the ground.

Abigail gave Florence a hug. "Yes, yes, it's quite exciting. But we need to be careful, for the boy's sake. We must act as though nothing is amiss, even to your parents and especially your brothers." She took Florence by the arm, leading her toward the door. "Go quickly up to the house. Enter by the kitchen entrance and up to my room. I will be along shortly."

Florence giggled. "This is so exciting. Just like one of your dime novels." She gave Abigail a hug and ran over to Patrick, gave him a kiss on the cheek and hurried out the back door of the stable.

Abigail stomped over to Patrick and whispered through clenched teeth, "How dare you lead her on like that. What lies have you told her?"

"I didn't tell her any lies." He looked away and then back at the ground. "I just didn't tell her the whole truth."

"And I'm sure God knows the difference." Abigail's sarcastic reply made him grimace, And," she added, "as usual I'm left to pick up the pieces."

Patrick took her hands. "Sis, I'm so sorry. I never meant for you to get involved with any of this. We should not have come. But I wanted to see you and pa one more time before the fighting started."

"That, and your spy mission." She shook her head and whispered, "You frustrate me so. No matter what you do, I can never stay mad at you." She wiped a tear from her cheek and hugged his neck as he drew her close.

After a moment, she pushed him away. She turned to Lisette and William. "Thank you both for your help tonight. Go back to bed and get what little sleep you can of what is left of the night. Oh, and if anyone asks, none of this happened."

Lisette chuckled. "Missy, I slept like a dead dog and never heard a thing all night long."

She gave Patrick a hug. "You take care. We need you back here safe and sound, you hear?"

She shook Sean's hand. "And you, son. Take care of my boy."

William gave Patrick a hug and nodded to Sean. He led his mother quietly out the back door.

Abigail felt light-headed and leaned against the carriage for support. The adrenaline from the excitement of the moment was suddenly gone, leaving her weak and exhausted.

Sean grabbed her arm. "Abby, uh Abigail, uh Miss McFerrin, are you alright?"

"Oh, these cussed corsets won't let a woman breath. Just let me sit while I tell you what I discovered on this morning's ride." There was no way she would let him or her brother know how she really felt.

They helped her to a bench. Patrick sat cross-legged at her feet. Sean stood a short distance away.

She tried to think of all she had heard. It seemed like the morning's ride was days rather than hours previous. Sean handed her a canteen. She took a long drink and began.

"This spy business is really rather easy, at least for a woman. I simply gave the governor a bit of attention, and he sang like a canary." She shook her head. "That man does like to hear himself talk."

She rubbed her temples as she put her thoughts into words. "As you probably already know, Colonel Edward Canby is at Fort Craig. He has a couple of regiments down there in the New Mexico Territory, but his men are spread quite thin."

The two men nodded in agreement.

"Colonel Green is commander of Fort Union on the Santa Fe trail."

Patrick nodded. "He's young, but Pa has spoken well of him."

She continued. "The governor is putting together his own regiment of Colorado volunteers up in Denver City under the command of Corporal John P. Slough. Father introduced me to him at a gala at the Tremont House last year. He was a lawyer at that time. He seemed to be a fair man, but out-spoken. They presently have about nine hundred men in training and hope to have a thousand by the end of the year. According to Larimar, they're a rowdy bunch and not very well disciplined."

Sean looked at Patrick. "Depending on the situation, that could make them even more dangerous."

Patrick nodded in agreement.

Abigail continued. "Especially when you add Slough's

second in command, John Chivington."

Patrick snorted. "Isn't that the blustery Methodist preacher we saw the last time we were in Denver City?"

"One and the same. He and his wife Martha were at that same gala. He's a huge man, and from all indications just as big a bully. He spent the entire night ranting about the 'no-good Indians' and how the 'only good Indian was a dead one'. I felt sorry for his wife, but liked her from the moment we were introduced."

She took another drink from the canteen. "My apologies. That is all the information I could gather without raising suspicion."

Patrick grinned. "That is a good deal more than we could have managed in such a short time. It reinforces what we suspected plus what I learned from the cowhands and William. You did quite well."

He turned to Sean. "Now we must go. I'm certain our cover is blown, thanks to Edward's suspicions. We only have a few hours before daylight. There's a good possibility we will be followed, and I want as much distance between us and them as possible. We'll follow the creek south to the Arkansas. That should hide our tracks. From there it should be safe to use the trail."

Abigail stood and they held each other for a time. He kissed her on the cheek and swung into the saddle.

Abigail snuffed the light in the lanterns and swung open the door.

Sean walked his horse to the open door. The setting moon illuminated his face in a pale blue glow.

Ice clung to the edges of her voice. "Goodbye, Mr. McKay. Take good care of my brother."

"I will," he replied with sadness in his voice. "Goodbye, Miss McFerrin. Thank you again for your hospitality. My only desire is that we were parting on different terms."

As he turned to go, Abigail whispered, "Goodbye, Sean."

He faced her with a broad grin spreading across his face.

"Goodbye, Abigail. We will meet again."

He lifted her fingers to his lips, brushing them with a kiss. He swung into the saddle and was gone into the night.

***

Abigail hurried to the house. Quietly she slipped in through the back door. She was relieved to hear her father's snoring emanating from his bedroom on the one side of the hall and Lisette's heavy breathing on the other. She tiptoed up to her room.

Florence was sitting up in bed waiting for her. "Where have you been," she whispered loudly. "Have they gone?"

Abigail hushed her. "I'm sorry I took so long. Yes, they're gone."

She struggled with the buttons on her dress. "Here, help me with this dress and get me out of this confounded corset."

They were interrupted by the sounds of horses in the front drive.

From the window, Florence exclaimed. "It's Edward and Luke and Joshua. What are my bothers doing here?"

Abigail slipped her nightgown over her head. "What do you think, silly? They're looking for you."

Abigail wrapped her robe around her and hurried down to the front door. Rubbing her eyes as if to get the sleep out of them, she asked, "Whatever are you doing here at this time of the night? All this racket would wake the dead."

Edward scowled. "Looking for you, and my sister, and your brother and that fancy friend of his."

"Why, Florence and I have been right here all evening. As for Patrick and Mr. McKay, they left hours ago. I believe I heard them say they were going north to Fairplay. Patrick wanted to get over Kenosha Pass as quickly as possible. For whatever reason, he wanted to visit someone in Denver City before they checked in for duty at Fort Union."

"Fairplay, you say?" he growled. "We'll see about that. I want to ask him about that blue uniform he's wearin'. There's somethin' mighty fishy about all this."

He wheeled his horse. "Come on, boys. We can make Fairplay by mid-mornin' if we ride hard."

Abigail leaned against the doorjamb. She whispered to herself, "Forgive me Lord for lying. I sure hope there's a special dispensation for spies."

She shook her head as she gently shut the door. She whispered to herself, "Paddy, what have you gotten me into this time?"

CHAPTER 13

They traveled in silence. Only the sound of horse's hooves on the rocks of the shallow stream broke the tranquility of the night. The setting moon had left a clear, blackened sky filled with pinpoints of light.

Sean was content to follow Patrick along the dark creek bed. It gave him time to ponder all that had happened the past two days. Two days? It seemed like two weeks since he had been in the sights of her rifle.

Sean's mind wandered as the shadowy, shapeless trees floated by. Abigail McFerrin. That slender five foot four inches of sass and wit and brains and charm – with flashing green eyes and auburn curls and lips that begged to be kissed. Why hadn't he kissed her last night instead of involving her in all this spy business. He bit his lip. How could a girl affect him so quickly?

He hadn't courted a girl since Mellissa back in Missouri. He was so young and in love – in love until she ran off with his best friend. Huh, some friend. He had sworn he would never let another woman get that close to him, never let anyone hurt him like that again.

Now, overnight, he had let someone break down those barriers, only to have he himself ruin it. This cursed war. How many lives and relationships had to be destroyed before its end?

Why hadn't he just kissed her and kept his mouth shut. Now she probably would never speak to him again, even if he could somehow get back there.

Yet she had whispered his name. Not Mr. McKay, but Sean. Maybe, just maybe there was hope.

High up on the ridge, Trout Creek Pass began to take shape in the pale light of morning. Patrick indicated the juncture where Cedar Creek emptied into the Arkansas River. He pulled up in a grove of Cottonwoods. He swung his leg over and stepped to the ground. "We can stop here and stretch our legs for a bit." Sean forced his legs out of the stirrups. His joints were stiff and his tired muscles ached.

Patrick seemed to understand without asking. "We should be able to make better time, now that we can use the trail. We'll be fine, providing we don't come upon some Union soldiers out on patrol. You doing alright?"

Sean rubbed his sore behind. "I've been better, but I'll live. I'm surely glad you know your way. I'm as lost as I could be."

Patrick chuckled. "This part of the country I know like the back of my hand. Now, down further south is a different story. That's why we need to hook up with Captain Madison and his men. I've never been south of Pueblo. Besides, Mace's Hole is an old outlaw hideout. We'll need his help to find it."

He began to unbutton his uniform. "Let's get out of this Union garb. From here on, we'll be better off as cowboys than lone Union soldiers. Should be a bit fewer questions asked."

Sean took little time stripping down to his flannel long-johns. "I won't be sorry to get this blue off my back. At the same time, I don't know much about cowboy-n. Watching y'all yesterday roping and riding sure brought that home in a hurry."

Patrick chuckled and shook his head as he adjusted his chaps. "You can ride fine and shoot straight. That's all I care about. Just let me do the talking. That southern drawl of yours is a dead giveaway."

He nodded to the knapsack of food. "We should have

time for a bite to eat. What did Lisette send with us?"

Sean brought out some ham slices and biscuits. "Leftovers from last night's feast. Looks mighty good."

They watched as an eagle floated on an updraft of morning air, each lost in his own individual thoughts. Sean broke the silence.

"How far we needing to go today? Will we make Canon City by nightfall?"

"We won't quite make it that far in one day. Not with the pack horses. We should make the gorge if we keep moving. We'll camp up in the caves, which should give us plenty of protection for the night."

***

Long shadows of the afternoon sun darkened the walls of the gorge. The horses picked their way among the jumble of rocks and boulders. Sean's body ached from the ride and the lack of sleep. Patrick began to ascend above the river's edge on a trail only visible to him. As the ribbon of water grew smaller below, Sean let his horse find her own footing. He tried not to look down. Much to his relief, he rounded a corner to find Patrick dismounting at the mouth of a large cave set back on a sizable ledge.

Patrick indicated the cave entrance. "Welcome home, at least for one night. There's a pool of fresh water inside and enough grass around the edges of the clearing for the horses and pack mules."

Before Sean could get the mules unloaded, Patrick had a fire going, coffee boiling and steaks sizzling.

Sean shook his head. "How did you know about this place? There's no way to see it from below." He added with a shudder, "And certainly no indication of a trail."

Patrick chuckled. "This place was my first home when we came out to this country."

Sean gave him a puzzled look.

"I was only two. Ma and Pa and Uncle Henry had come

out from Independence with Mr. and Mrs. Anderson. Edward was a year old and Jacob was three. They had gotten to Fort Bent later in the season than Pa had intended. Mr. Bent wanted them to winter at the fort, but Pa thought they could make it up the Arkansas to the valley before the snow came. They were up on the ridge when the blizzard hit. Uncle Henry remembered this cave and got everyone down here before they all froze."

Patrick paused and cleared his throat. "Abby was born here. Ma died the next day." He swallowed and stared into the glowing fire.

Sean broke the silence with a whisper. "I'm sorry." Patrick nodded.

Silently Patrick retrieved tin plates from a pack. He slipped his Bowie knife from its sheath. Deftly, he speared a sizzling steak from the hot skillet, sliding it onto a plate. He handed it to Sean before retrieving the other one for himself.

As Sean filled two tin cups with hot coffee, he asked, "How did your father know about the valley? Wasn't it still Indian territory?"

Patrick took one of the cups and smiled. "That's true. But Pa and Uncle Henry know how to work a deal. Uncle Henry was in the fur trade. Because he knew the land, he was part of Fremont's western expeditions. That's when he met up with William Gilpin and Kit Carson. It was after that expedition that he discovered the valley. He and Pa worked a deal with the Cheyenne, Arapaho, Utes and the government for the land from the Arkansas up Cedar Creek to the foothills of the Rocky Mountains."

Sean stirred the fire. Thoughtfully he said, "She really is a lady of the land."

Patrick laughed. "Abby? That, my friend, is an understatement. She can be a lady one minute and drive a hard bargain the next."

"Do you suppose she would give me the time of day with the way we had to leave?"

Patrick took a long drink of coffee before he answered.

"She definitely took a liking to you. There's no doubting that fact. However, we did leave her in a bit of a predicament. It will take some sweet talking, but she'll come around."

Sean stabbed the last piece of meat from his plate with the point of his Bowie knife. "What about Edward? After all, he's there and I'm here."

"Edward has a mean streak. Abby knows that. It would take more than sweet talk for him to get far."

The sound of horse's hooves and voices in the valley below grabbed their attention. Sean raised his hand to interrupt Patrick. Patrick quickly doused the fire with the remaining coffee. They crawled to the edge of the cliff. At the entrance to the gorge, a group of men were making camp in the last light of twilight.

Sean whispered, "Friend or foe?"

"We will need to get closer to be certain, but I would guess Union soldiers. Probably down from Fairplay."

"Looking for us?"

"Possibly."

Sean dreaded the answer, but had to ask, "Do we need to go back down the trail we just came?"

"I see no other option, but we'll need to go on foot. We need to get close enough to hear their intentions. They will not expect anyone to be above them, so their guards should be at either end of their camp."

Reluctantly Sean followed Patrick down the trail, making every effort to find firm footing and at the same time not allow any loose stones to slip under foot and go rattling down the side of the canyon. He was grateful that the waning moon gave enough light for the path ahead, but not so much that he could see the rocks below.

After a long slow process, Patrick signaled to halt. Crawling on their bellies, Sean could see down into the camp a hundred feet or so below. The stillness of the cold night and the canyon walls amplified the conversation of the dozen men warming themselves by the fire.

A squat, overweight fellow, from all indications the leader of the group, was giving the orders for the coming day.

"From what the old miner reported, Madison left Canon City yesterday. He's supposedly headed to Pueblo and then on down south to Peterson's ranch. We need to rest up tonight. Tomorrow we'll head out of here about sunrise. Once we get through this cussed gorge, we should make good time. We'll split up when we get close to Pueblo and come at them from both north and south."

He spat a wad of tobacco into the fire. "Main thing, I want Madison alive if at all possible. With a little *encouragement,*", he slapped the whip hanging from his belt, "he oughta tell us where the main Confederate camp is down in Mace's Hole." He yawned. "Now go get some shut-eye."

The men nodded agreement and began to settle down for the night as the leader conferred with a couple of his men.

Patrick and Sean backed away from the edge. Sean whispered, "It doesn't sound good. Is it possible for us to stay ahead of them?"

Patrick hesitated before he whispered his reply. "We can't travel as fast as they can, not with the pack horses. Madison could really use the supplies, so I hate to leave them."

He paused, then asked, "Do you think you can get back up to the ledge alone and get the horses saddled and packs loaded?"

Sean shrugged. "I don't see why not. Heck, we've been over this trail enough now, it feels like a walk in the park."

Patrick chuckled softly. "That may be a bit of a stretch. Besides, what else I'm goin' to ask you to do won't be so easy."

Sean steeled himself for the worst. "Go on. Let's hear your plan."

Patrick led Sean back to the edge of the trail. Pointing up river away from the camp, he whispered, "See the man leaning against that boulder?"

Sean nodded. "Yeah, he just lit up a cigarette."

Patrick continued. "He's been there since we got down

here and seems to be the only one guarding the horses. It'll be midnight soon. I figure they'll change guards then. It will take that new man's eyes a while to adjust to the dark. Your job, my friend, will be to distract that new guard long enough for me to knock him in the head, all the while making no noise."

"Holy ...." Sean muttered. After a moment's hesitation, he couldn't help but ask, "Then what?"

"Well, if we manage to pull that off without getting shot, I'll give you time to get back up to the ledge. Once you get the horses ready, you're going to start a landslide. There's a couple of boulders just down the trail a bit from the cave that should get things going. If our timing's right, I should have their horses untethered and ready to stampede back out of the mouth of the canyon."

"But...but where do I go with *our* horses?"

Patrick smiled. "Well, that's the tricky part. Just beyond the ledge the trail continues on up to the top of the ridge. Ride my horse, Patches. He's been up that trail a few times. If it's any consolation, the trail widens as you go up."

Sean fought the sick feeling in his gut. "I suppose I should thank you for that. What about you? How will we get back together?"

Patrick continued, "Again, if all goes as planned, I'll drive the horses as far away as possible. I'll pick out one of the better horses and ride up on the ridge on the other side." As an aside, he added, "If I get caught, I don't suppose it will hurt any worse to be shot as a spy and then hung as a horse thief, or vice versa."

Sean punched him in the shoulder. "Don't even think that."

Patrick took a deep breath. "Finally..."

Sean interrupted, "If all goes as planned..."

Patrick chuckled, "Yeah, that too. Finally, you follow the eastern ridge and along the river once it clears the gorge. You should get to Canon City about daybreak. Skirt around south of town. Then just keep heading east along the river 'til you get to Pueblo. There's a stage coach station on the south edge of town run by an old man by the name of Higgins. He's a friend of Pa's. Wait for me there. If I don't make it by sunrise the following day, get directions to Peterson's ranch and warn Colonel Madison."

Sean touched Patrick's arm. "The guards are changing."

Patrick nodded. "Give me to the count of a hundred and then let's get this plan moving." Looking up he added, "and Lord, we surely can use all the help You can give us."

Sean began his count as Patrick disappeared into the shadows. At one hundred, he started down the trail, his mind trying to form a plan of action. The guard's back was to him as he approached.

Sean cleared his throat. With the best western twang he could muster, he growled, "Pahdner, ya gotta smoke?"

The man whirled. "What the...?"

Sean caught his rifle as Patrick's rock smashed into the soldier's skull.

Patrick gagged him with his neckerchief and Sean bound his legs with his own chaps and hands with his belt. They clasped arms and went their separate ways.

***

The last of the moon's glow had faded beyond the canyon's walls as Sean strapped the last of the packs tight. He hurried back to the set of boulders that Patrick had mentioned, but try as he could, they would not budge. Frustrated, he searched for an alternative when he tripped over the root of a dead mesquite. He was about to utter a curse when it broke off in his hand and he realized he had just obtained a pry stick. Instead of a curse, he uttered, "Thank you, Lord."

Wedging the root under the edge of the smaller boulder and using another stone as a fulcrum, he began to rock the chunk of granite. With one last attempt, he put all his weight and strength on the end of the root. As he did, the wood snapped, sending him sprawling on his butt. The boulder teetered on the edge. With all the strength he had remaining, he braced his boots against it and pushed.

With a grinding of stone against rock, the edge gave way, taking the second larger boulder with it. Sean scrambled back from the receding trail as more and more of it tumbled down the side of the canyon.

From below came the crash of the falling rocks and the screams and cries of the men below. Faintly through the noise, he could hear the yelps and whistle of Patrick herding the soldier's horses out of the mouth of the canyon.

Sean checked the tether of the pack horses and mounted Patches. Whispering a prayer and then holding his breath, he urged the mare up the trail. Loose gravel rattled down the side of the cliff. His chaps scraped the canyon wall, then snagged a protruding mesquite branch, jerking him sideways in the saddle. The sudden jolt pulled horse and rider dangerously close to the edge of the trail.

Recovering his balance, Sean quieted Patches. A couple of swipes with his Bowie knife severed the branch. He urged the horses on, the packs scraping by, one by one. Then the clear, cold air of the open ridge greeted him. The open trail lay before him.

CHAPTER 14

The low-slung log cabin of Higgins' Station didn't impress Sean by its looks, but the lingering smell of frying bacon brought a growl from his empty stomach. He stretched his aching back as he kneaded his taut shoulder muscles. He had not slept except to doze in the saddle, pushing the horses as hard as he dared. He had eaten the last of the ham and biscuits mid-morning. He had given wide berth to anything that resembled civilization. At this point, he feared crossing a Union soldier's path more than an Indian's.

He took the horses around back of the cabin to a dilapidated barn. The stable boy gladly accepted a silver dollar to help him strip the packs and saddles off the horses and mules. Together they rubbed them down. Sean left him with instructions for hay and water.

Four Union soldiers stumbled out the front door as he rounded the corner. Sean waited until they were well on their way toward town before he stepped into the light of the flickering lanterns.

The interior of the cabin was one long, smoky room with a fireplace at each end. The smell of stale tobacco, sweat, and today's main meal hung heavy as the dusty cobwebs in the corners. Two tables of split logs stretched the length of the room, with rough benches on each side. A make-shift bar took up one corner. Sean figured the door in the far corner led to the kitchen.

Two old miners were playing checkers by the light of one of the fireplaces. The only other person in the room was a grizzled older man of ample girth cleaning whiskey glasses behind the bar. Dirty gray hair hung to his shoulders. A full, scraggly beard of the same color covered his face. From his size and appearance, this was not a man to mess with.

Sean considered his options. His weary body begged him to turn around and go sleep with the horses. His mind hoped Patrick would show up. Yet, he knew he really needed to get in contact with this Higgins fellow. Logic reasoned his best course of action seemed to be with this proprietor, in spite of his dour demeanor.

Sean took a deep breath to calm his nerves as he made his way to the bar. "Evenin'. I'd be much obliged for some hot victuals, if it's not too late."

The bartender replied in a deep gravelly voice, "If'n you got some money, I suppose we can rustle you up some grub." His gaze traveled from Sean's boots back up to his eyes. "Looks like you been doin' some hard ridin' today."

Sean nodded. "I can pay for whatever you can put together and a hot cup of coffee. It's been a long couple of days." Sean lowered his voice, glancing in the direction of the checker players, "And might a Mr. Higgins be around?"

The bartender set the glass he was cleaning on the bar. His hand moved to the musket leaning against the wall. He growled, "Who might be wantin' to know."

Sean opened his hands, moving them away from his side-arms. He tried to keep his voice steady. "Patrick McFerrin said to ask for him. I believe this is the right stage station."

The man relaxed as a grin spread across his face. "Paddy McFerrin? James McFerrin's boy? Well why didn't ya say so sooner. Hell's bells, boy, any friend of the McFerrin's is certainly welcome here. You not only have the right station, but yer talkin' to Willy Higgins." He patted the rifle at his side. "Sorry. Usually nobody asks for 'Mr. Higgins' unless there's trouble a-comin'."

Sean shook Higgins' extended hand. "Sean McKay. Pleased to meet you, suh, eh sir." Sean bit his lip for allowing himself to revert back to his southern drawl.

Higgins smiled and shook his head. "That's alright, son. I figured you was a southern boy." He indicated the bench at the end of the table. "You sit yourself down and I'll have Maud rustle you up some grub. She can fry you up some potatoes and eggs and a slab of bacon. I think there's some gravy and biscuits left over from supper."

Higgins came back with two steaming mugs of coffee as the two miners finished their game. He barred the door behind them and then sat across from Sean.

He stroked his beard. "What's Paddy up to these days? I hear tell he went off to learn soldierin' at West Point after he and his pa had a fallin' out."

Sean tried to mask his surprise at the last statement. There was no way of knowing the extent of the old man's knowledge of their position. With no little trepidation, he decided to share the situation. He hardly had any choice but to trust this new "friend".

A large woman interrupted his thoughts as she set a loaded plate in front of him. He thanked her profusely. Between bites, he began his story.

"I was riding down from the ranch with Patrick. Last evening, uh…" He ran his finger around the lip of his cup before he continued. "We got, uh, separated from each other up at the gorge above Canon City. He'd said to ride on ahead and wait for him here if the need should arise."

Higgins took a drink of coffee. He pulled a stub of a cigar from his breast pocket. He looked Sean up and down as he lit it. A puff of smoke curled up toward the rafters before he spoke. "Any chance you might be headin' down to Peterson's ranch?"

Sean choked on a mouthful of eggs. After he had

recovered and drank some coffee, he mumbled, "Might be."

Higgins leaned back on his bench in thought as Sean mopped up the last of his gravy with a piece of biscuit. He straightened up as if he had made up his mind what needed to be done, but first posed a question. "How many horses do you have with you?"

"Four, sir. Two saddle horses and two pack mules. I left them out back with your stable boy."

"Two saddle horses?" he asked, staring at Sean through his bushy eyebrows.

"Yes, sir." Sean hesitated. "One of them is Patrick's. He had to, uh, borrow a horse." He gave the old man a side-long glance, "A Union soldier's horse."

Higgins chuckled as he shook his head. "This just gets better and better."

He combed his scraggly gray beard with his fingers. "Well, boy, we'll figure something out in the mornin'. For now, you go find yourself some clean hay out in the barn and get some sleep. You look like warmed over death."

Sean was too tired to argue. He saw no choice but to trust the old man. He thanked Higgins for the meal and did as he was told.

***

She rode ahead of him, her petticoats covering the sides of her steed, her auburn curls flying in the wind. Each time he would catch up with her, she would laugh and spur her horse ahead of him, just out of reach.

Suddenly, a pain wracked his shoulder...then another. He groaned. Was it a shot from Edward's pistol or possibly a bullet from a Union rifle? He wasn't sure.

"Wake up! Sean, wake up!"

Instinctively, Sean grabbed the handle of his knife. He sat up, shaking his head to clear the cobwebs of sleep from his mind. In the pale light of dawn, he could just make out the features of his intruder. "Patrick?"

"Sean. Yeah. It's me. It's ok."

Sean relaxed. "Thank God. I wasn't certain whether I'd ever see you again."

Patrick chuckled. "From the way you were moanin'and goin' on, I don't think it was me you were looking for. Bad dream?"

Sean took a deep breath, sheathing his knife. "More or less."

Patrick continued. "We haven't much time. I've got the horses ready. The first stage of the day is due any time, accompanied by a troop of Union soldiers. We need to be long gone before it gets here."

Sean gathered his gear and tied it on behind his saddle. He nodded toward a strange horse tied to a post. "Are we taking an extra ride with us?"

Patrick shook his head. "Nah. That's the pony I, uh, 'borrowed' from our soldier friends. Higgins said he'd get it back to them. There's not much doubt they'll be by this way, once they gather up their horses."

Sean smiled. "Then your plan worked?"

Patrick nodded. "I drove their horses out onto the plain, then headed up on the ridge. It just took a bit longer than I had hoped. I stopped by the ranch of a friend of the family south of Canon City for a bite to eat and a little rest, then headed on down here. I'm just glad you made it OK."

An old fellow was talking with Higgins in front of the station. Dirty gray braids hung to his shoulders from under a beaver hat. A bear-skin coat wrapped his body from shoulder to ankles. Higgins gestured toward his companion with the stub of his cigar. "This here's Lester Gooding. He'll get you down to Peterson's ranch and on down to Mace's Hole, if need be. Y'all be careful now."

Patrick and Sean nodded to their new companion. He spat a wad of tobacco into the dust and nodded back. They expressed their appreciation to Higgins. Then, with a jingle of spurs and a word of encouragement to their horses, they headed south into the frosty morning air of the Colorado high plains.

***

The sun was sinking into the broad saddle of Hardscrabble Pass as they entered the canyon of the same name. A bear of a man stepped from behind a boulder, rifle at the ready. The setting sun reflected from the barrels of several more guns scattered on the ridge above them. Gooding made a sign to the man. After a short discussion, he waved them on.

Dusk was settling over the valley as they neared the encampment. Beyond a pond, the log cabins of Peterson's ranch nestled at the base of a cliff.

Three log buildings had been built in an open u-shape with just enough space at the corners for a man to pass. A low-slung porch connected all three.

All conversation ceased from the men gathered on the porch as Patrick and Sean dismounted. Two continued to clean their rifles in silence as a third laid his across his lap. A short, stout fellow lit a cigarette while another that reminded Sean of a brown bear grunted and spat a wad of chew that landed inches from Sean's boot. This was a time and a place where any stranger was a foe until proven otherwise.

From the shadows a low voice growled. "Paddy? Paddy McFerrin, is that you?"

A tall, lanky man dressed in black stepped into the light. Patrick exclaimed, "Lucas Tanner, you ol' son of a gun. Mighty good to see a friendly face."

Lucas glanced around at the men looking on. "These are the men Peterson's been waiting for. They're good." The men relaxed and conversations resumed.

He walked with them around the side of the buildings. "Rumor has it you're ridin' with Madison and his 'Forty Thieves'. Is that true?"

Patrick and Sean both chuckled. "Actually, it's the San Elizario Spy Company, but yes, that rumor is true. However, for the sake of our necks, we would appreciate you keep that fact to yourself."

Patrick stopped, nodding in Sean's direction. "This is my good friend and," he mocked a whisper, "fellow spy."

Lucas shook Sean's hand with vigor. "Any friend of Paddy is a friend of mine." He slapped Patrick on the back. "Just be cautious or he'll lead ya into a heap of trouble, let me tell ya. Now go get yourselves some victuals and come back up to talk to Peterson. I'll tell him y'all are here."

CHAPTER 15

Abigail hung the last ornament on the tree, a delicate crystal star from the Venetian glass blowers. At least that's what the shop keeper in Louisville had assured her. She wasn't so sure, but the refraction of light from the oil lamps sent a shimmering rainbow of colors around the room.

Abigail closed her eyes and breathed in the profusion of fragrances of the spruce tree before her, the cedar boughs on the mantel and in the centerpiece of the table, and the pine wreaths on each side of the deer's head above the hearth.

Lisette bustled in with a huge tray. "Nary a one of you touch these until our guests arrive. That includes you, Miss Abigail."

Abigail inhaled the added aroma of fresh-baked sugar cookies and hot spiced wassail. "I hardly think anyone would miss just one."

Lisette placed the tray on the side table. "I would, if no one else. I've counted every one." She mumbled to herself as she adjusted the centerpiece, "Of course, 'tis a pity that a few were a bit dis-formed and weren't quite pretty enough to make the tray." She glanced at Abigail. "They're on a plate out in the kitchen."

Abigail stepped back to admire their handiwork.

"William, you made a fantastic choice. Wherever did you find such a perfect tree?"

William adjusted one of the candles. "I spied it up on the ridge above Deer Lake when we drove the herd up to summer pastures. I figured I better cut it this year, 'cause it would be too tall after."

James harrumphed. "I'm still not sure about bringing live trees into the house. Greenery boughs are one thing, but a tree?"

Abigail shook her head. "Really, Father. If it's good enough for Queen Victoria, it certainly should be good enough for us. Why, it looks just like the pictures of Prince Albert's Christmas trees in Godey's Lady's Book. I've had dreams of a tree like this ever since I saw them in Aunt Maud's magazine."

James smiled and nodded. "It is a beautiful sight."

Abigail gently un-wrapped the final decoration. The silver dust glued to the wings of the papier-mâché angel sparkled in the firelight. "Father. Would you put the angel on top?"

Her father sighed as he held the delicate piece of art in his rough hands. "This was the one thing your mother insisted on bringing west with her. Wherever we were at Christmas, her angel had to be there. She would put it on the mantel or in the center of the table. It seems only right that it crown your Christmas tree."

Abigail and William steadied him as he climbed on a dining chair to place the angel at the top of the tree. He stepped carefully back down, then hugged Abigail to him as the four of them stood back to admire their handiwork. Lisette whispered, "I just wish Master Patrick could be here. Christmas was always his favorite holiday."

Their reverie was broken by the jingle of sleigh bells.

***

James clinked his glass with his case knife to quiet the boisterous conversations. He cleared his throat and nodded to the opposite end of the table.

"Francis, it is always our pleasure to welcome you and

Mildred, Edward, Florence and Luke to our table on Christmas eve." He laid his hand on Lisette and Thomas' arms who sat on each side of him and smiled at Abigail and William. "It would not be Christmas at the *MC* without you present. It is, however, regrettable that your Joshua and our Patrick could not be here. Francis, if you would, please say grace so that we might partake of this delicious spread before us."

As Mr. Anderson began his usual lengthy prayer, Abigail glanced around at those seated around the table.

Old Thomas was just as solid as the first day she could remember anything. He had always been there, as far as she was concerned. Yet now, his hair was almost completely white, his shoulders bowed and his hands trembled slightly. Even though he had been a freedman for almost twenty years, he still acted the part of a servant, her father's aide to the day he died.

Father was, well, Father. He was quite handsome; tall and strong. He could be a bit intimidating until you got to know him. For the first time, she noticed some gray streaks in his dark brown hair and in his trimmed beard. She was glad he kept his beard trimmed, unlike Mr. Anderson's full shaggy whiskers.

Lisette was really quite beautiful, especially on a day like today. She had pinned her jet-black hair up like Abigail had shown her following her trip back East. Her hair was a pleasant contrast to the high-necked emerald-green satin dress father had gotten her on his last trip to Santa Fe. No one would ever think her anything but a French lady; that is, until she spoke. She never could or would forsake the sounds of her beloved New Orleans.

William had his mother's laughing eyes and long, dark lashes. It was a good thing for him he had Father's nose, chin and large stature. Abigail blushed when she thought that. No one ever said those words, yet everyone who knew the family thought them. Only William's hair gave indication that Negro blood coursed through his veins.

She could not reason why her heart skipped a beat when she glanced at Edward. Admittedly, he was quite handsome. He would be the pick of every young lady when he entered the room, with his wavy, shoulder-length blond hair, broad shoulders and narrow waist. His muscles bulged in his linen shirt even as his hands were clasped in prayer. He could be a complete gentleman at times, yet she had seen his moods become violent at the slightest provocation. She had witnessed his aggression. That's what scared her.

Luke was a complete contrast to his older brother, which is probably why Edward bullied him unmercifully. He had been ill as a baby, and even now at fifteen was frail and almost effeminate. Abigail hoped he would have the opportunity to go back East to study, for he had little chance to succeed in this rough country.

Abigail had always been a bit afraid of Mr. Anderson. He was loud and gruff, and on more than one occasion she had seen him remove his belt and whip his sons for the slightest infraction. He espoused to be a devoutly religious man, quoting much scripture, but his actions often did not coincide with his speech.

Mrs. Anderson, on the other hand, was truly the mother Abigail had never known; kind and loving and caring. There was no place she felt more safe than cradled in Mrs. Anderson's ample bosom.

And finally, there was Florence. Florence had been born the summer after they had settled in this valley. She was the sister Abigail would never have, her confidante, her dearest friend, and, to Abigail's chagrin, not the sharpest quill in the case.

"Amen"

Everyone gave a sigh of relief.

James resumed the position of host. "If everyone would pass their plates to their left, I will carve the turkey, if Francis, you would do the same with the ham. Then we can pass the remainder of these fine dishes."

He continued. "Edward, am I to understand this fine bird came to us by way of your shotgun sights?"

Edward puffed out his chest. "That would be correct, sir. I shot it in the slough just above where Cedar Creek enters the Arkansas. I got it and two of his friends."

Mrs. Anderson sampled the ham before her. "Thomas, I do so admire the way you cure your pork. Ours always comes out too salty."

Thomas nodded. "I appreciates the compliment, ma'am. I'm thinkin' Miss Lisette has a ham and a large slab of pork belly wrapped up for you to take home with you."

Lisette tapped her fork on her plate. "Thomas, shame on you. That was to be a Christmas gift."

Mrs. Anderson smiled. "No worry. I'll act surprised and be mighty grateful."

James asked no one in particular, "Have you heard from Joshua?"

Mr. Anderson straightened in his chair. "Yes. We received a letter day before yesterday. He's settled nicely into his accommodations in Denver City. I appreciate your introducing him to Mr. Larimar and the governor. I was not impressed with Gilpin, so encouraged him to enlist in Larimar's regiment."

Mrs. Anderson dabbed the corner of her eye with her napkin. "I do miss him at this Christmas time, but both he and Francis felt it important that he serve our country and our new territory. What have you heard from Patrick?"

James finished his bite of turkey before he answered. "We have not heard from Paddy since the fall festival. He had mentioned his plan to go down to Fort Union, as it is of major military importance on the Santa Fe trail. Governor Gilpin also mentioned it is a key supply depot for the rest of the Union forts of the southwest."

Edward scowled across the table at Abigail. "Well, I understand that a bunch of Texas rebels are planning a spring campaign to take over the New Mexico Territory and even come up north into our Colorado. I, for one, plan to join *our* army over in Denver City as soon as the passes open back up.

We need to defend our territory from that rabble from Texas."

Mr. Andrews nodded in agreement. "In my opinion, we never should have made Texas a state. They wanted to be a republic, let 'em be a republic and see how long they last."

As the debate continued around the table, Abigail whispered to Florence. "You've been awfully quiet today. Have you heard from Paddy? I can't believe there's not been a single letter. I just hope he's alright."

Florence pouted. "Not a word. He comes back to see me for two nights and then not a word."

She sniffed and played with her creamed corn with the tines of her fork. "Oh, Abby. I feel just awful, but I've just got to tell you." She turned away. "Oh, you're just going to hate me."

"Florence. I could never hate you. Tell me what?"

"Well, you know if Patrick was here, I'd have eyes for no one but him. But he's not. I don't even know for sure where he is." She continued to play with her food.

Abigail leaned closer and whispered, "And?"

Florence shrugged her shoulders. "And I met this handsome Union soldier when I went with Pa over to Fairplay to get supplies. He's come courting a couple of times and I think I'm beginning to like him. Oh, Abby is that wrong. Am I a..." she looked around and whispered, "a hussy?"

Abigail giggled. "No, you're not a hussy. Besides, Paddy should know you're not gonna wait for him if he doesn't even write. Just be ready with an explanation, if he shows up at your door some morning."

James interrupted their conversation. "Now that we are all as stuffed as this poor bird was, shall we adjourn to the parlor? Luke, I do hope you brought your guitar. I trust the rest of you children are not too grown up to lead us in some Christmas songs?"

Luke tuned his guitar while Thomas added a log to the fire. Starting with "Deck the Halls" they sang through their repertoire of carols, Florence's tender voice on Soprano,

Abigail with her husky alto, William adding a rich baritone and Edward's deep bass, with Luke supplying a high light tenor. They ended with Joseph Mohr's "Silent Night" as Lisette and Mrs. Anderson carefully lit the candles gracing the boughs of the tree. Then Mr. Anderson solemnly read the Christmas story from St. Luke's Gospel.

After a brief silence, Florence giggled. "What are we waiting for? Let's get the gifts."

Soon the packages and boxes were distributed. Florence handed Abigail a package. "I hope you like it."

Abigail tore the paper aside to reveal a gray fox hat and muff. "Florence, these are beautiful."

Florence rushed to explain. "They came from St. Louis. I know you can't wear them when you ride, but…" she leaned forward and whispered, "they can come to good use when Edward comes tomorrow to take you for a sleigh ride. He's already asked Pa."

"Then, yes, they will come to very good use." She looked across the room at Edward, who was blushing from ear to ear.

"Now it's your turn." Abigail handed her a hat box. "I'm not sure where or when you will have the opportunity to wear it, but I couldn't resist it when I saw it in a millinery shop in Lexington."

Florence squealed as she pulled out the little red hat with an ostrich feather stuck in the brim. "Put it on me and let me see how I look." She strutted in front of her brothers and squealed again at her reflection in the hall tree mirror. "I can't wait until spring when I have the chance to walk down Broad Street in Denver City on some man's arm." She put her fingers to her lips. "I can't believe I said that."

"Nor can I," scolded Mrs. Anderson.

Abigail's next package was from Edward. Nestled in the folds of a silk neckerchief was a pair of deerskin gloves. Edward's eyes twinkled. "They're quite soft and lined with rabbit fur to keep your hands warm, say for a sleigh ride on a cold winter's day."

She smiled and replied coyly. "I'm sure they would, should the occasion ever arise."

He blushed again.

Next was a small package from Luke wrapped in oil cloth and tied with twine. Inside was a leather journal with the words *My Thoughts* embossed in gold on the front. Embarrassed, he mumbled, "You pen such pretty words. I hoped you might like to write your thoughts on a daily basis."

"Oh Luke, that's sweet of you to say."

Edward rolled his eyes and mimicked her. "Oh, that's so sweet of you to say," as he punched his brother in the arm.

Abigail scowled at him. "Edward, just for that, you have to go last. Luke, you go next."

Luke carefully unwrapped the large box before him. He beamed as he dug through the folds of newspaper to reveal a leather-bound collection of the plays of Shakespeare. As he opened the cover of *A Midsummer' Night,* he exclaimed, "Abby, these are wonderful."

She smiled. "I'm glad you like them. Father ordered them from New York City months ago. They only arrived last week."

She nodded to William.

He handed her a leather riding crop. "First, here is my gift to you. That's for the next time you find yourself in a race with someone like that scum Grady." He then made quick work of his packages; a new lariat from Abigail, chaps from the Andersons which he promptly put on. Their father had given both he and Abigail leather hats.

Edward looked at Abigail. "May I go, now?" He asked sarcastically.

She nodded. "By all means."

He opened the wooden case which revealed a pearl handled bowie knife. He gently removed it, letting his fingers trace the markings on the handle and along the fine edge of the blade. "Abby, this is beautiful. It's perfectly balanced. Thank you."

She smiled. "You're welcome. I'm glad you like it."

Mr. Anderson stood. "I regret to interrupt such a fine time, but we really must go. It will be after sunset now before we can get back to the ranch. James, thank you for a very pleasant day."

As the Andersons piled into the waiting sleigh, Edward held back, as he had ridden his own horse. He called out to his father, "I will be along shortly."

He led Abigail back inside the house and quietly shut the door. "I have one more gift for you." He handed her a small jewelry box.

Abigail took out a cameo brooch set in black onyx surrounded by gold filigree. "Edward. This is too much. I can't accept this."

"Please. Take it. Let it be my apology for the way I acted at the festival."

Their intimate moment was interrupted by a knock on the door. A courier waited patiently. "I have a letter for Miss Abigail McFerrin."

Puzzled, Abigail replied, "I'm Abigail McFerrin."

"This is a letter from your brother, Patrick. He paid me handsomely to ensure that you should receive it today, Christmas Day, 1861."

She took the letter, calling for Lisette to give the young man some of the leftovers from dinner and a mug of hot wassail. With trembling hands, she broke the seal, revealing a single page with hand-drawn tracery around the edges connecting wreaths at each corner.

Edward waited in the shadows as she began to read.

Dearest Sister,
Happy Christmas to all at MC.
All are well here.
I trust this Warm Message is received in good time.
Wintering at M.H. Not F.U.
Supplies and Information lacking
SM sends his regards.

My Love and Appreciation,
← Patrick →

Abigail gasped as Edward snatched the letter from her. He held her at arms length as he read it, then snarled, "So Paddy really is a rebel. M.H. would be Mace's Hole, an outlaw encampment. And your beloved Sean McKay sends his regards. I just hope I can send my regards his way in the form of a musket ball."

He pushed her away, causing her to stumble over a foot stool. He angrily wadded the letter into a ball and tossed it at the blazing logs in the fireplace. Through gritted teeth he hissed, "Happy Christmas, Miss Abigail." He slammed the door behind him. She could hear him whipping his horse as he galloped down the lane.

Abigail crawled to the hearth, retrieving the letter as the flames began to singe the edges. She was sitting on the floor sobbing when Lisette burst through the door.

"Miss Abigail, what in tarnation is going on in here?"

Abigail handed her the letter while dabbing her eyes with the sleeve of her dress. "I received this from Paddy. Edward grabbed it from me and read it. He was angry, assuming that Paddy is fighting with the Confederates. He was especially upset that Mr. McKay sent his regards."

Lisette smoothed the wrinkled page. "Well, Missy, it would seem that there is more to the message than the message."

Abigail shook her head. "Lisette, I'm in no mood for riddles."

"It's no riddle, but the oldest spy trick in the book."

She held it for Abigail. "See here? It's called invisible ink, easy to make, easy to use. The heat from the fire must have brought it out."

Abigail held the page closer to the fire, and words began to appear as if by magic. Along the tracery on the left of the page, *Need assistance;* across the top, *Joining Sibley in spring;*

down the right side, *Meet me at Peterson's ranch on February 1.* Within the body of the letter was added the words, *Need supplies and horses,* and *Information lacking regarding fortification.*

Abigail chuckled. "Now that I'm aware, Paddy gave plenty of clues...the *warm message,* and the arrows on each side of his name pointing to the edges of the page. However, I don't know that I would have figured it out, had Edward not tossed it at the fire."

Lisette put her arm around Abigail's shoulders. "God works in mysterious ways."

Abigail nodded. After considering for a moment, she asked, "Is the courier still here?"

"Yes'm. He's going to stay the night with William and plans to ride out in the morning."

"Good. I'll have a message to send back with him." Then she added. "Lisette. Let's keep this between us. I'll share the letter with father, but without the added message. He didn't want Paddy to leave, and he certainly won't want me to go."

Lissette looked sternly at Abigail. "Miss Abigail, you certainly are not considering taking these horses and supplies down there yourself, are you. My William, or one of the ranch hands can go."

Abigail bit her lip. "Lisette, you know William can't go riding into a Confederate camp, even with horses and supplies. Besides, Father needs him here to run the ranch. I'll take Running Deer and Little Fox with me. We'll be fine."

Lissette shook her head. "Your father is not going to be happy that you're getting involved with this," she muttered to herself as she left the room.

Abigail thought to herself, *but involved I am. Paddy, what are you getting me into?*

CHAPTER 16

Sean dreaded the prospects of returning to Peterson's ranch. The place made his skin crawl. He hated even more the thought of Abigail there. He reined up beside Patrick. "Are you sure meeting her at Peterson's is a good idea. Could we not have met her at Higgins' Station?"

Patrick shook his head. "Higgins is being watched. Lieutenant Madison thought the ranch would be a safer place."

Sean shivered, but not because of the north wind. "I just don't much care for Peterson or any of his men."

"They're just a bunch of old mountain men who have lost their livelihood and way of life, not unlike the Indian. Besides, four walls and a roof are better than the caves and tents at Mace's Hole."

Sean muttered to himself. "Not much. At least one can get away from the lice and fleas and filthy men at the Hole."

Sean thought back over the months they had spent in Maces Hole since the fall festival and the men they had been training. "What do you think of the recruits we've been training," he asked.

Patrick stroked his beard with his gloved hand. "They're a bit of a motley crew, but we've brought them a long way in a short time." He chuckled. "I wouldn't say any of them are West

Point material, but they'll follow orders and fight well when the time comes."

Sean grimaced. "And will we ever really see battle. Or are we destined to be outlaws and desperados, robbing supply trains and harassing scattered Union boys?

"Oh, I think we'll see action soon enough, at least if Madison has his way. I figure he'll lay out his plan at this meeting at Peterson's. We'll do our part, if Sibley will do his."

Sean took a drink from his canteen. "I like Madison. He's a born, no-nonsense leader with a quick wit and keen insight. I hear he fought in the Mexican War. He couldn't have been more than a kid."

"Yeah, he's done a lot in thirty years. I heard, after the war, he tried his hand in the gold fields of California before settling around Tucson. Even was a deputy sheriff for a time."

Sean added, "Yeah, and the story of his warding off an Apache attack by fortifying his ranch house has already become something of a legend. I sure wouldn't hesitate following him into battle."

They rode on in silence, each lost in their own thoughts. Sean couldn't help but worry about Abigail. Yet they were in desperate need of supplies and fresh horses.

He bit his lower lip. He longed to see her again, yet dread of the encounter lingered in the recesses of his mind. Her message had simply been that she would meet at the appointed time and place. She had not even mentioned his name.

Would she speak to him? Would she look at him? Would she even acknowledge his existence, as tense as their parting had been?

Patrick broke the silence as if he could tell what Sean was thinking. "Don't worry. She'll be happy to see you. Mind you, she will undoubtedly give you the cold shoulder at first, but it will not take long for her to thaw. Just give her a little time and encouragement."

Sean blushed. "Has it been that obvious?

Patrick's laugh echoed from the barren canyon walls.

"You have talked of little else but her comfort and safety since we received her return message." Sarcastically, he added, "Besides, she would not consider leaving the ranch in the middle of winter for just her brother. Now come on, move that nag of yours along. She should be there waiting for us."

Sean had just settled back in his saddle, when the sound of a rifle shot and the ping of the musket ball ricocheting from a boulder ahead of them brought them both to attention. They raised their arms as they pointed their index fingers to the sky, the sign for the "Lone Star State".

Patrick waved his hat to the sentries now visible on the outcropping of rocks on either side of the entrance to the canyon. "Security has definitely been improved since last fall."

"I'm just glad it's them and not me on guard duty," Sean replied. The cold north wind whipped at his coat. He pulled the collar tighter around his neck. "That wind has got more than just a bite to it."

The clouds hung low, shrouding the Greenhorn Mountain peaks and turning the afternoon sun to dusk. Dark billows hovered over Hardscrabble Pass. The pond in front of the ranch house was frozen solid. The gloom of the coming storm was settling over the compound.

Smoke curled up from the fireplace chimneys at each end of the larger center cabin. For the first time, Sean noticed the three small windows under the eave above the porch roof. He assumed they were for light and ventilation in a loft above the main room. He considered investigating that possibility. It would have to be better than the two side cabins which served as bunk houses. Sean wiped his nose in recollection of their previous visit. Each building consisted of one large room lined with bunks. They reeked of stale tobacco, urine, and dirty bodies.

The hulking shape of Peterson filled the doorway to the main cabin as they reined up at the edge of the porch. He nodded. "Howdy, boys. What's the word from Madison?"

Patrick nodded back. "He should be here sometime

tomorrow." He indicated the clouds gathering above them. "That is, providing this storm blows through by then."

Sean reined up beside his friend. "What about the supplies coming down from the *MC*? Have they arrived yet?"

Peterson shook his head. "Not seen anything of 'em yet." Sean gave Patrick a worried look. Peterson continued. "Go get you something to eat and some hot coffee. Then come back here and we'll decide if we need to send out a search party."

They led their horses through a fissure in the canyon wall into the meadow where the workings of Peterson's ranch took place. A cook fire crackled around a large iron pot and licked around a half of calf roasting on a spit. Sean and Patrick each grabbed a tin plate and a coffee cup as snowflakes filtered down through the pines.

CHAPTER 17

Abigail brushed the snow from her coat and chaps. She and the two ranch hands, each leading eight horses loaded with packs leaned into the wind. Zeke and Terrance were good men, devoutly loyal to both her and her father.

The snow flurries which had begun at dusk had blown into a blizzard as the twilight turned into the black of a moonless night. She regretted that she had not made camp as they had suggested. Because of her stubborn nature, she had put them and the mission in jeopardy.

She had told herself it was because she wanted to get to Peterson's because of her brother. She kicked her horse, as much in frustration with herself as to make him continue against the wind. Try as she would to deny it, the desire to see that tall, broad-shouldered man from Missouri was as much her incentive.

Running Deer and Little Fox appeared out of the swirls of white. Running Deer rode beside her. "Must get out of wind. Will get lost in blowing snow. There is opening to canyon ahead. We find shelter and make fire to keep warm."

Abigail tied a rope around her waist and gave the end to Little Fox. She made sure Zeke and Terrance had done the same, then waved the Indian forward.

Slowly they inched along the canyon wall. The wind buffeted from all directions. The blinding, swirling snow encased her in a shroud so that she could not see either the man in front or behind her.

Abigail had never been so cold. Try as she might, she could not keep the blanket wrapped around her. Her feet were frozen in the stirrups and all feeling was gone from her fingers. She shuddered at the memory of a ranch hand two years previous who had lost all his toes and four of his fingers to frost bite.

A cold blast hit her broadside. She struggled to stay in the saddle.

A shout, a whisper, she wasn't sure which, carried in the wind. "Grab my arm!"

She felt her senses leaving her. She was so cold, she no longer cared.

Again the voice. "Hold on. I've got you."

Arms enfolded her, tugging and pulling at her. Was this what it felt like to die? So cold and helpless. She was floating through space. Then all was dark.

***

Sean held her close, wrapping the blanket around her as best he could. Her body was cold and lifeless. There was no way for him to know if she was still breathing. "Please, God, help her be strong. Help her to be…" he swallowed, "OK." He would never forgive himself if anything happened to her because of him.

He gave the reins of her horse to Little Fox and rode beside Running Deer as he led them into camp. A shout brought men to help with the horses and the near frozen men. He handed Abigail down to Lucas and followed them into the warmth of the main cabin.

***

The fog of her mind lifted slightly. Abigail shivered against the warmth of the blazing fireplace. Her hands and feet tingled and burned as Sean and a tall stranger rubbed them in bowls of snow. A huge man with a shaggy beard and wild hair helped her drink some strong warm liquid that burned her throat on its way down, but immediately warmed her gut.

Through the mist she asked, "Are you Saint Nicholas?"

The man bellowed a laugh. "That's got to be the first time anyone's ever mistook me for Santa Claus. No, Missy, the name's Peterson. Welcome back from the frozen tundra of death."

Abigail shook her head in an attempt to clear the cobwebs from her mind. Instead, she felt herself drifting away. But this time, her mind took her to a place where the warmth of the sun cradled her in a bed of wildflowers in the meadow above the ranch house back at the *MC*.

***

Abigail pried her eyes open a slit only to be blinded by the light. Again, she wondered if this was death. She snuggled down into the warmth of the cocoon that enveloped her. At least this death was not frigid cold.

A familiar voice broke into her dream world. "Well, well. Are the two of you gonna sleep away the entire day?"

Abigail bolted awake, shielding her eyes from the sunlight streaming through the small attic windows. "Paddy! Where am I? What am I doing here?"

Her "cocoon" jumped up, cracking his head on a rafter with a groan.

She turned to see Sean in his long-john's kneeling beside her, then realized she was dressed the same. She pulled the buffalo blanket around her. "Mr. Mckay! What is the meaning of this?"

Sean looked sheepishly at Abigail and pleadingly at Patrick. "I meant to be gone before you awoke."

He hurried to further explain. "You were half frozen when we got you here last night. Lucas helped me rub the life back in your hands and feet. I only laid beside you to warm you up. I thought it better here in the attic by the chimney than down amongst the ruffians below." He added with a shrug. "I can assure you, Miss Abigail, uh, McFerrin, that there were no improprieties taken."

Patrick handed each of them a steaming cup of coffee. "Calm down, Sis. Sean saved your life last night. From what Peterson said, he got all of you here in the nick of time."

"Zeke and Terrance, Running Deer and Little Fox are all

OK?"

"They are all fine."

Abigail shook her head. "I should have camped when we saw the storm approaching. I thought we had time, but it was on us in such a hurry."

Patrick nodded. "Storms are like that, here in the foothills and high plains. Many a man has gotten caught just like that."

He continued. "The scouts had reported that y'all were not far. But when you weren't here when the blizzard hit, me and Sean headed out to look for you. We got separated. I'm just mighty grateful to God and to Sean that he found you. I found my way back here just after y'all got settled down. I figured things were pretty well under control."

Abigail finally looked at Sean. "Mr. McKay, uh, Sean, I do owe you a debt of gratitude and an apology." Her tone softened. "Thank you, sir."

Sean bent down and kissed her hand. "It was my pleasure, ma'am. Welcome to Peterson's Ranch. Now, if it's alright with y'all, I'd like to get some clothes on and eat some breakfast. I'm starving."

Patrick stroked the stubble of his beard. "You might want to hurry. Lieutenant Madison should be here by noon."

CHAPTER 18

All conversation ceased as Madison entered the room. Abigail was intrigued by his appearance. He was one of those people that seem larger than life. When he came into the room, he seemed to fill the room with his presence. His hat was cocked at an angle, yet he was not in any way flamboyant. Ramrod, straight back. Unmussed uniform. A gentleman, ready for a joke, yet no-nonsense. He was a man any woman would follow into a party or man into battle.

Abigail followed Madison with her eyes as he took his place at the head of the long table. He nodded and the men resumed their individual conversations.

The warmth of the hot coffee and the blazing fire in the fireplace did little to dispel the cold of the previous day. She wondered if she would ever be warm again.

Was she completely crazy? After risking the lives of her friends, what was she thinking. She was just a woman. How she hated that thought. She watched the camaraderie between Sean and Patrick. She longed for that same friendship, yet she also knew full well that she *was* a woman, and she was proud of that as well.

She looked at the men around the table. These were rough men, desperate men. Experienced in fights and battle. Even though they had, even this morning, treated her with genteel respect, she knew they had and would fight and even kill their enemy without thought. Could she do that? The thought clenched at her gut and caught in her throat. Yet, the excitement, the anticipation in the room was captivating and invigorating.

And why was she here? For Patrick...for Sean...for the cause?

She loved her brother. They were not twins, but she felt that close. Growing up without a mother, they had learned to depend on each other. Yet there had been plenty of times he had made stupid decisions that she would not and could not support.

And Sean? What was there about this stranger that had so suddenly come into her life and become a constant part of her thoughts. As much as she tried to ignore those thoughts, they persisted. And now, he had saved her life.

And then there was Capt. Madison. She knew nothing of him, but what little Sean and Patrick had mentioned – simply the leader of a rebel spy ring – little more than a bunch of outlaws.

As if on cue, he looked her way and nodded before continuing his conversation with the man on his right. He certainly was not without good looks and charm. He would, she supposed, be the epitome of a Texan; not quite six foot; dapper in his well-tailored uniform. His dark brown hair was neatly trimmed, as was his mustache. He was clean shaven except for a triangle of beard under his lower lip, which gave accent to the cleft in his chin. Piercing brown eyes that seemed to dance with laughter, could wash over you with kindness, or bore a hole in you.

And the "Cause"? She had no desire to get caught up on either side of the conflict. Neither side was right. She hated what the Federal government was doing to the Indians. She had seen far too much of their lies and deceit. Yet, just as despicable was the whole matter of slavery. Her trip back east had opened her eyes to that.

Yet, as she observed the banter and camaraderie of the men around the table, she could not deny her envy. She longed to belong to a group like this, to be a part of something bigger than herself. She knew she needed to leave, get on her horse and return to the safety of the ranch without looking back. But something held her. The desire for adventure; the desire for a cause; the desire to belong.

***

Madison passed cigars to the fourteen of his men plus Sean and Patrick lounging around the table. "Gentlemen. Fine Carolina cigars, compliments of our friends in Washington."

Sean glanced at Abigail as Patrick struck a match to light their cigars. She was leaning on the edge of the fireplace, sipping a cup of coffee. Every indication pointed to her disinterest, but Sean could tell she was taking in every word that was being said.

He marveled at her beauty, even in men's clothes. He closed his eyes and imagined that he could still feel her body against his own under the buffalo robe. His heart raced and his body warmed at the thought.

Their eyes met and she smiled. His heart and lower body jolted. He wasn't sure how to deal with his feelings. No woman had ever affected him like this. The fact that he had almost lost her last night grabbed him in the pit of his stomach.

She turned toward the open door and the sun fell full on her face. He looked at her fine features and then around at the rugged faces around the table. She did not belong here. How he wanted to take her away from this place, this time, this conflict.

He laughed to himself and turned away. Take her away? To what and where? He had no home. He didn't even know if he had any family left. Probably not after this war.

No, she deserved more than he could ever give her. He turned to Patrick. "You know, she does not belong here. This is no place for a lady."

Patrick glanced at his sister. "I agree. Since the storm has passed, I have instructed Zeke and Terrance to get things ready for the trip back to the ranch. They need to leave at daybreak tomorrow."

They turned their attention to Madison as he began to speak.

Madison took a long drag from his cigar and blew a series of rings into the air. "Gentlemen, things are heatin' up. All those politicians on both sides of this skirmish who thought this conflict would be over in a matter of days were sadly mistaken. It's only just begun."

He indicated the man next to him. "The good news is that Lawrence here and a half a dozen of you good men intercepted the stage bound for Fort Garland. The cigars y'all are puffin' on, plus the mail and a month's payroll, were lifted off that stage."

A raucous cheer and applause erupted around the room.

Madison continued. "The bad news is that a company of Union soldiers came down from Fort Lyon and attacked our camp at Mace's Hole. They captured forty of our young recruits and hauled them off to Denver City."

The cheers turned to groans. Sean leaned into Patrick. "At least, the two dozen recruits we've been training for the past three months had already headed south." Patrick nodded his agreement.

"With the loss of that camp and the supplies there-in, we are especially appreciative of Miss Abigail McFerrin, who risked life and limb, and if I understand correctly, near frozen appendages, to bring us much needed supplies and a couple dozen fresh horses." He raised his coffee cup. "Miss McFerrin, we salute you."

Abigail blushed as she acknowledged their raised glasses and cups.

Madison took another drag on his cigar. "Now for the business at hand. As some of you already are aware, General Henry Sibley has proposed a New Mexican campaign to President Davis and subsequently won approval. He has amassed a sizable force of Texas Rangers and New Mexican volunteers to sweep up the Rio Grande valley, take Fort Craig, Albuquerque and Santa Fe for the Confederacy, with the intent of taking Fort Union."

He took a drag from his cigar. "With Fort Union under Confederate jurisdiction, we could control all Union supplies to their troops in the Southwest. It would also give us a foothold to further campaigns into the gold fields of Colorado and California. From there, we would have the opportunity to open the California ports to the Confederate cause. Even as I speak, Sibley has begun his march from Fort Thorne toward Fort Craig."

He tapped his cigar on the edge of the table to knock off the ashes. "We will leave here at daybreak tomorrow. Skirting Walensburg, we'll go over Cordova Pass to gather our troops outside Trinidad. Our objective is to meet up with Sibley in Santa Fe by early March."

Madison reclined back in his chair, tapping his finger on the table as he seemed to collect his thoughts. He leaned forward as he looked around the table at his men. "I had desired an attack on Fort Garland with the purpose of gaining additional supplies prior to our march on Santa Fe. With the capture of our recruits at Mace's Hole, that is out of the question. However, there is one objective that is of great importance."

He cleared his throat before he continued. "We are lacking any substantial information regarding the fortifications and number of troops at Fort Union. It is imperative that we have that information once we join forces in Santa Fe and cross over Glorietta Pass."

A tense silence filled the room as the men looked at each other and then down at the table. Lucas uttered what all of them had been thinking. "Any of us going into fort Union would likely be walking into a fox's snare."

The crackling of the fire was the only sound in the room.

Madison once again leaned forward. "Gentlemen, are we not called the 'Santa Fe Gamblers and the 'Forty Thieves'? Has no one an idea?"

From the back of the room came a soft voice. "Could not a lady in petticoats infiltrate any man's lair?"

Sean and Patrick exclaimed in unison. "Abigail. No!"

CHAPTER 19

After a stunned silence, the room erupted into animated conversations. Sean and Patrick rushed to Abigail as Madison looked on.

Patrick took his sister's arm. "Abby, you're not really considering this, are you? I absolutely forbid it. Your place is back with Father and the safety of the ranch."

Sean added, "Abigail, only yesterday you almost died bringing us horses and supplies. That's enough."

Abigail smiled at both of them, then turned to her brother. "I only asked the question to consider the possibility."

She rested her hand on Sean's arm, but looked directly at Madison. She raised her voice so as to be heard above the others. "Yet, I will pose the question again. Could not a lady be accepted where it might be difficult for a man?" All conversations ceased and everyone's eyes shifted to Madison.

Madison took a long draw from his cigar, watching the smoke curl toward the rafters. He looked over at Abigail as he stroked his beard. When he spoke, it was authoritative, yet thoughtful. "Miss McFerrin, we do greatly appreciate your delivery of horses and supplies. That act certainly did not come without a good amount of risk."

He looked at Sean, then at Patrick. "However, I do

question your understanding of the perils and dangers that are embodied in your proposal. Spies are imprisoned at best and shot or hung at worst. I would hesitate to send any of my men, as brave as they are," he paused as he looked around the room and nodded toward Sean and Patrick, "including your brother and Mr. McKay, on such a mission. I cannot and will not ask this of you."

Sean looked pleadingly at Patrick as Abigail moved away from them. Patrick whispered through clenched teeth, "Abigail, don't."

She ignored them as she stepped to the end of the table opposite Madison. With quiet determination, she directed her comments to Madison as if there were no others in the room. "Sir, I do appreciate your concern. However, this occasion, should we agree to its feasibility, would not be the first or the last when a woman has come to the aid of a cause."

Madison took a long drag from his cigar. Slowly he blew out the smoke. He tapped his finger on the table in front of him. "It is true. Many a woman has aided a cause." He hesitated, then continued. "In the Holy Scriptures, Rahab of Jericho hid the Israelite spies, and Deborah, the Judge led an army into battle. Even in our more modern times, our own George Washington used women as spies during the Revolutionary War."

Madison looked at Patrick and then back at Abigail. "I will again remind you of the dangers involved. Are you of a certainty this is your desire?" He hesitated, then added, "And, then, I would ask, why?"

Abigail looked at the men around the table. She took a deep breath and let it out slowly before she began. "Sir, I am a Coloradan. I am neither a Unionist nor a Confederate. My family has strong roots in the South, but I find slavery despicable. Yet the Federal government would 'civilize' this great western land, which means they wish to rape and plunder it."

She cleared her throat. She smiled at Patrick before she continued. "My brother has pledged his support to his good friend and to you and the rebel cause. I wish to do the same. If I can be of service, that is my wish."

Madison pushed his chair back away from the table. Thoughtfully, he stood, turning his back to the group as he stared into the blazing logs in the fireplace. There was no sound in the room save for the popping and crackling of the fire.

Slowly, he turned, placing his palms on the table. He looked directly at Abigail. In an almost fatherly voice, he again asked, "Are you positive this is what you want to do?

Abigail swallowed and nodded. "If I can be of service, that is my desire."

Madison smiled and nodded to her. "Very well said." He straightened up as he dropped his cigar butt on the floor and ground it under his boot. He sat down and looked around the table at his men. Gesturing with his fingers, he said, "Gentlemen, make a place for the newest member of the 'Forty Thieves'."

Sean's heart sank. He gasped and Patrick muttered a curse under his breath. They hovered over her like mother hens. Abigail ignored them. She sat in the proffered chair, her attention on Madison.

Madison stood, pacing as he stroked his trimmed beard. Sean watched him closely. In the short time he had known this man, he had come to respect his quick wit, sharp reasoning, and intuitive leadership. Sean had no qualms of following him into battle. But this involved Abigail. This was different. He waited, almost afraid to breathe.

Madison turned abruptly. He leaned on the table with both hands. He looked directly at Abigail. He asked softly, "Miss McFerrin, again I ask, are you certain you wish to become involved with this endeavor?"

Sean whispered over her shoulder, "Abigail, please say no."

Abigail folded her hands on the table in front of her. She looked directly back at Madison. "Yes, sir, I am certain."

Madison took a deep breath, smiled and shook his head.

"Well, we are not known as the Santa Fe Gamblers for nothing."

He looked at Patrick, then at Sean before he continued. "Very well. Miss McFerrin." For the next few weeks, you are Miss Lora Dartmouth from St. Louis. You are on your way to visit your grandfather, Harold Dartmouth, the proprietor of the mercantile in Santa Fe and co-owner of the El Farol Cantina."

He turned to an old Mexican on his left. "Miguel, you will take Patrick with you to visit your family in Taos. Then get on down to Santa Fe to let Dartmouth know that his 'granddaughter' is coming for a visit. You will remain there until Miss McFerrin, alias Miss Lora, arrives."

He nodded to a slender man with a handle-bar moustache and spectacles. "Tobias, you're the only Northerner in this bunch. You have two days to make the new Miss Lora Dartmouth a Northern lady abolitionist." He paused and rubbed his temples as he smiled at Abigail, "And do what you can to help her lose that southern accent."

That comment brought a round of laughter from the men.

He continued. "Once Tobias thinks Miss Lora is ready, Lucas and Sean, you will take her back up to Pueblo."

Madison ignored Sean's startled look. "You will take her to a house on High Street. It's a house of 'ladies of the night' run by Miss Lenore Abernathy, a good friend of mine."

He disregarded the chuckles of the men and spoke directly to Abigail. "She will outfit you with any attire you will need for your trip. Ensure she also equips you with a derringer and concealed holster."

He then nodded to Sean. "And lastly, Mr. McKay, while you are in Pueblo, you will outfit yourself in apparel befitting an Eastern lawyer. In Pueblo, that could pose a conundrum, but do what you can. You will be escorting Miss Lora on the stage to Santa Fe with letters and contracts for Mr. Dartmouth to sign, with a stopover at Fort Union."

He folded his hands and gazed intently at Abigail.

"Miss McFerrin, does this seem to be a feasible and

acceptable plan?"

Abigail smiled. In her best southern drawl she said, "Why, suh, it would seem to be delightful." Then changing her demeanor completely, she added in the most refined manner she could summon, "Miss Lora Dartmouth is at your service. It is with great pleasure that I bring greetings from our brave Union supporters in St. Louis."

Madison smiled and nodded. "Then we have our assignments. Mr. McKay, please remain for a moment. The rest of you are dismissed."

Abigail touched Sean's arm as she passed to join a quite unhappy Patrick at the door. With trepidation, Sean took a seat on Madison's right.

Madison offered Sean another cigar and struck a match to light it. As the last of the men exited the room, he cleared his throat and began.

"You do not agree with my decision?"

Sean contemplated his answer. "Abigail is a strong young woman. That is my concern, for she is quite young and rather impetuous. She favors adventure, but I fear that she has no idea the danger for which she has volunteered."

"You care for her, do you not?"

Sean felt the heat of a blush rush to his face "That I do."

Madison chuckled. "That fact is rather evident, which is why I desire that you accompany her. I need someone to watch out for her, to protect her if the need should arise. I could have sent Patrick, but they look too much alike, and he would have the tendency to be over protective. I could have sent a stranger, but I need for her to feel comfortable. That left you.

"However, you must not show your attraction to her, at least not to the rest of the world. Let her appear to be the strong one, you the weak. You are her lackey, not her protector."

"Lackey! I'm to be her lackey?"

Madison laughed. "Okay, perhaps not lackey, but the dutiful servant of her grandfather with no interest in her personally. Be there for her if she needs you, but don't get in her way."

Not without apprehension, Sean nodded. "I understand."

CHAPTER 20

The gray February day matched Sean's mood perfectly. He mumbled a curse as the first flakes of snow swirled out of the low clouds. He picked his way around the muddy quagmire that was the main street of Pueblo.

Lackey, indeed. The terminology still grated on Sean's nerves. How was he supposed to protect her if no one was aware that he was there to protect her?

A bell tinkled above the door to announce Sean's entrance into the only tailor shop in town. A spindly man with a nose much too long for his face was unpacking a bowler from a wooden crate. A small oriental lady was bent over a treadle sewing machine in a back corner.

The man bowed slightly. In a squeaky voice that reminded Sean of a mouse in a trap, he said, "Welcome to Tyler's Tailor shop. Is there something for which I might help you?"

Sean fought the strong urge to laugh. The man not only looked like a mouse, but sounded like one too. Instead, a plan began to take shape in his mind.

"Yes, I believe you might. May I see that hat you just unpacked?"

Sean modeled the hat in the mirror and liked what he saw.

The reflection in the mirror was the beginning of the transformation from a cowboy to an eastern businessman.

Sean decided it was time for him to try out his new identity and character. "Kind sir, my name is Zebadiah Donner. I am in need of a suit for an upcoming business trip; something conservative and unassuming, if you will."

Tyler laid his finger beside his long nose. "Six foot two, I would say?"

"Three. Good estimate."

As Tyler walked around him, Sean felt a bit like a horse at an auction. He considered asking if the strange man wanted to see his teeth, but thought better of if, for fear he would say yes.

Tyler stepped back. "I believe I have just the suit for you, one we tailored for a businessman a few weeks back. Not sure what business he was in. Got shot at the poker table over at Willie's before he come to get it."

Tyler went to the back room and reappeared with a dark brown frock coat with striped trousers and maroon silk waist coat. He held it up to Sean and nodded. This should do, with a few minor alterations."

Sean was pleased. "That should do fine, except for the waist coat. Might you have something a bit less flashy? I have no desire to bring attention to myself."

Tyler brought out one a bit lighter in color, a high collar shirt and tie, with the promise that all would be ready by the end of the day.

Sean was pleased as he picked his way across the muddy thoroughfare to the barber shop for a shave and a trim of his heavy black mane into that of a clean-cut businessman. He hoped to find a pair of spectacles at Doc Greeley's next door to finish out his new persona.

***

Lucas guided Abigail around puddles of muddy water down a side street of Pueblo. She brushed a snowflake from her nose. She pulled the collar of the wool coat closer around her neck against the cold wind. Apprehension and doubt tugged at her mind as she struggled to keep up with Lucas.

At the end of the street, a two-story clapboard house stood out from the adobe buildings, log cabins and tents that lined the street. It was, by far, the gem of the bustling mining town.

He led her up the steps of the sweeping front porch and rang the ornate bell in the center of the large center door. Moments later, that doorway was filled with the hulking body of a huge black man. Bulging biceps strained his white shirt and tapered waist coat.

Lucas nodded and asked, "Is Miss Lenore in?

The man replied in a deep, bass voice that reminded Abigail of thunder from a distant mountain pass, "Miss Lenore does not accept guests from two until five in the afternoon on week days. You may return after the dinner hour, if you wish." With no further adieu, he started to close the door.

Lucas interrupted him. "Please sir. We have a letter from Lieutenant Madison for Miss Lenore."

He frowned and hesitated. Then, with an air of reluctance, he stepped aside and motioned for them to enter.

Abigail had heard of bordellos, but had certainly never been inside one. She had expected something gaudy. To her surprise, it was as if she had stepped into the foyer of one of the fine homes of Charleston.

The curve in the mahogany stairway blocked her view of the upper hall. A door below the stairs opened into a hallway leading to the interior of the house. She peeked through the open pocket doors into the drawing room which was tastefully appointed. A harpsichord with an inlaid top was centered in an alcove with brocade curtains at the windows. On each side was a carved rosewood settee with matching parlor chairs.

The rustle of taffeta announced a woman's entrance from the interior of the drawing room. The black man stepped back and bowed slightly. "Gentlemen...Miss Lenore Abernathy."

Abigail was entranced by the lady's beauty and demeanor. Miss Lenore was about Abigail's height and stature.

She carried herself in a regal way, more like a duchess rather than a madam. Her dark brown curls were pulled back and held in place by combs studded with pearls. Her complexion matched the purity of the jewels.

The cut of the dark blue dress accented her trim waist. White lace outlined the plunging neckline that converged at a large cameo brooch nestled in the cleavage of her ample bosom.

She smiled as she entered. "A letter from George...pardon me, Lieutenant Madison?" She took the letter from Lucas and nodded to the black man. "Thank you, Francis. These men are friends of Mr. Madison, so they are friends of the house."

He nodded. As he ducked through the lower hallway door, Abigail was sure he flexed his muscles as a warning to her and Lucas.

Miss Lenore chuckled. "You must forgive Francis. He has been my bodyguard for as long as I have been in business. He also ensures that no one gets too rowdy, shall we say, during business hours."

Miss Lenore unfolded and began to read the letter from Madison. Abigail turned and was shocked at the image she saw in the mirror of the hall tree beside the front door. Even Lisette would not recognize her, with her hair tucked into the hat pulled down over her eyes. Baggy trousers and a long coat completely disguised her gender. What would Miss Lenore think when she found out that she was not a man? From the image before her, how could anyone transform her into a lady?

Abigail did not have long to wait. Miss Lenore looked up from the pages and smiled. "So, Miss Lora Dartmouth, you need some ladies' apparel? When you came in, I thought you were much too pretty a lad to be coming here for business." She chuckled, "However, my younger girls will be disappointed."

Abigail blushed and stared at the floor.

She continued, "And Lucas. I much appreciate your delivery of the Lieutenant's letter. May I offer you a courtesy of the house?"

Lucas stuttered. "I thank you, ma'am, for the offer. But I was instructed to return immediately upon delivery of the letter..." he grimaced as he looked at Abigail, "...and the package."

Miss Lenore nodded. "That is all well and good. However, do go around to the back door. I will have Nora, my cook, put together some food to take with you for your return trip."

Lucas nodded to Abigail and wished her luck before slipping out the front door. The older woman's tone softened. "Now, don't fret, girl. I'm sure we can supply your needs."

She looked to the top of the stairs and raised her voice. "You can come out now, girls. The lad's a girl and needs our assistance."

Seemingly from every corner of the house, girls appeared, seven in all.

"Girls, I'd like to introduce Miss Lora Dartmouth. She's a friend of Lieutenant Madison. Alice, you remember Mr. Madison, do you not?"

One of the older girls at the top of the stairs giggled. "I surely do. The nicest of gentlemen, and quite generous, if I recall."

Miss Lenore nodded. "Miss Dartmouth needs some traveling clothes." She smiled at Abigail and then back to the girls, "A lady's traveling clothes, that is – from corsets to bonnets and everything in between." She glanced back at the letter. "Tomorrow, she will be taking the stage to Santa Fe, with a stop at Fort Union."

She seemed to be checking off a list in her mind. "She'll need a traveling dress, cape and bonnet, with accessories. Keep the hoops to a minimum. There's not all that much room on a stagecoach. She will also need at least one, possibly two day dresses and one evening gown, nothing too risqué. She's a 'respectable' lady, you understand."

The girls giggled at the inside joke.

"We haven't much time. Let's see what we can come up

with. Use my room to gather her things."

Miss Lenore stopped Abigail as she passed her on the way up to join the girls. "And for you, my dear, we shall start with a hot bath." she whispered to Abigail. "I mean no offence, but you smell far more like a horse that's been smoking cigars than a lady."

Abigail took off the hat and shook out her hair. "No offence taken. I can assure you, a bath will be most appreciated."

***

Clothes and accessories covered Miss Lenore's bed and settee by the time the sun shone low through the western windows. Abigail felt like a china doll being dressed, undressed and dressed again by school girls on holiday. She had been apprehensive at first, but everyone had been extremely nice. She was not sure whether it was the novelty of the situation or Madison's reputation, but she appreciated the attention and assistance.

All was packed into trunks, except for the things necessary for the coming morning. The girls scattered as the bell for the evening meal sounded, leaving her alone with Miss Lenore.

Abigail stared at her reflection in the full-length mirror. The dark green traveling dress fit perfectly. The high neck and the cuffs of the long, puffed sleeves were trimmed with off-white lace. Matching buttons graced the front of the blouse from throat to waist. A brown cape and bonnet with a dove's feather lay on the settee along with gloves and a purse.

Miss Lenore adjusted the comb in Abigail's curls. "This has been quite a transformation from the young boy who entered my door this morning. You are a very pretty young lady."

Abigail turned to face her. "How can I ever thank you and your girls?"

"My dear, it has been our pleasure – a nice distraction

from our mundane existence on a cold winter's day." She lowered her voice and glanced to ensure the door was closed. "Anything for the cause. I am not privy to your plans, nor do I wish to be. However, I would suspect there is some danger involved. Do be careful."

She pulled a key from the depths of her bosom. Unlocking a drawer in the desk, she produced a derringer in a small holster along with a small case of cartridges. "With that thought in mind, slip this in the hidden pocket of your purse. With luck, you will not need it, but it will be there in case you do."

In an instant, her demeanor changed and she was all business. "Now, if you will excuse me, I must get the girls ready for the evening. I will send one of them up with a tray. I think it best for you to remain out of sight. Word of a lady of your good looks would spread like a prairie fire in this town."

Abigail thanked her once again, and the matron was gone. Shortly, April brought her a tray with a bowl of stew, hot cornbread and a decanter of wine. Then she was alone with her thoughts.

She shook her head in wonder. Only four days past, she was freezing in a snow storm. Tonight she is sleeping in the bedroom of a madam in a bordello.

She ran her fingertips along the filigree edge of the silver tray. Four days past, she would not have been caught dead in a house of ill repute, let alone have a conversation with one of *those* women. Today she called them friends and was wearing their clothes.

Four days past, she had awakened in the warm arms of a man she hardly knew. Tomorrow she would embark on what could be a dangerous adventure with that same man.

She was unsure whether the excitement she was feeling within her was from the thoughts of being with Sean, the anticipation of their mission, or the strong wine. The one thing she was sure of, however, was no dime novel from New York City could compare with her present reality.

A tap on her door startled her from her reverie. A folded note had been slipped under the door. When she cracked open the door, the hallway was empty.

She broke the seal and read the short, cryptic message.

Stage leaves at 8:00 in the morning.
Meet Mr. Zebadiah Donner in lobby at 7:00 sharp.
S. M.
Burn this after reading.

Abigail read and reread the note several times. The reality of it all came crashing down on her. She was meeting a stage in the morning to spy on the enemy. What had she been thinking when she volunteered for this mission? Suddenly she wished she was on her way back with Zeke and Terrance to the safety of the ranch.

And who was Zebadiah Donner? And why was she meeting him instead of Sean?

She read the note one last time. With trembling hands, she touched the edge of the note to the flame, then watched it turn to ash in the fireplace.

***

Abigail wished she felt more alert, but she had gotten little sleep. All night, her imagination would not allow her to ignore the unfamiliar noises of a brothel. That, and the thoughts of the dangers of the impending adventure had caused sleep to remain elusive.

From the top of the winding stairs, she observed a man in a brown frock coat standing in the doorway to the drawing room speaking softly to Miss Lenore. His back was to the stairway, but he somehow looked familiar. However, she could think of no one she knew with close-cropped hair and who wore spectacles.

As she reached the bottom step, Miss Lenore caught her eye. "My dear, I do hope you were able to rest. You have a long grueling trip ahead of you." She touched the man's arm. "Mr. Donner is here to escort you to the stage. Francis took your trunks earlier this morning."

Abigail gasped as the man turned to face her. "S...!" He interrupted her before she could utter his name. "Miss Lora, we should be going. I've heard the stage waits for no one."

Miss Lenore took them each by the arm and steered them toward the door to the left of the stairway. "I apologize for showing you out the back door. There are few citizens out this early, but we do not want anyone to see you exiting my humble abode."

She handed each of them a covered basket. "Nora has prepared a little something for your journey. Now, you really must leave or you will be late."

As an afterthought, she added. "By the way, when you next see Lieutenant Madison, give him my regards. Please inform him, when he comes to see me again, he will need to come to Denver City. I'm moving the girls to a new house on River Street. What with the new territorial government and this silly war, the move is my only economic option."

Abigail hugged her neck and Sean made much ado of gallantly kissing her hand. "Our most humble and heartfelt gratitude for your hospitality," he said.

She winked at him. "You, sir, are certainly welcome at any time. Now, go."

As they skirted the out buildings and entered High Street a block south, Abigail questioned him. "Just what did you mean by 'her hospitality'? Did you spend the night there? Did you spend the night alone, or with...?"

He gave her a side-long glance as he guided her around a puddle. "I was in the room next to yours, and yes I was quite alone. Were you?"

"Sean McKay, how dare you even ask such a question."

He stopped mid-stride and was suddenly quite serious. He looked around and then whispered through clenched teeth. "Miss Dartmouth, the name is Zebadiah Donner. Do not let that

slip again. Our lives very well may depend on it."
They continued to Higgins' Station in silence.

CHAPTER 21

The incessant rocking of the Concord stagecoach came to a shuddering stop. The driver called out, "Ten minutes. Ten minute stop while we change teams. Ten minutes, no more, no less."

Sean stepped down and in turn helped Abigail descend the steps of the swaying conveyance. As their fellow travelers looked for a bush large enough to shield them as they relieved themselves, Sean filled their canteens from the well and brought a cup of water for Abigail.

"Miss Dartmouth, I do hope the journey has not been too strenuous."

Abigail stretched her back and rolled her shoulders. "I have heard much of the rocking motion of the Concord stagecoach. Aunt Martha, after riding from St. Louis to St. Charles, compared it to an infant's cradle. If that be the case, I shall never rock a baby in a cradle again."

Sean nodded. "The first ten minutes were quite tolerable. After that, I felt as though I were on a ship in the middle of the Atlantic."

Abigail continued, "And I don't wish to be one to complain, but the accommodations both in Walensburg and Trinidad left a bit to be desired."

Hennessey, the old grizzled driver of unintelligible age looked up as he hitched the last of the new team of horses to the coach. "Missy, I'm afeared you won't see much better at Fort Union. Last time I was there, the bedbugs outnumbered the soldiers at least a hundred to one."

Sean immediately wanted to scratch in all the wrong places.

Captain Wallace spoke up as he strode around the back of the carriage, followed closely by his young lieutenant. "That should not be true by this time. The new fort should be completed by now."

Phelps, Hennessey's guard, looked down from the roof of the coach where he had been checking the straps holding the trunks and mail bags. "New fort? Since when? I was just at Fort Union not mor'n a year ago."

Captain Wallace answered, "Colonel Canby ordered it this past summer after the rumors of invasion by the Texas rabble. He deemed the old fort indefensible and wanted a new fort, a fieldwork, in its stead."

Hennessey interrupted the conversation. "Ten minute's up. All aboard."

Sean helped Abigail up the step and settled himself across from her as the remainder of the passengers climbed on board. Sean thought it interesting how quickly a person can learn other's stories when trapped knee to knee and shoulder to shoulder for hours on end.

Jesse Turner, the rancher's son, settled down beside Sean. He was a thin lad with big hands and big feet. Sean figured him to be about fourteen or fifteen. According to him, his folks had come out to Taos in '58. He had stayed back in Ohio to help his grandfather. When the old man passed away, the boy headed out to join his folks.

Next to him was James O'Connell. His older cousin, Ezekiel was riding up on top with the baggage. Sean hadn't heard Ezekiel say much, but James liked to talk, especially about the green hills of bonny Ireland. When asked why he left, he had answered, "Tis better for ye to take yer chances in this here land o' plenty, than starve to death over thar. Then we heard of gold in California, so me and 'Zekiel just kept headin' west."

Sean had asked him why California and not Colorado. His answer, "Tis warm in California and I hear tell sun always shines. I'm tired o' bein' cold." Sean agreed that wasn't a bad thing.

The young Lieutenant settled beside Abigail, trying his best to be polite and proper so as not to fall on her as the stage jolted to a start. Captain Wallace barely got his girth in the door as Hennessey snapped the whip over the teams' heads.

Sean had been concerned when Lieutenant Wilson and Captain Wallace joined them in Trinidad that morning. Now, he thanked the fates, or God, or whomever for sending them at this time and in this place. Already from the conversation just previous, he had gained new and valuable information.

He gazed at Abigail as she stared vacantly upon the passing scenery. She had been noticeably quiet the entire trip. He had wanted to apologize for his harshness that first morning, but there had been no opportunity to talk privately. The concern that she would be able to carry off this charade weighed heavy on his mind.

Sean glanced up and caught Lieutenant Wilson looking at him. Sean had the feeling that he should know him, but try as he would, he could not place him.

Wilson looked away, then turned back and asked. "Mr. Donner, you look quite familiar. Did you perhaps go to West Point?"

Sean willed himself to not look at Abigail as he heard her gasp. *Of course, West Point, Travis Wilson had been in the Engineer Corp two years ahead of him.*

Sean forced a laugh. "No, I can assure you I've never been to West Point. However, you may have known my brother, William. He graduated a couple of years ago. We look somewhat alike, but Pa always said that he was the fighter and I was the pencil pusher."

Wilson nodded. "That's more than likely the case. I don't remember the name, but I do seem to place him in the class behind of me. He was a good marksman, as I recall."

Sean thought this would be a good time to change subjects. "You spoke of a 'fieldwork' fort. I am not familiar with that term."

Lieutenant Wilson's face brightened, anxious to share his knowledge. "A fieldwork is an earthen fortress which can be built fairly quickly, usually on the field of battle. In the case of Fort Union, the original fort had no true fortifications, being a supply depository rather than a military presence. Yet it is of extreme importance in distribution of supplies to all the other military forts throughout the rest of the Southwest."

As an afterthought, he added, "As a man of numbers, I believe you will be quite impressed with the engineering feat of what many civilians as yourself would call a Star Fort."

Captain Wallace leaned forward. Coldly, he said, "Lieutenant, I'm sure you've bored this gentleman quite enough."

He addressed Sean. "Mr. Donner, I am curious why you and such a lovely lady would be traveling in these parts at such a dangerous time."

Sean slowly removed his spectacles and cleaned the lenses on the ruffle of his shirt sleeve. He returned them to his nose and proceeded to look over them as he answered.

"Sir, you have every right to question our intentions, as it would seem quite unusual for a journey at this time, as you have said." He glanced at Abigail. "Had we any idea of the enormity of the situation here in this wild country, we would not have left the safety of St. Louis."

Absentmindedly, he brushed his fingers along the top of the leather case. "However, Mr. Dartmouth, my employer, had need of my assistance in Santa Fe. I am carrying several important letters and contracts. Against my wishes and judgment, Miss Dartmouth wished to accompany me in order to see her grandfather."

Abigail sat up, touching her fingers to her lips. "Captain Wallace, I so appreciate your concern. Yet, with all the tales of Indians and now this unfortunate disagreement with our Southern states, I have seen no problems. And regarding this insurrection, surely God cannot side with those who would force other humans to be their slaves." She shrugged her shoulders. "Besides, Santa Fe seems a far distance from Georgia and Virginia."

Wallace sat back in his seat. "Well said, Miss Dartmouth. I only wish I had your confidence in our Union forces and the weakness of the enemy cause."

Sean smiled. Looking directly at Wallace he said, "Regarding my interest in Fort Union, I am a spy."

Abigail gasped, Wilson sat erect, Jesse snorted in his sleep, James snickered and Wallace's hand instinctively dropped to his sidearm.

Sean continued as if nothing was unusual. "You see, Spiegelberg and Brothers out of Santa Fe have the sutler's contract at Fort Union. The Spiegelbergs are competitors of Mr. Dartmouth. Now, it seems that there might be some ill feelings between William Moore, who is in charge of the post sutler, who supplies goods for the soldiers, and Major Paul, the fort commander. Part of my mission is to investigate the possibility of Mr. Dartmouth obtaining that contract away from the Spiegelbergs."

Everyone relaxed. Wallace shook his head at Sean. "Sir, please do not use the word 'spy' during a time of war."

Sean put his hand on his chest. "Sir, I do apologize. I did not consider my choice of words."

"No apology necessary. When we arrive at the fort, I will speak with the quartermaster, Captain Granger. He may be of assistance to you."

Sean leaned back in his seat and winked at Abigail. She rolled her eyes and turned toward the window, but a quick smile teased the corners of her mouth.

Chapter 22

The bite of a northwesterly breeze kicked up swirls of dust between the patches of prairie grass and sage brush. Abigail wrapped her cloak more tightly around her shoulders as she gazed through the open coach window at the arid landscape. This windswept land had little in common with her valley above the Arkansas.

For a moment, she allowed her mind to take her back. She wondered if Zeke and Terrance, Running Deer and Little Fox had gotten back to the ranch safely. She also worried about her father and his concerns for her as well as for Patrick. She shook her head, trying to force herself to concentrate on the mission that lay before her.

The winter sun had several hours ago begun its descent and even now had begun to fill the western sky above the snow-capped peaks of the Sangre de Christo Mountains with hues of purple and red. Her travel-weary body was startled to attention by the guard's trumpet blast announcing their arrival.

Fort Union was abuzz with activity as the stage swayed to a stop in front of the sutler's cabin just outside the main gate to the fort. From what Abigail could see, it was the proverbial ant hill, as men worked on the embankments and a steady stream of horses, mules, men and wagons took their turns entering and leaving the entrance to the fort.

From her perspective, it looked more like a mound of dirt or major mole run rather than a fort. The sloping sides were surrounded on the entire perimeter with a wide ditch. It reminded her of the paintings of medieval castles encircled by a moat. It certainly had none of the clean lines of the Adobe structure at Fort Bent.

As Sean helped her to the ground, a young officer appeared. "Miss Dartmouth and Mr. Donner?"

Abigail nodded.

"I am Lieutenant Donavan. Major Paul had received word that you would be arriving today. Duties have kept him from meeting you himself, so he has sent me to do the honors." He addressed Abigail. "Mrs. Paul has requested you spend the night in their guest chamber."

Turning to Sean he added. "They are planning a dinner this evening for the two of you and Captain Wallace and Lieutenant Wilson. With all the unrest and rumors at present, we don't get many civilian visitors. Mrs. Paul is looking forward to the opportunity to entertain."

He added, "Mr. Donner, we should be able to find you a bunk in the non-commissioned officers' barracks. I trust that will be sufficient."

Sean nodded as he claimed his satchel and saw to Abigail's trunks.

She touched his arm. Briefly their eyes met. Sean whispered, "Are you ready for this?"

She smiled. "The time has come." She only wished she felt as confident as she sounded.

Lieutenant Donavan turned to a young man standing to one side. "Private Dorsey, take Miss Dartmouth to the Major's quarters. Gentlemen, if you will follow me?"

Sean gave her one last backwards glance as he turned to accompany the other men.

The young private helped Abigail climb to the seat of a buckboard. This gave her the opportunity to observe more clearly her surroundings as he adjusted her baggage in the back of the wagon.

This "new" fort was really nothing more than an earthen berm with several angles or points, surrounded by a wide ditch. It had been laid out in the flat valley not far from Wolf Creek, a sufficient distance from the two mesas on either side. The sutler's store and what Abigail assumed to be a warehouse were a short distance on the road leading away from the fort. Rows of tents filled the flat between the fort and the creek.

The private explained the situation as he released the brake of the wagon. "The Major's home as well as the Quartermaster, Captain Granger, and his wife's home are still back at the old fort."

Puzzled, Abigail asked, "Why the necessity for a new fort?"

Private Dorsey shrugged. "The original fort was really just a collection of buildings. It was meant to be a depot and distribution center for supplies rather than a military complex. Defending it from any sizable enemy assault would prove difficult, if not impossible. Besides, most of the buildings were poorly constructed. Many are rotting and falling down and all the barracks are damp and infested with bedbugs and lice."

As they cleared the crest of a hill, Abigail understood what the young man was saying. The settlement resembled a small village of tumble-down cabins. Dorsey reined in the team at the front door of one of the two decent houses in the area, where a large woman awaited their arrival.

***

Sean fought his claustrophobic tendencies as Lieutenant Donovan led them down the narrow passageway to the barracks. The ceiling was only inches above Sean's head. He was forced to duck under each doorway.

A musty smell hung in the air from the damp walls where mold had already begun to grow. The dirt floor was coated with an inch of slime from the crunch of many boots. The flickering kerosene lamps attached at intervals along the wall gave only enough light to give a shadowy, ghostly nuance to the tunnel.

Lieutenant Wilson caught Sean's glance and gave him a sympathetic grin. He leaned in and whispered, "Not the most elegant of accommodations, but I suppose it keeps one out of the wind and weather."

Sean nodded and tried to smile.

The officers' quarters were constructed a bit higher in elevation to ensure better drainage, and rough-hewn boards provided a semblance of a floor. Bunks were built three high into the walls. Sean wished for a tent out in the open, but said nothing.

He and Wilson found empty bunks near each other and followed the rest out into the open courtyard. Wilson chuckled as Sean gulped in deep breaths of fresh air. As they joined the group, Lieutenant Donovan was introducing Captain Granger, the Quartermaster.

Granger led them up to the parapets where they could get a better view of the entire area. From this vantage point, the position of the fort and its construction seemed logical to Sean. Suddenly, all those hours of study back at West Point regarding basic field defenses began to make sense.

Proudly, with a sweep of his hand, Granger began to explain the fort's architecture.

"Gentlemen, what you see before you is a marvelous work of military ingenuity, that, I am very proud to say, has been constructed in just over six months of intense labor. Due to its design and construction, it is, for all practical purposes, impenetrable."

Sean calculated area and scope. *Difficult, but hardly impenetrable.*

Lieutenant Wilson asked the question, Sean thought for his benefit as much as for his own, "I am impressed by the design and construction, but wonder why the urgency of the project? Would not a permanent structure be more desirable?"

Granger nodded. "A strong Adobe style fort such as Bent

has built up north on the Arkansas has its advantages. However, construction of such a structure cannot be completed in a short span of time."

Sean nodded. *Basic field defensive strategy.*

Granger went on to explain. "After Captain Sibley resigned his post here and sided with the Southern cause, Colonel Canby became concerned for the defenses here at Fort Union. The original fort was never meant to be more than a supply depot. A fieldwork was the logical solution. Since the rumors are that Baylor has 'liberated' the southern portions of the New Mexican and Arizona Territories and made them part of the Confederacy, and Sibley has begun a march up the Rio Grande, this construction was a very wise choice."

Sean looked around him again. Much work had been done, but much was left to do. *Hopefully, too little, too late.*

Granger continued with the details as he led them around the parapet. He pointed in the direction of the setting sun. "Just a mile over that rise is the old fort. This location was chosen for its accessibility to the water of the creek and its distance from each bluff.

"The structure is a basic square with bastions on each side for quarters and storage, making it octagonal in shape. The entire area covers seven hundred and fifty square feet. The parapets are seven feet from the interior floor of the center courtyard and eight to twelve feet on the exterior to the bottom of the ditch. An abatis of sharpened cedar stakes is firmly embedded along the exterior slope."

Again, Sean nodded. *I must admit, it is a well-planned endeavor.*

Captain Wallace asked, "And how long have you been in charge?"

"I took over in October from Captain Grover, who drew up the original plans and began the initial construction. We have pressed on diligently from that time and are quite near completion."

As dusk was approaching, the workmen were gathering

their tools for the end of their work day. Sean noticed a group of men under armed guard. He asked, "Do you have prisoners working on the construction?"

Granger seemed to notice Sean for the first time. "That, we do. Southern sympathizers. And who might you be?"

Wallace motioned toward Sean. "That's Zebadiah Donner. He's a spy."

Wallace and Wilson both chuckled at Captain Granger's astonished look. "A spy for Harold Dartmouth, that is. He's here with Miss Dartmouth, the gentleman's granddaughter. It seems he'd like to see what possibility there might be of gaining the sutler's contract here at Fort Union."

"Ah, Harold Dartmouth down in Santa Fe. I've heard he's a fair and trustworthy man. I must admit, I'm none too pleased with the present contract. Mr. Donner, we will need to have a conversation after the Major's dinner this evening. Now, gentlemen, we will have need to continue this discussion in the morning. We are expected to be present at the Paul's within the hour. One does not keep Mildred Paul waiting."

As Sean rode over to the old fort with Lieutenant Wilson, he went over in his mind the information that had fallen in his lap in the last few hours. He wondered how long this streak of good luck would last. And he wondered how Abigail was faring.

***

Major Gabriel Paul may have been the commander of the fort, but Mildred was in complete charge when it came to dinner parties. She had confessed to Abigail, "In this God-forsaken land, there are few opportunities for pleasantries. My dear, your presence is a welcome respite."

Major Paul sat at the head of the table, but Mrs. Paul held court at the opposite end, glowering at the waiters if anything was handled improperly. Abigail had been placed between Captain Wallace and Captain Granger to Major Paul's right. Seated directly across the table was Lieutenant Colonel J.

Francis Chavez, a very handsome man of undoubted Mexican descent, with jet-black hair, a handle-bar moustache that curled on the ends, and dark brooding eyes whose gaze never seemed to leave her the entire dinner.

Abigail felt a tinge of pity for Sean, trapped between Mildred Paul and Captain Granger's wife Gertrude. She was confident he would enchant them with his charm.

She only wished he would share a little of that charm with her. He had barely touched her since that morning in the loft at Peterson's ranch and had said few words since he barked at her on the street in Pueblo.

Abigail smiled at Granger and did her best to act interested as he finished a story of some battle which had occurred during the Mexican War. She glanced at Chavez, who was not amused by the story, but held his tongue.

Abigail was relieved as the last of the dessert dishes were removed and the sounds of instruments being tuned floated in from the main hall. Major Paul leaned over to address her.

"Miss Dartmouth, I have spoken with Mr. Donner. I do hope it will not pose an inconvenience, but I have requested the stage postpone its departure one day. I am sending Mrs. Paul and Mrs. Granger with you on down south to Las Vegas in the New Mexican territory. The rest of the women and children left after Christmas. Now that the new fort is almost completed and the bulk of the supplies and equipment have been moved, it is not safe for them to stay here. It will be later this summer before our new quarters will be ready."

He added, "And I do strongly encourage you to remain in Las Vegas until we put an end to this Texas rabble."

Abigail had not wished to keep up this charade for another day, but saw no alternative. "We will be delighted to remain here." She nodded to Mrs. Paul. "I will gladly do what I can to help Mrs. Paul pack for the trip."

Sean gave her an encouraging glance and conferred with the ladies on each side of him.

They moved to the main hall, where the music flowed

from one dance to another with Abigail in demand for each. Lieutenant Colonel Chavez seemed to win a place in line quite often. Abigail appreciated his dancing abilities as well as his conversation. It did not take her long to realize he was her best source of information. She found herself on his arm in the commander's garden as the clock struck the hour of midnight.

***

The noonday sun warmed Sean's shoulders. However, the sun's rays did not penetrate nearly as deep as the searing thoughts of Abigail leaving the party on Chavez's arm. Sean mumbled a curse. Why did he let her affect him this way? Besides, she was just doing her duty. He cursed again. But why did she have to do it so well?

From the ledge jutting out from the mesa, all aspects of the fort were clearly visible. He tried to concentrate as his pencil flew over the sketch pad in his attempt to capture the details of the encampment as well as the information he had gleaned.

The sound of falling rocks drew his attention to the trail below. Lieutenant Wilson was on his way up.

Sean tore the page from the pad. He stuck the folded paper into his long-johns and quickly started a new sketch. What was visible to Wilson when he sat down beside Sean was the branches of a dead tree and a bald eagle soaring high overhead.

He handed Sean his canteen. "I hate to interrupt Mr. Michelangelo, but the fort is in an uproar. A messenger has just arrived from down south. Sibley's troops have defeated Canby at Valverde Ford. They've begun the march up the Rio Grande, with little or no resistance. Major Paul wants his wife out of here as soon as possible. The stage leaves in an hour."

CHAPTER 23

After a tearful goodbye, the two wives settled into the seat across from Abigail. Boxes and trunks surrounded them, along with two additional mail bags.

Sean checked to ensure Abigail was comfortable. She looked tired. He at first was concerned. Then the thought crossed his mind, wondering how long she and Chavez had "talked" last evening. In disgust, he climbed atop the carriage to join the other men.

To his chagrin, Colonel Chavez stepped out of the sutler's cabin with a small package. With a flourish, he stepped up to the coach door. Sean could only hear part of the conversation, but it was enough that Chavez had a parting gift for "Miss Lora" and how much he had enjoyed the previous evening. Sean gritted his teeth and looked away.

His attention was drawn to the parapet. Captain Wallace and Captain Granger were in deep discussion. Lieutenant Wilson caught his eye. Sean returned his wave.

Sean liked Wilson. It was unfortunate that they were on opposing sides of this conflict. He regretted his need to deceive his new friend. He just hoped they would never meet on the field of battle.

Jesse and the two miners were curled amongst the

baggage. Sean attempted to get as comfortable as possible with a mail bag as a back rest. He felt the derringer to ensure it was in its small holster and shifted the corner of sketch paper from where it was poking him in his navel.

Hennessey cracked the whip over the heads of the team. The team strained against the reins jerking the stage to a stuttering start. Then it settled into its rocking rhythm.

***

Abigail smiled as she broke the seal on the package. A hint of Chavez' cologne lingered on the wrapping. The folds revealed an intricate, folded fan.

Mrs. Paul looked at Mrs. Granger and then at Abigail. "Colonel Chavez is quite a handsome man. I dare say, he could charm the knickers right off, if given a chance."

Abigail looked over the top of the unfolded fan. She caught herself just as she was about to make a comment in her southern drawl. Instead, she commented sweetly, "The gentleman is charming." She added demurely, "And was always a gentleman. I assure you, the knickers never came off."

Mrs. Paul sputtered. "I did not mean to cause offense."

Abigail returned the fan to its wrapping. "None taken."

Abigail leaned back in her seat, visions of the previous evening filling her mind. Each man that had been her dance partner was forthcoming with tidbits of information, eager to impress her.

Captain Wallace had expressed his concern with the dampness of the storerooms. He would never have built the fort that close to Wolf Creek.

Even last evening, Captain Granger was anxious regarding Canby's ability to thwart an invasion. If Sibley was able to get by Canby and march north, Granger wondered aloud if they could get the supplies and especially the ammunition moved to the new fort in time for a full-scale attack.

Abigail had complimented Major Paul on the number of men at his service. He had been quick to respond that he only had four hundred fighting men and some of them were ill trained due to the need for their use on the construction. Much to his displeasure, he had requested reinforcements from Gilpin's Colorado volunteers, as unruly as they were. However, he doubted they would arrive in time due to the distance and the snows remaining in the mountain passes.

Lieutenant Donovan was unhappy with the use of the southern sympathizers being used on the construction details. He did not trust their work. They also posed a threat during a possible attack.

But it was Colonel Chavez that had given the most insight into the overall attitude in the camp. His troops were as well trained as any of the Americans, and they had done more than their share of the work in the construction. However, discrimination against their ethnicity ran rampant throughout the officers, including Paul. Due to that, morale was low.

Overall, things were not as good as they seemed on the surface. Abigail hoped what information she had been able to gather would be of help. She wished she had been able to talk with Sean, but the opportunity never arose. Now she feared they would be retained in Las Vegas rather than completing the journey to Santa Fe.

Her hand instinctively went to the derringer in her purse when a shout rang out from the men on the roof of the carriage.

***

Phelps' shout startled Sean from his dream. With disappointment, he realized that he had been cuddling a mail sack instead of Abigail.

Hennessey reined the team to a hurried stop. Across the road, a felled tree blocked their advance. Steep granite walls rose on each side, giving them no room to maneuver around the obstacle.

Looking over their shoulders, Sean muttered the obvious. "This would seem a perfect place for an ambush."

Phelps nodded, his rifle at the ready.

A voice from the boulders echoed off the walls. "You there on the stage, lay down your guns. We have you covered, but want no one harmed." Sean felt a wave of relief at the sound of Lucas' voice from Peterson's ranch. He quickly counted six heads looking down their rifle barrels, one with red curls protruding from under his hat rim.

Lucas continued, "We'll relieve you of the strongbox under your seat, as well as that sack of mail. We also are to understand that you are carrying two passengers from St. Louis headed for Santa Fe. We wish for them to accompany us the remainder of their journey."

Hennessey looked back at Sean. "Donner, what's the meaning of this?"

Sean tried to look astonished. "I would assume these men desire to hold Miss Dartmouth for ransom. I feel it would be best to accommodate their demands rather than endanger the officers' wives."

The old driver shook his head. "I don't like this one bit. Are you sure they will do Miss Dartmouth no harm?"

Sean tossed the mail bag, strong box and Abigail's trunks behind the coach. To Hennessey he replied, "I have sworn to protect Miss Dartmouth and deliver her safely to Santa Fe. You must do the same for the other ladies."

Sean climbed down and helped Abigail to the ground. Abigail turned back to the ladies. "Mrs. Paul, thank you for your hospitality. Please give my regards to your husband and to Colonel Chavez. Mr. Donner will assure my safety."

A rope from a hidden source pulled the log to the side of the road. Hennessey cracked his whip and the stage bolted around the obstacle and was gone.

The dust had not settled before six young men scampered down the hillside. Patrick flung off his hat and wrapped his arms around his sister. Without letting go, he extended his hand to Sean. "Tis good to have you back with us. I've been worried sick."

Lucas interrupted their reunion. "Sorry to break up this

little party, but we had better skedaddle out of here purty quick. There's horses saddled for y'all up on the ridge. It won't take long 'til a pack of our Union buddies'll be up here lookin' fer us. They don't much like their mail and cash box tampered with."

Abigail changed into some riding clothes while the boys packed up the loot. They were gone none too soon. As they cleared the ridge, shouts and shots echoed through the canyon. Only the ensuing darkness and rough terrain separated them from their pursuers.

About midnight, they made camp in an outcropping of rock at the base of Sipapu Pass. Everyone needed to rest. From the sag of her shoulders, Sean was sure that was especially true of Abigail. Patrick and Sean made a quick lean-to of branches to shelter her from the wind while Lucas built a small fire. After a quick supper of dried beef jerky and coffee, Abigail curled up under a saddle blanket. Within minutes, she was snoring softly.

Patrick poured Sean a cup of coffee. He nodded toward his sister. "How did she do?"

Sean thought of Chavez, but held his tongue. "She handled herself quite well. We have not, however, had the opportunity to compare our findings."

Patrick nodded. "With any luck, we will cross over the pass tomorrow. Madison will be waiting for us in Taos."

"Are the Union scouts still following us?"

"There's a good chance they are. However, we could not go any further in the dark. We will strike out again at daybreak. If we can beat them over the pass, we will be in friendly territory."

He looked at Sean. "Friend, you look exhausted. Get some sleep."

Sean crawled into the lean-to beside Abigail. Within minutes he too was snoring.

CHAPTER 24

Gray clouds had hidden the sun from the start of the day. High above the tree line, all was a gray-white desert of rocks and snow. Abigail had no idea the time of day. Her mind was as numb as her body. She simply watched as her mount struggled to place one hoof in front of the other.

Far below, Abigail could just make out a dozen riders in blue uniforms. She tried to envision the various scenarios if the Union scouts caught up with them. Would there be a shoot-out? As they were out-numbered, would they be able to hold their own? What if she and Sean were captured? Would they be hanged as spies? Would they reach the safety of Taos, or freeze to death in this icy wasteland?

As cold as she was, she wasn't certain she cared. She looped the reins over the saddle horn and sat on her hands to try to warm them. Her toes had long since lost any feeling. Ice hung heavy on her scarf from her breath.

Twice the mare she was riding stumbled. Abigail patted her shoulder and tried to give her words of encouragement, but her voice was lost in the wind. Each time the horse regained her footing and continued to plow through the waist-high drifts.

Patrick rode up beside her. He looked like some kind of snow creature, covered from head to toe with frozen, white powder. He shouted, "We're over the top. Don't give up. We'll be at the tree line in about another hour."

The hour seemed like an eternity, but the shelter of the trees was a welcome respite from the wind. They stopped long enough to rest the horses and warm themselves as best they could without a fire. Patrick encouraged her to eat some jerky, but she was too cold.

The report of the rear scout confirmed that the Union soldiers were gaining on them. Once again they were on the move. But now the descent was easier on the horses and gradually the air became warmer and the snow less a hindrance. Late in the afternoon the sun broke through the clouds. The feeling began to return to Abigail's extremities. She was even able to remove the soggy scarf from around her neck.

Sean rode down from where he had been riding with the rear scout. The news was not good. At the rate they were going, the Union forces would be within shooting distance before nightfall and they would have the advantage of an uphill position. One of the New Mexican volunteers knew the area and proposed a plan.

As the sun slid toward the western horizon, the weary Confederate party made their way through a draw between two cliffs. Once through the passage, they quickly divided, back-tracking behind the crest of each hill.

Patrick positioned Abigail behind a large stump at the far end of the draw. She reminded him, "You will remember that I can pick off an apple from a stump at a hundred yards."

He nodded. "Yes, but have you ever killed a man?"

Subdued with that thought, she quietly followed his directions.

The sky was a brilliant red, the shadows long and darkening when Abigail heard the rattle of rocks under the hooves of the Union horses. She readied her rifle. A volley of shots rang out. Lucas' deep voice echoed from the ridge, "You're surrounded. Lay down your guns."

From her left came the scuffing of boots on gravel. Below

her, two dark figures were about to draw bead on the backs of Patrick and Sean. She cocked her rifle and called out calmly, "Gentlemen, if you value your lives, you will do as our man said and lay down your guns."

The two men lowered their rifles to the ground, then raised their hands. When they turned, Abigail found herself face to face with Lieutenant Colonel J. Francis Chavez.

CHAPTER 25

Shopkeepers and patrons huddled in small groups watching the unlikely parade proceed down the main street of Taos. The eleven Hispanic Union scouts with Chavez were loosely tied together. Lucas led the way. Sean and Patrick rode on the right and left of Abigail at the back.

The warmth of the late February sun was a welcome relief from the cold of the mountain pass of the previous day. Their entry into Taos caused quite a stir, as Chavez was well known, loved by some and not so much by others.

Madison had set up his center of operations in a cantina on the square of the dusty little town. The tequila burned Sean's throat on its way down, but warmed his gut as he and Abigail waited to one side while Madison talked with Chavez.

Savory aromas filled the air from the platters of roasted beef, shredded pork and stacks of fresh tortillas the proprietor of the cantina laid before them. Soon their empty stomachs were filled to the maximum.

Chavez leaned back in the chair across from Madison. He looked at Abigail and nodded. "Senorita Dartmouth, I am not easily fooled. I was truly convinced you were in danger."

Sean interjected sarcastically, "And that she was, until you were forced to lay down your arms." Chavez smiled,

Abigail scowled, and Madison chuckled.

Madison looked around at the dusty streets and then back to Chavez. "Sir, for the moment, you and your men are our guests. We do not have fancy accommodations, but we will do what we can to make you comfortable." He added with a grin, "Other than the fact that you will be under guard. Presently, however, I need to hear the reports of my men," he nodded at Abigail, "and woman."

He motioned to one of his men. "Take the Colonel and his men down to the stables at the edge of town. Make sure they have plenty of clean straw, enough to eat and several bottles of tequila." He shrugged his shoulders in apology. "I'm afraid it is the best we can offer under the circumstances in this little hellhole of a town."

After Chavez was led away, most of the men that had been around the table at Peterson's ranch lounged nearby. Madison indicated the two chairs across the table from him to Sean and Abigail. "Now Miss Dartmouth and Mr. Donner, shall we begin?"

Sean held the chair for Abigail and sat beside her. He did not understand his nervousness. They had accomplished their assignment. Yet, somehow, he felt much as he had when Patrick and he had been called into the provost office at the Point after a late night on the town.

Madison seemed to understand their apprehensions. "Please, you are in no way under fire here. Certainly, we understand the danger in which you were placed and appreciate beyond words any information you may have gleaned."

He turned to Abigail. "And I do apologize for the uncomfortable ride over Sipapu Pass. It can be treacherous at this time of year." He nodded to Patrick. "However, we could see no better way to extricate you from the stage."

He leaned forward. Looking at Sean, he asked, "Now, the first question must be, in your opinion and from the information you were able to gather, is this Fort Union worth all the fuss?"

Sean took a long swallow of the strong liquor before him

and began. "First, let me say that Miss, uh, Dartmouth handled herself very nicely."

Madison chuckled. "I believe that might be an understatement. It is not every day that a Lieutenant Colonel will traverse a snow-covered mountain to rescue a damsel in distress. We thank you Miss Dartmouth. And Mr. Donner, we note your concern. Now Sean, please continue."

Both Sean and Abigail blushed. Sean stood, unbuttoned his vest and shirt to retrieve the folded sheet of sketch paper. With some difficulty, he flattened the wrinkled page, spreading it out before Madison. Even through the trip over the pass, the drawings were intact.

Sean began. "Definitely, Fort Union is a keystone for either the Union or Confederate presence in the southwest. With its location at the junction of the two branches of the Santa Fe Trail, it is the spigot that controls the flow of supplies and equipment to the rest of the western territories."

He tapped a spot on the table off the edge of the page. "The old original fort is not really a fort at all. Rather, it is a cluster of bug-infested, decaying cabins built on an open plain. Canby was certainly correct in his evaluation that it is indefensible. Therefore, his decision to build a fieldwork was a wise choice. This new fort, if you will, is approximately a mile east of the original location."

He indicated his drawing. "You see before you my rough sketch of that fieldwork. Strategically, this was an excellent idea on Canby's part. A fieldwork is a perfect answer to an immediate problem, and I must say, Captain Grover and presently Captain Granger have done a superb job of construction since its beginning last summer. As you well know, an attack against a fieldwork, under the best of circumstances, is difficult."

Madison nodded. "So, the second question would follow the first. Is an attack feasible?"

Sean continued. "The fort is not without its flaws. Since the major part of the structure is underground, it is quite cramped, dark and damp and for the most part undesirable. It would suffice as a short-term solution. However, I, for one, would rather be shot than have to stay down in those catacombs for any length of time."

Abigail leaned forward as though to add to the conversation. Madison nodded to her, "Miss McFerrin, if you have anything to add, please don't hesitate."

Abigail glanced at Sean, then looked back at Madison. "I don't know anything about fieldworks and construction. I can only relate some of the comments from the various men with whom I danced. However, what was said would verify what Mr. McKay has stated.

"Captain Wallace, the field inspector, as well as Captain Granger expressed concerns that the storerooms were damp. Granger was fretting like an old woman that his supplies would rot, and the magazine was too damp to hold the ammunition. At present, everything is still stored at the old fort."

Sean nodded in agreement. "Wallace and Lieutenant Wilson each questioned the location of the fieldwork in such close proximity to Wolf Creek."

He continued. "Again, I would commend them on the speed of the construction. However, that too leads to a fault. The work has been done by unskilled labor and in some cases forced labor. In reality, the work has been quite shoddy. They are forcing Southern sympathizers who are awaiting trial to work on the construction. We could assume there is not a great deal of pride in their work. In addition, I'm quite sure those men would gladly fight their captors, given the chance."

Sean referred back to his drawings. "It is true, due to its design, it could not be easily breached." He indicated crosses on the drawing. "However, I counted only ten 12 pounders and some of them are in poor condition."

He shook his head. "At best, a frontal attack would be costly in lives spent." He took a sip of tequila. "However, there is one most glaring flaw, and yet one I believe they have completely overlooked." With his glass still in his hand, he pointed with his little finger at the far side of his drawing. "If my calculations are correct, the fort is still within range of artillery on the mesa above the fort. From the vantage point where I sat to draw these sketches, I could see directly into the center of the compound." Again, he drug his finger along one side of the drawing. "Add to that, the construction on this side is especially vulnerable. Any kind of heavy field artillery could be devastating."

Madison nodded. "So what is their fighting manpower?"

Sean looked over to Abigail. She folded her hands in thought before answering. "Part of my information came from Mrs. Paul and the rest directly from the Major as we danced. They are both worried. He mentioned that at present he only has about four hundred fighting men, and due to their use as laborers, they are ill-trained."

She gave Sean a side-long glance before she continued. "However, the best information came from Colonel Chavez. There has been blatant discrimination against him and his New Mexican volunteers, causing many to desert or fail to reenlist. Along with that, all the troops are owed back pay. Morale is extremely low."

After a moment of thought, she added, "Major Paul has requested reinforcements from the Colorado volunteers. He seems to think they will be his only salvation."

Patrick interrupted. "Gilpin's rabble is mainly a bunch of miners. They're ornery as mules and mean as bears waking up after a winter's nap. We best get there before they do."

Madison stood with his hands braced on the table. "Miss McFerrin, Mr. McKay, you have both done a fantastic job. This is far more information than I could have ever hoped for.

"As for Colonel Chavez and his troops, from what Miss McFerrin has said, they are loyal to their leader more than the Union cause." He looked over at his lieutenant. "Lucas, have our quartermaster take enough out of the strong box that was confiscated from the stage to pay Chavez' men their back wages. Then send them back to their homes with their promise they won't come back to fight for the Union."

As an afterthought, he added, "Chavez we'll need to keep with us. We'll trade him when the time comes." He stood, addressing the men lounging in the area. "We leave for Santa Fe in the morning. Y'all are dismissed."

He leaned toward Sean and Abigail. "The two of you did a mighty fine job. Miss McFerrin, there's a boarding house down that side street run by a Mrs. Brady. She's got a hot bath and bed waiting for you.

"Sean, there's a barber shop down the street with a bath house in the back. Soon as you get cleaned up, the boys and I'll want to buy you a drink. Now git, both of you."

***

The bath more than refreshed Abigail, it gave her a whole different outlook on things. Her body begged for her to let the feather mattress cradle her to sleep, but her mind would not allow her to rest until she had taken care of a matter.

She considered digging into the trunks for a dress. Instead she shook the dust from her riding clothes and put them back on. She left the rifle on the bed, but slipped the derringer in her belt. She shouldn't need it, but as of late, she wasn't sure about anything.

Dusk had settled over the dusty main street. It would be dark before she had time to complete her mission. Two of Madison's men were smoking in the doorway of a saloon. She returned their greeting but did not stop to talk.

Four men sat around the fire in front of the stable. One of them softly picked at a guitar while another played a mournful tune on a harmonica.

Abigail addressed no one in particular. "I realize it is late. However, I wondered if I might have a word with Colonel Chavez?"

One of the men unlocked the stable door. She handed him the derringer. "You best keep this out here, just to be safe."

She stepped into the dim interior, lit only by a single

lantern hanging from a peg in the center of the run. As her eyes adjusted to the light, a figure emerged from the shadows.

"Ah, Senorita Dartmouth, your presence is an unexpected pleasure. I do hope it is not to gloat."

Abigail looked down at her hands. "Sir, I assure you I am not here to gloat, but rather to apologize."

Chavez bowed. "There is no need for an apology. You did not ask me to follow you nor ask for my protection. This is war, after all. It is much better that we were taken prisoner than to be shot."

Abigail felt foolish, yet needed to continue. "Sir, I am glad that neither you nor your men were shot. My apology is for the other night at Major Paul's. I did not want you to think I was in any way leading you on."

Chavez played in the dust with the toe of his boot. "Miss Dartmouth, or whoever you really are, I greatly enjoyed your attention and your company the other evening. I don't regret the time I spent with you in the Paul's garden, and, if my memory serves me correctly, I did not share any great secrets with you. To be honest, I don't regret following you and ending up here in this stable. It's better than that damp, dark fieldwork they call a fort."

He looked up at Abigail. "Again, this is war. Before many days, the men you are with will do battle with those I was with. I'm happy, in this instance, that I will not be part of that battle."

He held out his hand. Abigail allowed him to hold hers. "You are a good woman and these are good men. I thank you for your concern and thank you for your apology. I wish you God speed and safety."

Abigail turned to go. "And I wish the same to you, sir."

When Abigail stepped into the night air, she realized Sean had joined the four guards at the fire. He asked, "May I walk with you?"

She nodded.

They walked a ways in silence before she asked, "So you were spying on me?"

"No, not spying. Concerned, yes. I should have known you could take care of yourself."

She took his arm and looked into the night sky. "We made a good team. I must admit, although I was apprehensive, I enjoyed the adventure.

She hesitated. "But what do I do now? Where do I fit in?"

Sean stopped. He took both her hands in his before he answered. "We do make a good team. However, we will have to wait and see what adventures God and the future have in store for us."

***

Santa Fe turned out to simply be a bigger dusty version of Taos. Madison set up his headquarters at the El Farol cantina, and they waited, and they drank tequila, and they waited. By the time Sibley got to Santa Fe, the Colorado Volunteers had gotten to Fort Union. Madison was livid, but there was not a thing he could do about it. The timing was past and now the real battle would begin.

CHAPTER 26

March 28, 1862 dawned unusually cool. Sean draped a blanket over Abigail's shoulders. "It almost feels like snow is in the air. I would think it quite late this far south."

Madison sighed. "Cool weather makes for a more pleasant battlefield, I suppose."

Patrick, Sean, Abigail and Madison watched in silence the animated and exuberant troops passing before them in Santa Fe's dusty main street. The proprietor of the El Farol cantina placed a tray of tortillas, scrambled eggs and bacon before them. A senorita brought four steaming mugs of thick, black coffee.

Patrick nodded toward the soldiers in the street. "How many troops did Major Pyron bring up from Albuquerque?"

Madison sighed again. "He has a battalion of the 2nd Texas Mounted Rifles, plus Major John Shropshire, with four companies of the 5th Texas Mounted Rifles. That's about two hundred fighting men and two six pounders plus some support personnel. They're a bit bedraggled from the march."

Sean asked what they were all wondering, "With your hundred, what's our odds?"

Madison filled a tortilla with eggs and bacon and took a bite before he answered. "From what our scouts have reported,

Major Slough left Fort Union on the twenty-second with about a thousand men and eight artillery. Chivington is a couple days ahead of him with 450 of his Colorado volunteers.

"Pyron plans to move us up to Anthony Johnson's ranch today. That's at the western end of Apache Canyon. I figure we'll meet Chivington someplace in the canyon tomorrow."

"Chivington's Pike's Peakers could be brutal," Patrick commented.

Sean added, "But the Texans are mighty fine fighters."

Madison nodded. "Both of you are correct. Chivington's men are rough and tough, but untested in battle. The Texans have already been through a great deal, but they've not lost a battle."

"Yet," Patrick slipped in.

Madison shrugged. "It should be an interesting fight."

Abigail had been quiet to this point. She asked nonchalantly, "Where do I get to fight?"

Sean choked on his coffee, Patrick glared and Madison laughed. All three men looked at her and in unison exclaimed, "Nowhere!"

"Why? I can shoot as straight as any man out there in that street."

Emphatically Patrick answered, "You're staying right here in Santa Fe."

She retorted just as emphatically, "I am not. I haven't come all this way to sit on the sidelines and watch."

Madison held up his hands to quiet the other three. "Miss McFerrin, I appreciate your enthusiasm and I have no doubts regarding your ability to shoot. But under the circumstances, your presence on the battlefield would cause more of a distraction than an asset. However, if you do not become squeamish at the sight of blood and gore, I'm quite sure Doc Bailey would value your assistance. It would get you as far as Johnson's ranch, and I'm regrettably confident there will be men wounded."

Abigail scowled, but reluctantly agreed.

***

It seemed as though the dust still hung in the air from the move to Johnson's ranch even as dawn broke over the foothills of the Sangre de Christo Mountains. Long shadows of Saguaro cactus gave the essence of sentinels watching and waiting for the battle to come.

This was a harsh land, a desolate land. For the first time in many weeks and months, maybe even years, Sean felt homesick for the green pastures and tall oaks lining the lane leading to the stately white house of Great Oaks. He shook his head to clear the images of the burned-out shell from his mind. That space in time was gone forever. Only the future remained.

Sean filled a tin cup with what had a slight resemblance to coffee from a pot from the nearest campfire. He wondered what the future would be after today, and tomorrow, and after this cursed war. He had no home, no family, no land. And then there was Abigail.

He watched her as she helped Doc Bailey and the orderlies set up cots and an operating area in anticipation of the results of the carnage to come. He cussed at himself. Why did his heart beat faster every time he saw her, or even thought of her? She intrigued him. She fascinated him.

But she was out of his league. Oh, they had made a great team. He even let himself dream, for just a moment, of a life together, but he knew that was not possible. He had nothing to offer her, even if he survived all this. No. His purpose was to protect her now, so she could go back to her ranch and the life that was her destiny.

The shouts of the officers jolted him from his reverie. He checked his rifle and ammunition. When he looked up, Abigail was gazing at him across the compound. He flashed a reassuring smile back to her, then turned to join his comrades.

***

Abigail watched until Sean was lost in the sea of soldiers.

She bit her lip to keep the tears at bay. In spite of her bravado, she was afraid; afraid for Patrick, afraid for Sean, afraid for herself.

It was one thing to waltz into Fort Union and dance with the enemy in the form of Major Paul, Captain Wallace and Colonel Chavez, pumping them for information. Even now, the thought of holding a gun on Chavez seemed like a surreal dream. But today, the two men she loved the most in life were in danger of real bullets fired from real rifles.

She put her fingers to her lips. She had just put into words thoughts she had not allowed herself to admit. She loved him. She loved Sean. She actually, really loved him.

Of course, she loved her father, and William, and Patrick. And there had been other boys she liked. She even liked Edward as if he were a brother. There had been dozens of young men who had come courting during her stay at Riverglade Plantation. There were plenty of them she liked. But love?

Her knees felt weak. She sat less than gracefully on an empty crate. Her mind led her through scores of horrific scenarios. What if she never saw him again? What if he died today, a Union musket ball torn through his heart? She had overheard her father's gory stories of arms and legs lost as the aftermath of battle during the Mexican War. What if Sean ended up like that on Doc Bailey's operating table later this day?

She jumped when Doc Bailey touched her arm. "Miss McFerrin, are you OK?"

Abigail took a deep breath. "Yes, I just needed a moment to rest."

"If you are sure you can handle this, I would like to go over the operating procedures."

Abigail nodded. She looked once more at the receding soldiers, breathed a prayer for their safety, and followed Doc Bailey into the surgical tent.

CHAPTER 27

The rutted road of the Santa Fe Trail followed the bank of Glorietta Creek through the cactus, scrub brush and scrawny pinion pines. The columns of soldiers came to a halt at the entrance to Apache Canyon. Sean watched eagles and vultures circle overhead, as if in anticipation of what was to come. Soldiers muttered impatiently as the sun marched toward its zenith. Sean pulled a handkerchief from his back pocket to wipe the sweat from his eyes.

Patrick removed his hat to use as a fan. He shook his head in exasperation. "Marking time is the worst. 'Tis a bit like waiting for a bear to pounce."

Sean glared at him, "Not the best of analogies."

Patrick shrugged. "Maybe not. But it's still true."

Sean shifted his rifle to his left hand and returned the handkerchief to his pocket. He gazed up the road ahead of them to the point where it curved out of sight into the canyon. He tried to visualize the enemy in his mind.

He had hunted bear, and deer, and even a cougar that had been killing the young calves back at Great Oaks. And he had had more than a few fights with his half-brothers, and seen his fair share of brawls while at West Point. He shuddered. But he had never killed another man. Could he today? Would those years of training at West Point carry him through in a real battle?

It was as if Patrick could read his mind. "I wonder how many of these soldiers will be fighting their first battle…like us."

"Several, I suspect," Sean replied. "I'm glad we have the Texans with us," He nodded up the line. "Looks like we may not have too much longer to wait. Here comes Madison."

Madison addressed his men. "Pyron sent four advance scouts into the canyon last night. He's been waiting for them to return." He shook his head. "They haven't. We're not gonna wait any longer. We're about to advance on up into the canyon – into the unknown. Good luck, gentlemen."

Sean and Patrick fell in beside Madison. The rising altitude brought a refreshing shift in the air temperature. Arid flat land and cactus gave way to boulders and tall Apache Pines. The canyon broadened, narrowed, then broadened again. A bridge over Apache Creek slowed their progress before entering a narrow valley.

Rumors and jokes were bantered about among the marching men that the enemy had fled. Madison commented. "If we continue at this pace, we should reach Pigeon's Ranch before dark." He explained, "Pigeon's Ranch is actually a stage stop about halfway through the canyon. It's at the height of the pass. From that point, we would be fighting from the upper advantage."

The march came to an abrupt halt. All joking ceased as the advance scouts reported the proximity of the enemy. Battle lines were formed. Madison's San Elizario Spy Company brought up the left flank. Captain Grigsby led a company on the right, while Pyron advanced in the center. The two artillery companies were brought forward as the first Union troops came into view over a slight rise.

Sean's pulse quickened. He shifted his rifle to the ready. He took a deep breath to calm his nerves, gripping his rifle to stop his shaking hands. He wasn't sure if it was out of fear, or the excited anticipation of the coming battle. He hoped it was the latter.

Initially, the volleys of the cannons halted the Union advance. However, it did not take long for Pyron to realize the ineffectiveness of his artillery in the broken terrain of the canyon.

The order was given. Sean dropped to a knee and took aim across the open expanse. Madison yelled, "Fire." Sean's ears rang from the deafening roar of the rifles up and down the line.

Sean gazed through the cloud of smoke. He was almost relieved that there was no visible sign of destruction from his shot.

A cloud of smoke rose from the opposing line. Seconds later, the report echoed from the canyon walls. Sean felt, as much as heard, a musket ball whistle past his right ear. A piercing scream from a soldier down the line startled him. Blood oozed from between the man's fingers.

With determination, Sean rammed a musket ball home. He took careful aim. There was no longer any hesitation. "Fire." His target fell backward – no longer a man, but rather the enemy.

A blue haze hung over the valley, as volley after opposing volley echoed from the granite walls. Projectiles whistled through the air, breaking limbs from trees and sending sprays of rocks from boulders, with neither side making any progress.

The loading and firing, loading and firing became an automatic response. The barrel of Sean's rifle burned his hand. Each time he thought he had found a target, two flashes of fire would take its place.

In a lull of the firing, Madison shouted and pointed to the ridge above them. No sooner had the words left his mouth than the man to his left slumped forward, blood quickly spreading through his coat where a bullet had pierced his shoulder.

The man next to Sean screamed as a shell exploded the rock in front of him, blinding him with the scattering fragments.

The call to retreat was sounded. Sean guided his wounded comrade toward the rear while he and Patrick covered each other's retreat.

Pyron formed another defensive line at a narrow section of the canyon. The fighting intensified. Sean was impressed by the stamina of the Texans, but Chivington's troops were relentless.

During a lull, Madison wiped the black of the spent gunpowder from his face with his shirtsleeve before taking a long drink from his canteen. "So much for an easy fight. Those Pike's Peaker's are ruthless."

A comment came from down the line. "Ah'd swear they's got a charmed life. I shoot one, and he sits right back up and starts shootin' back." Sean shook his head, muttering his agreement.

Madison shouted as he dropped to one knee and aimed his rifle toward the ridge. "They're flanking us again!" Sure enough, snipers had gotten a foothold in the boulders above them and were punishing the line with enfilade fire.

A messenger pulled Sean and Patrick to the back of the line. "Pyron needs you." They followed him to the rear where the Major was directing orders.

Over the din of the battle he asked, "You boys know anything about explosives?"

Patrick looked at Sean and shrugged. "Just what they showed us at the Point."

Pyron motioned behind them. "We've got to make another retreat. That bridge we crossed over Apache Creek. We need it ready to blow once we get the cannons and men across. Take those two kegs of gun powder and get it ready."

Sean and Patrick each grabbed a keg of powder and coil of fuse. They ran back the quarter of a mile to the creek as fast as the fifty pound kegs on their shoulders would allow.

The bridge span was not much, maybe fifteen feet. The creek some twelve feet below ran full from the melting snows of the mountain peaks towering above them.

Sean indicated the center support. "If we can take out that beam, it should take the section with it. I'll try to wedge the kegs in between those supports while you get the fuses ready."

Sean cussed himself for not bringing any extra rope with him. He stripped out of his shirt and proceeded to tear it into shreds, using them to hold the containers in place. The cannon, followed by the retreating troops rumbled overhead as Patrick attached the fuses to the kegs.

Sean pulled Patrick over the west end of the bridge as the rear guard covered them. From the protection of a boulder, Patrick lit the end of the fuse. It sputtered to life.

Sean held his breath. Seconds ticked by. Patrick shook his head. Through gritted teeth he said, "It didn't..."

Kaboom! The center of the bridge rose in a flash of light. Splinters of decking flew into the gray dusk of evening. The span shuddered, then crashed into the rushing water below. Sean and Patrick scurried with the rear guard to join the rest of Pyron's troops.

A few of Chivington's cavalry jumped the span of the creek, but for the most part, the divide halted the Union onslaught. As darkness thickened, a truce was called in order to care for the wounded and bury the dead.

Exhausted, Sean sat on a boulder and leaned on his rifle. To no one in particular, he asked, "Remind me – what did we accomplish today?"

Wearily, Patrick slumped to the ground beside him. "Well, if nothing else, you and I didn't get wounded or shot dead. That's something, I suppose."

An old soldier took a long drink from his canteen. "This is war, boys. Today, we gained some ground, then lost it and more. Therefore, today's battle will be chalked up as a victory for the Union. Tomorrow, we do it all again." He spit a wad of tobacco into the dust. "For now, let's go get something to eat."

Sean helped Patrick to his feet. They joined the others making their way back to Johnson's ranch.

CHAPTER 28

Abigail adjusted the lantern's light. She wiped the gushing blood from the boy's shoulder. Doc Bailey wiped his bloody hands on his caked apron. With the tip of a knife and his index finger he retrieved the musket ball. It clanked into the pan with the myriad of others like it.

Abigail had long ago lost count of the men, young and old, that had been laid out before them. She had cringed and gagged at the first few; a grazed temple, a shoulder wound, a shattered elbow, and one whose right eye was damaged by a shattered rock. It was the one who died on the table and the young boy whose leg could not be saved that haunted her.

With difficulty, she straightened her back. She searched through the bloody rags for one clean enough to wipe the sweat from Doc's brow. He had been tireless, never wavering, never hesitating. He seldom spoke except to give a direction or whisper a word of encouragement.

He looked up and whispered, "Thank God." There wasn't another body waiting to be stretched out before them on the crude operating table. He slumped in exhaustion onto an empty crate. An orderly brought both him and Abigail a tin cup of steaming black coffee.

Abigail rested her hands on the edge of the table. She

raised her eyes toward the tent opening. Instead of an orderly with another wounded soldier, Sean's outline filled the space in the canvas. His face and hands were as black as the night behind him. His pale torso where his shirt had been was streaked with dirt and dried blood. His eyes were tired and bloodshot.

Abigail had not seen anything so beautiful in all her eighteen years. She gasped and began to cry. Her knees went weak. She crumpled into his arms.

Doc Bailey looked up with weary eyes. "Get her out of this hell hole. Take her someplace where she can wash off the blood and gore from this day. Then get her something to eat and something stronger than coffee to drink, if she will."

He added softly, "She was a mighty fine trooper today. I've never had better help and couldn't have done what we did today without her."

Sean nodded. He carried her through the camp to where Patrick had found an empty tent. Abigail stirred as Patrick brushed his rough fingers over her cheek. He nodded toward the tent. "There's a bucket of hot water and a clean towel inside. Seth found your trunk of clothes. It's in there as well. Sorry, sis, there's no tub available."

She smiled. "None expected. The hot water and some lye soap will do just fine."

As Sean set her feet on the ground, she looked down at what was left of her dress. "And do me a favor. When I get out of this dress, please burn it. No amount of scrubbing will ever get it clean."

She entered the tent. In the dim light of the single lantern hanging from the center tent pole, Abigail stripped down to her corset and pantaloons. She handed what was left of the bedraggled dress to Patrick through the tent flap.

Then, starting at her hairline, she started scrubbing. The rough towel tore at her skin and the soap stung her eyes, but she didn't care. She would have peeled the first layer of her skin away, if that would be what it took to remove the caked blood from her hands and arms.

She wished for a mirror, but there was none in the trunk. There was, however, a hair brush, so she did what she could to untangle her curls, letting them fall to her shoulders unobstructed. She slipped one of the plain day dresses over her head, ignoring her petticoats and her shoes.

Sean, Patrick and four other young men seated around the campfire jumped to their feet as she stepped through the tent flap into the light. She waved her hand for them to be seated. Then the aroma of the bubbling stew teased her nostrils and she almost fainted. Her hands went to her stomach. "I...I'm famished."

Sean and Patrick each grabbed an arm and helped her to an empty crate. Sean did the best he could to clean a tin plate with the sleeve of his shirt...a shirt that Abigail noticed was a couple sizes too small, so that his muscles and chest stretched the fabric to its limits. He piled the plate with stew while Patrick filled a tin cup half full of coffee and topped it off with whiskey.

She ate in silence, listening to the conversation around the fire.

"It has been a devastating day."

"The first defeat the Texans have experienced since leaving Mesilla."

"Those Colorado miners were ruthless, relentless."

"They have to have charmed lives."

"Grigsby and some of his troops got cornered. They ended up being taken prisoner."

"Thank God reinforcements are on the way. Lt. Colonel Scurry left Santa Fe with eight hundred additional troops; five companies of the 7th Texas Mounted Rifles under Major Powhattan Jordan and nine companies of the 4th Texas Mounted Rifles under Major Henry Raguet."

"And three additional cannons."

"They should get here sometime after midnight."

Patrick shook his head. "I overheard Madison and Pyron talking a bit ago. The rumor has it Colonel John Slough left Fort

Union with nine hundred. They should join Chivington by morning. Our little skirmish is about to turn into a major battle."

"What about Sibley?" One of the men asked.

Another mumbled, "He's undoubtedly drinking himself into a stupor down in Albuquerque."

Sean added as an after-thought. "Sibley has great ideas. We're sleeping in tents of his design."

One of the older men muttered, "Jus' too bad he's such a piss-poor leader."

Patrick broke in. "Scurry's a good soldier. I know men who have fought along-side of him. They have nothing but good things to say. He'll do a good job here."

Sean shook his head. "It is a pity we could not have moved faster. If we could have pushed through the pass and taken Fort Union before Chivington got his Colorado volunteers down here from Denver, none of this would have been necessary."

They sat staring into the dying embers. One of the men shook his head. He mumbled more or less to himself, "Not a good day. There's thirty shallow graves up at the entrance to the canyon."

"And forty good men with bullet holes," another added.

"What about the wounded men?" Abigail asked.

Patrick reassured her with a tired smile. "They are being well taken care of. They've been taken into Santa Fe. The Catholic church there has been turned into a hospital."

Abigail's thoughts went to the young man who had lost his leg. She whispered a prayer. As if in answer, the embers popped, sending a shower of sparks into the dark sky.

One by one the men excused themselves. Patrick looked over at Abigail. "Sis, will you be OK?" She smiled and nodded. He looked over at Sean, "I'm going to go check on the horses. Get some sleep."

Sean helped Abigail to her feet. She looked up into his face. She whispered, "This sounds silly," she hesitated, "but I don't want to be alone. Will you stay with me tonight?"

He put his arm around her and led her into the tent. He spread a blanket over a clean pile of hay and draped another one over them. She curled up into his arms, feeling safe for the first time since watching him march away that morning.

***

Sean slipped his arm from under Abigail. He wasn't sure either of them had moved all night. He tucked the blanket around her and slipped through the tent opening. The chill of the morning air sent a shiver through his body. The sky over the mountain range glowed red as the sun peaked out from the cut of the canyon.

"Mornin' sleepy-head," Patrick said, holding a skillet over the embers of the campfire. "How's scrambled eggs and salt pork for breakfast?"

Sean rubbed his eyes, then looked down at his hands still black from the previous day's battle. "What do you mean, 'sleepy-head'? I hardly had time to fall asleep. Besides, the sun is barely awake."

The smell of the frying pork set his stomach to growling and mouth to watering. "Eggs? Where'd you get eggs?"

Patrick divided the mixture between two plates, tossed in a handful of flour into the skillet and drained a cup of milk. "Pour us a couple of cups of coffee. This gravy will be ready in a minute." He stirred the creamy mixture until it was thick and bubbly, then poured it over the eggs and pork.

"A rancher was here early with eggs and goat's milk. I got the last four eggs and two cups of milk. Thought I'd save the last egg and some of the milk for Abigail." He nodded toward the tent. "I figured she'd need all the sleep she could get."

Sean gratefully accepted the plate of food. "She had quite a day." He stirred the gravy into the eggs and pork. "She sure ain't like any woman I've ever known."

Patrick chuckled. "It's true, there's not many quite like her."

Abigail tossed aside the tent flap and stepped through the

opening. Stretching, she looked at her brother. "Will the two of you quit talking about me like I was some kind of horse-flesh."

Embarrassed, Sean jumped up and offered her the crate where he had been sitting.

She accepted his offer. "Besides, how's a girl supposed to sleep with the smells of frying pork filling the air?"

Patrick scurried to fix her breakfast while Sean poured her a cup of coffee.

She asked softly, "Will there be more fighting today?"

Patrick handed her the plate of food. "Colonel Scurry and his men got here sometime after midnight. The official word is for us to be ready to fight at any time. The scuttlebutt is we'll march back up the canyon tomorrow morning."

He chuckled as he mopped up the last of his gravy with a hardtack. "Besides, he's got to have time for his engineers to patch up the bridge me and Sean blew up yesterday."

Abigail stood and handed her empty plate to Patrick. "Thank you for breakfast. Now, I suppose I should see how I can assist Doc Bailey."

Sean stepped to her side. "Abigail, you did more yesterday than any woman should ever be asked to do. I was intending to ask for a leave to take you into Santa Fe later this morning."

Abigail shook her head. "No. As long as you boys are determined to blow holes in each other, my place is here helping to patch up those holes."

She turned her back on them and made her way to the surgical tents.

CHAPTER 29

Sean checked his rifle, ammunition, Bowie knife, and canteen one more time. Stars faded into the red glow of morning. The wait for the word to move out went from anticipation to tedious.

Sean more than once considered breaking ranks to find Abigail. The thought of marching into unknown dangers without at least saying goodbye was almost unbearable. Her words at breakfast the previous day still stung his mind.

But he had spent the day in strategy meetings, while she helped Doc Bailey. Then he had pulled night guard duty. She had retired to her tent by the time he had returned.

His thoughts were interrupted by a poke in the arm from Patrick. "Looks like we have a visitor."

Abigail was making her way between the rows of cheering men. White lace accented the deep blue dress, filled out from beneath with petticoats. A petite bonnet held her auburn curls in place.

A broad smile spread across Sean's face. Patrick leaned over and said, "It would seem that our Southern belle has come to wish the troops well."

She stopped before them and dropped into a deep curtsey. In a deep drawl she said, "Gentlemen, ah couldn't possibly allow the two of you to march into glorious battle without wishing you God-speed. That would be terribly inconsiderate under the circumstances."

Patrick bowed. "Ah, sister, only you would put on such a fine performance.".

She kissed him on the cheek and whispered, "After the previous devastating battle, I thought a few words of encouragement might help. Besides, I had not had the opportunity to wish you well." He returned her kiss.

When she looked up into Sean's face, her tired, sad eyes betrayed her. He reached out, taking her hands in his. Gently he asked, "Does this mean you will be traveling to Santa Fe?"

She smiled and curtsied. "Why, suh, ah will be more than happy to return to Santa Fe when you and my dear brother can travel with me."

She added softly, "If I cannot fight beside you, then my place is here to aid Doc Bailey." She kissed him on the cheek. "Take care of yourself and watch over Paddy."

Once more, he watched her walk away as the signal to move out was given.

***

The sun had not quite reached noon when the first shots rang out. Sean looked down the lines formed along Glorietta Creek in the valley just west of Pigeon's Ranch. Madison's troops including he and Patrick were under the command of Major Raguet on the left flank. Major Shropshire had his troops scattered among the trees on the right. Scurry's troops and his artillery formed the center thrust.

Volley answered volley, with no apparent movement from either side. Sean could not help but wonder if it was not just a huge waste of musket balls. For the first half hour, it seemed that some tree branches and a few boulders were the only casualties.

Then, as the sun reached its zenith, Pyron motioned for Madison to begin a maneuver to their left. Using the bank of the creek as a protection, they began to flank the Union soldiers. Sean caught glimpses of Shropshire's troops doing the same through the trees on the right.

The fighting intensified. Screams from the wounded on each side pierced the constant roar of guns. The Union forces were pushed back to the protection of the adobe buildings of Pigeon's ranch. Scurry ordered a three-prong attack, with Raguet, Pyron, and Madison attacking the Union's left, Shropshire the enemies right, and Scurry continuing up the center.

Sean and Patrick, with men scattered on each side, battled from tree to tree and boulder to boulder. Slowly they gained the higher ground of the ridge above the ranch. From their vantage point, they could clearly see the valley below.

Sean and Patrick, with a dozen other marksmen, settled in behind a stone ledge while others protected their position. Sean took careful aim and an artilleryman collapsed against the barrel of his cannon.

Patrick fired, and a soldier fell headlong from the roof of the stable. One by one, the marksmen counted their targets. No longer were they firing at the unknown, but rather specific targets within their sights.

As the shooters devastated the Union line, Scurry advanced down the road, pushing the enemy before him.

***

Abigail wiped the perspiration from her eyes with the back of her hand. Since they had heard the first volleys of guns just before noon, there had been a steady stream of wounded. Reports regarding the battle varied, but things seemed to be going in favor of the Confederates. Abigail could not tell it from what she and Doc were seeing. A seemingly endless parade of bloody bodies were laid on the crude operating table.

A badly wounded soldier writhed before them. Doc had just begun to clean the dirt and dried blood from the man's shoulder when shouts and the sound of gunshots echoed through the camp.

An orderly stuck his head in through the tent flap. "We're being attacked! Union troops from up on the mesa are descending on us like flies."

Doc Bailey looked across the table at Abigail. He shook his head. "There's not more than a couple dozen men left here to guard the supplies. With the main battle being fought miles up the canyon, we have no chance of defending our position."

He nodded toward the entrance of the tent. "You must leave now. You cannot be found here, to be killed or taken prisoner. Run up in the hills behind the ranch until this is over."

"And what about you?"

"I will keep doing what I'm doing as long as I'm able. Now, go!"

Abigail took a deep breath, gritted her teeth, and shook her head. "We can't let this man die. As long as you are here, I am here with you."

Doc shook his head in resignation. "You're a very good woman, and brave beyond sensibility." He bent back to his task.

Abigail did her best to concentrate on the procedure before her, even as the shouts and shots grew louder and encircled their tent. Suddenly, the tent flap was ripped back. Abigail looked up into the face of a Union soldier.

"Edward!"

"Abigail?"

Edward stood in stunned silence. He swallowed and asked, "What are you doing here?"

She wanted to respond with a sarcastic comment, but she was too tired and afraid. She simply said, "Trying to save this young man's life. Please, let us do that. Please."

Edward put his fist to his pursed lips. "Abigail, Abigail, Abigail, why are you not back at the *MC*? Why are you in this God-forsaken place?"

She could only whisper pleadingly, "Please."

Edward turned, giving orders as he walked away. "Leave this tent and those other two there. We have no use for any more wounded. Round up what prisoners you can find for us to take back with us. Push the wagons together and burn them. Then we best rejoin Chivington up on the mesa before the rebels realize what has happened."

Abigail and Doc listened as flames roared. The earth shook with the explosion of the ammunition wagons.

Doc was putting the last of the stitches in the man's shoulder when the tent flap flung open once again. Edward peered in. With a grim face, he said, "Abigail, go home, please go home."

Abigail mouthed the words, "Thank you," and he was gone.

***

Dark gray clouds roiled over the tops of the mountain peaks. A cold wind whipped the standards. The Union forces had retreated to a narrow passage in the canyon. Individual squadrons of the Union rear guard had taken positions in the trees and boulders up the slopes on each side.

Sean watched as Madison led ten of his men on a flanking maneuver. Sean and Patrick, with five of the marksmen, took a position in a grove of pines. Using the trunk of a tree to stabilize his barrel, Sean took careful aim. A Cavalry officer plummeted off the back of his horse.

As the recoil of his weapon slammed into his shoulder, an excruciating pain ripped through his side. He slumped to his knees in agony. Blood oozed through his fingers clutching the tear in his shirt which became a growing sea of red. The blast from Patrick's rifle deafened him. From the corner of his eye, he saw his assailant slump from behind a log to his left.

A volley from that same area forced them all to dive for cover. Patrick grabbed Sean's coat, dragging him down the slope to the protection of a ledge of granite.

To their dismay, they watched as Madison and his troops were surrounded by the enemy. The constant barrage from the upper position kept them cowering in their shelter. They were forced to witness their leader being led behind the enemy's line.

Sean groaned in agony. His side felt as though a hundred needles were driving into his flesh. The scene before him swam before his eyes as nausea clenched at his throat. For an instant, he wondered if this was what it felt like to die.

Patrick forced him to focus on him. He did what he could to clean Sean's wound with the little water that remained in his canteen. As he worked, he explained the situation, "The ball has pierced your side and exited cleanly. I'm afraid it's left a shattered rib in its wake."

Patrick tore his own shirt into strips. With them, he wrapped his friend's wounded torso. Once the nausea passed, Sean was able to get his legs under him, and they rejoined the rest of their comrades.

As dusk settled, the Union forces continued to retreat. Scurry pulled back to Pigeon's Ranch. He congratulated his men for their hard-fought victory. But it had not been without its cost. They buried Major Shropshire, Major Raguet, and thirty of their fellow soldiers in the meadow behind the ranch house.

***

The wind had an icy edge to it. Flakes of snow freckled their coats. Patrick was half-carrying Sean back toward camp when they received the news. As they cleared the final curve in the canyon trail, the valley spread out below them. The totality of the devastation struck home. Only the medic's tent and the two tents of the wounded remained standing. The entirety of their precious supply train lay in a smoldering pile of ashes.

***

Abigail interlaced her fingers with Sean's. She held his hand firmly against the rough boards of the table. He moaned through gritted teeth. His muscles bulged against the pain.

Sean's body cringed as Doc Bailey drained the canteen of water over the wound, dabbing it with a used bloody rag. Doc muttered, "My apologies, son. I have nothing left but dirty creek water with which to clean your injury. All my supplies are gone."

Patrick uttered a curse from where he held Sean's shoulders steady. "They left neither cup intact nor flask of whiskey unbroken. There's not even a blanket that hasn't been burned."

Abigail whispered, "At least they left Doc and me here to do what we can."

She looked up at her brother. "Edward was here. He's the one who gave us a reprieve."

He sighed. "So Edward joined up with Chivington." He shook his head. "That's what this war has done. Brother against brother. Friend against friend."

Doc looked over at Patrick. "Do you have a Bowie knife?'

Patrick nodded.

Doc shook his head. "I can't stop the bleeding. Without any supplies, I see no alternative but to cauterize the wound. Otherwise, he could bleed to death."

Abigail gasped. She had seen her father use the procedure on a cowboy with an arrow through his arm. The thought of Sean having to endure that kind of pain was nauseating.

Doc continued his instructions. "Heat the blade in the embers of the fire until it just begins to glow. Then bring it to me."

Patrick did as he was told. Abigail looked away rather than look into Sean's eyes.

Sean looked up at Doc Bailey. "You're going to burn me with the blade?"

Doc nodded as Patrick returned with the glowing blade. He picked up a wooden rod from his utility tray. "Bite down on this."

Abigail bit her lower lip to fight back the tears. She kissed him on the forehead.

Sean moaned and squeezed her hand as the hot steel seared his skin. His body convulsed and then went limp.

Abigail stumbled from the tent. She fell to her knees, sobbing uncontrollably. Patrick knelt beside her, holding her in his arms as snow swirled around them.

CHAPTER 30

Fog shrouds the willows in ghostly veils of gray, swirling above the water's edge. A small boy stumbles over the gnarled roots. He is running, running, running from what and to what he has no idea, only that he must keep running.

Out of the mists, the Corinthian pillars of Great Oaks shimmer in the moonlight on the opposite bank of the river. Grim silhouettes of his mother and brothers stare out at him from darkened windows. He tries to swim across, but the icy current tosses him back to shore, leaving him shivering in a pool of melting snow.

Tramping feet of marching soldiers shatter the silence of the night. Torches pierce the dark. Shouts of hatred bark like the howls of coyotes. Vines of flames grow round and round the columns and climb the walls. The house, the windows, the faces, melt into a mound of burning wagons.

The heat from the glowing embers scorch the skin of the boy turned man. He calls out, but there is no response. His skin burns. His clothes become drenched from his sweat.

A beautiful girl riding a black stallion races atop the waves of the river, her gossamer gown flowing in the breeze behind her. She stops to kiss him on the forehead.

A soldier turns and fires. The girl dissolves into the smoke of the rifle. "Abigail, Abigail, Abigail!" the man cries. "My beloved Abigail."

The soldier takes aim again. A ball burns his side. He screams...and all is black.

***

Sean struggled to open his eyes, but the light blinded him. He tried to shield his eyes with his hand, only to have his attempt rewarded by a stabbing pain in his side.

"Good Morning."

He struggled once more to open his eyes against the glaring light. Was that the voice of an angel, or just another part of his dream?

From the shadows, she spoke again. "How are you feeling?"

He gingerly turned toward the voice. Reality slowly cleared the cobwebs from his mind. Through his parched lips he whispered, "It's not hot enough to be hell, but I hurt too badly for it to be heaven, so I must be back on earth" He looked around the room, "but where on earth I'm not sure."

Abigail stepped from the shadows. The cool of her fingers brushed his cheek. "Thank God your fever has finally broken. Welcome back to the land of the living."

The cool drink she pressed to his lips felt like rain on a dry, cracked lakebed after a drought. "Where am I? How long have I been here?"

Abigail smiled. "This is the afternoon of the third day. You're in the guest room in the home of Mrs. Louisa Canby."

Sean shook his head in disbelief. "As in Louisa Canby, the wife of General Canby?"

This time Abigail laughed out loud. "One and the same." She offered him another sip of water. "As father has been known to say, 'life can often make strange bedfellows'. Louisa opened her home here in Santa Fe to us after that first dreadful night. She has worked tirelessly beside Doc Bailey and me in her drawing room turned operating room. She has organized wagons from the surrounding ranches to bring our wounded from the battlefield. Not without merit have our troops given her the name 'Angel of Santa Fe'."

Sean relaxed into the pillow at his head. Behind closed eyes, visions reappeared. He asked softly, "What things might I have said during these past days?"

She again brushed her fingers by his cheek. "What one says in the delirium of a fever cannot be held against one. Rest now. I'll bring up some broth a little later."

Her comment only made Sean wonder more what he might have said over the expanse of the last three days. Visions of the girl on the black stallion lingered in his thoughts as he drifted off to the first restful sleep in days.

CHAPTER 31

A rooster heralded the morning from his perch atop a fencepost. Kittens chased their tails while their mother sunned herself on the warmth of the flagstones. The rays of the rising sun gleamed from the polished surface of the oak table centered on the patio.

Sean and Patrick made a place for Madison between them. Doc Bailey gave the final instructions to the orderlies packing the last of the crates beside the back door. Everyone around the table stood as he led Louisa Canby to the table. Abigail refilled the coffee mugs and took her place beside Mrs. Canby.

They bowed their heads as Louisa said grace. After the "Amen", she nodded to Madison. "Welcome back, Captain Madison, and congratulations on your promotion."

"Thank you, Ma'am. It's mighty good to be back. It's not every day one receives a parole and a promotion at the same time."

Abigail took a sip of coffee. "I understand Colonel Chavez was part of the trade."

Madison nodded. "Yes. It didn't seem quite fair, trading a Colonel for a Captain, but I was not one to complain. Ironically, he was not any more eager to return to Fort Union than I was eager to leave. The place is really quite depressing."

He watched the rooster pecking at some unseen insect. He shrugged and added, "A little southern charm would have done the place a world of good."

Mrs. Canby sat back in her chair. "Speaking of southern charm, on behalf of myself and the other Union wives who chose to remain in Santa Fe, I must express my appreciation to you and your men."

She began passing bowls of scrambled eggs and grits, then continued. "When our soldiers retreated from here in the wake of your coming, several of us decided to stay, rather than leave our homes empty. We did not anticipate the actions of the local criminal elements nor the looting that would occur. It is not often one welcomes the occupation of the enemy, but such was the case. You returned order and safety to our city, and truly lived up to the term of southern gentlemen. For that we are grateful."

Madison shook his head. "Ah, my dear Mrs. Canby, it is to you we are eternally grateful. You opened your home to our wounded. You organized transportation for them from the battlefield when we were not able to provide that ourselves. I even have heard reports that you revealed the whereabouts of hidden caches of food and supplies and blankets. Through your kindness and compassion, many lives have been saved that would otherwise have been lost. You truly are the 'Angel of Santa Fe'. You have captured the hearts of far more men than your husband will ever capture souls on the battlefield."

Mrs. Canby smiled. She shook her head. "I'm no angel, only an instrument of God's mercy. God sometimes puts us in unusual situations." She looked from Sean to Abigail. "He brings us together in difficult circumstances." She gestured to the tents of the wounded in the meadow beyond her home. "Whether friend or foe, the wounded must be cared for. They are, after all, the sons of some dear mother. How could I do less than what I have?"

She toyed with the flapjack on her plate with the tines of

her fork. She touched Abigail's arm even though she spoke to Madison. "I understand you will be leaving soon."

Madison replied, "Yes, we will be leaving at first light tomorrow to rejoin General Sibley in Albuquerque. It would seem your husband would prefer we return to Texas as soon as possible."

Mrs. Canby dabbed the corners of her mouth as if to give herself time to collect her thoughts. When she spoke, it was as if to all of them, yet at the same time to herself. "'Tis a pity we cannot get along. We are a great country, you know. I have had the privilege of serving with my husband from the shores of the Potomac to the beaches of the Pacific in the new state of California. We are a great country."

There was a bitterness in her voice as she continued. "Yet, I have seen many atrocities in the name of democracy, many injustices in the name of freedom…to the Indians and the Mexicans as well as the black slaves. I've heard all the pros and cons, of state's rights and civil rights, of southern rights and northern rights. But there is nothing right about brother fighting brother, and father fighting son; of family fighting family and neighbor fighting friend."

She dabbed a tear from the corner of her eye with her napkin. "One day, we will be reunited as one country. Until then, I wish each of you Godspeed. I cannot wish you victory, but I can wish you Godspeed."

She stood as the grand lady she was and announced, "And now, gentlemen, if you would clear the table of my china, I would ask that you return my dining table and chairs to their proper place in the east room, and I wish you adieu."

The men rose and in unison bowed to their hostess. She acknowledged their gesture, then bent and whispered to Abigail, "Walk with me, if you would."

Abigail and Mrs. Canby walked arm in arm, down the path between the crocuses and daffodils struggling to poke their heads through the cold ground. Mrs. Canby did not break the silence until they had settled themselves on a wrought iron bench beneath a tall pinion pine. She took each of Abigail's hands in hers. "Selfishly, I would ask that you stay here, rather than leave with the others tomorrow, but I know that is not something you can do. You see, I had a daughter, Mary, who would be just about your age. She died while we were in California."

Abigail whispered, "I'm so sorry."

Mrs. Canby continued. "You remind me of myself at your age, so I would like to think Mary would be like you, a strong, brave, courageous young lady. So, I will tell you what I would tell her...be kind, be generous, be true to yourself, and be true to your God. And," she added, "take care of those two young men. They both love you very much."

Abigail felt herself blush.

"Now go join your friends, and may God be with you."

Abigail whispered, "And also with you."

***

The light from the lantern flickered over the maps spread before Colonel Green and Captain Madison. Green had given numerous orders to his officers, leaving only Madison, Sean and Patrick remaining at the table. The colonel peered into the shadows where Abigail had been standing. "Miss McFerrin, you may as well join us. You are as much of this group as any man here."

Sean grinned as he pulled out a chair for her.

Green continued. "Gentlemen, we could enumerate the 'what if's' of the past days; what if the Colorado volunteers had not arrived when they did; what if Sibley had sent the needed supplies and reinforcements; what if we had captured the Union supply train instead of losing our own. There are always the 'what if's' of battle. The bottom line is that, in spite of our hard-fought victory up in Glorietta Pass, our Colorado campaign is devastated and at an end. Tomorrow, I will be taking what is left of our army to join Sibley in Albuquerque and try to get us back to Texas without losing any more men."

He rubbed his temples with his fingertips. "However, Captain Madison, I have another assignment for you and your men. While Canby and most of the troops from Fort Union and Fort Garland are busy escorting us back to Texas, I need for you to go back up to Peterson's Ranch. Your assignment is to harass the union forces, especially the communications between Fort Union and Fort Garland, confiscating as much Union gold in the process as possible. We will expect you to join us in San Antonio by winter."

He turned to Abigail. "Miss McFerrin, I wish to thank you for your valuable assistance these past few months. Captain Madison has had nothing but praise for you." He slipped an envelope from beneath the maps. "This letter came for you this afternoon. I apologize that it has taken this long to reach you, as it appears to have been sent several weeks ago. It actually came with the last of the parolees from Fort Union. I believe it was passed along by a lieutenant Edward Anderson."

"Edward?" With trembling hands, Abigail took the letter. Her fingers traced the woven texture of her father's stationery. Patrick held the lantern as she broke the *MC* seal. She silently read over the short message. Then, with a trembling voice, read it aloud for the others to hear.

> *Dear Miss Abby,*
> *Shortly after you left, Master James became ill.*
> *Mr. Anderson brought Doc Adams over from Fairplay.*
> *He says your father has had a stroke.*
> *Please come home when you can.*
> *Love,*
> *Lisette*

Abigail put her hand to her mouth. She felt as if someone had hit her in the stomach, knocking the wind from her lungs. She gasped as she crumpled sobbing into Patrick's arms. "Oh, Paddy, not Father, not strong, healthy, vibrant Father."

She stared back at the letter through her tears. Madison

said gently, "We'll depart first thing in the morning for Peterson's Ranch. From there, Patrick, you will have leave to take your sister home."

Madison and Green left quietly, leaving the three alone at the table. Sean broke the silence. "I should leave also. I'll get things ready for an early departure in the morning."

Abigail laid her hand on his arm to stop him. "No, don't go. You are part of us. You are part of me. Please stay."

She turned to Patrick. "What should we do?"

"We have no alternative. If Madison is willing to give us the time off, we must go back to check on father. After that, we will see."

He patted her arm. "Father is strong. He will pull through this like he always has. There is no use in fretting until we see the situation for ourselves."

Abigail looked at Sean. "Will you come to the ranch with us?"

"Should I?"

She nodded. "Patrick will need you. I will need you."

He put his fingers to her cheek. "Then I will come."

CHAPTER 32

Sean peered down the barrel of his rifle into the light of the fireplace. He wanted to ensure it was clean after their day of hunting. Patrick looked up from where he was sitting cross-legged on the hearth, a sketch pad spread on his lap.

Abigail entered through the hall door and sank into the leather settee, the firelight illuminating her tired eyes. "He's resting peacefully. Lisette has finally gone to bed as well."

Sean handed her a cup from the side table. "Lisette left this for you. Some tea laced with a little whiskey, I believe. She thought it would help you sleep."

Sean admired Abigail's stamina as much as he was concerned about her health. The trip up from Santa Fe had been difficult on all of them. The snow had not melted completely over La Veta Pass which had made travel tedious. Twice they had to make detours to avoid Union troops.

James had been very happy and relieved to see them. From Sean's point of view, he looked fine. However, he still was having some trouble speaking, and he used a cane as his left leg remained weak under his weight.

Abigail motioned to her brother. "Let's see your work."

Patrick laid the pencil aside and turned the pad for her to see. "Just a sketch of the stag Sean killed up by Sugar Lake this morning."

She smiled. "As always, you have a way of capturing the essence of the scene. And I'm sure Alfred and Lisette will appreciate the fresh venison."

Sean took the pad. "This is fantastic. I didn't know you could draw like this. And what does this mean below the drawing, 'As the deer panteth for the waters, so my soul panteth after Thee'?"

Patrick took back the pad. "The words are from the Psalms in the Bible, young King David's thoughts while running from Saul." He sighed, then glanced at Sean. "Not unlike our avoiding union soldiers on our trip up from Santa Fe, yes?" He looked at his sister, then back to the page. "I've always liked to draw. It's just another one of the many things that irritated Father."

Abigail spoke softly, "He was very glad to see you."

Patrick stared into the fire. "I suppose."

Sean wanted to ask, but was afraid to. As long as he had known Patrick, there had been a tense silence when the subject of his father arose.

As if Patrick knew what he was thinking, he began to speak. "I was never quite the son Father wanted me to be. I liked to read and write and sketch. I couldn't ride and rope and shoot like he thought a man out here in the untamed west should be able. Not like William."

Sean shrugged. "I don't know, you did pretty well riding that bronc last fall at the festival."

"Yeah, but you'll remember, Edward rode better."

Sean added, "And you shoot darn straight, if you ask me. You saved my life."

Patrick shook his head and stared into the fire.

Abigail broke the silence. "After all we have been through the past couple of months, this past week has seemed nicely tame." Patrick and Sean both chuckled.

Abigail continued softly. "You both could stay here. You don't have to go back."

Patrick looked up. "Another one of the things Father accused me of was never finishing what I started. Even if I'm not sure what we're fighting for." He stared into the fire, then added, "If I ever did. And even if I think we don't have a chance of winning, too many of my friends have died. I have to see this through."

Sean continued to clean his rifle. He wanted to console his friend. He searched for the right words. After all, it was his fault Patrick was involved. It was because of him that Patrick was in this situation. But no adequate words came.

Patrick got to his feet. Picking up his sketch pad, he nodded to Sean. "Get some rest. We leave in the morning."

Abigail turned to Sean. "How is your side?"

"There is still some pain, but it has healed nicely. I can't say I appreciated the treatment, but I know it was for the best. I will have a nice scar to show my grandchildren."

She looked away. "You could stay here. You could use the excuse of your wound. Madison would understand."

He shook his head. "You know that is not possible. Just like Patrick, I have to see this through."

"Then I will go back with you. Father is recovering nicely under Lisette's care and watchful eye. And William is having no problem running the ranch."

Sean smiled. "Madison warned me you would say that." He pulled a letter from his coat. "Madison gave me this to give to you before our return. It is instructions for further surveillance he would like for you to do for him. Although I do not know the specifics of the orders, and our larger campaign in Colorado has been thwarted, there is still need for information regarding enemy troop movement, supplies, etc. There is a blacksmith and a store keeper in Fairplay who are southern sympathizers. Any information is to be funneled to them."

He brought the letter to her and sat beside her. With the path that lay ahead of him, he knew he should not share with her what filled his mind, but he could not stop himself.

He took both of her hands in his. "My dearest Abigail,

I've loved you from the moment I looked down the barrel of your rifle. I loved you as we thawed you out at Peterson's Ranch. I loved you as I jealously watched you dance with Colonel Chavez at Fort Union. I loved you as you nursed me back to health in Santa Fe. And I love you with all my heart right now."

He shut his eyes as he continued. "There was a time when my family had land and wealth and prestige. Now, all I have to offer you is my love, but that I offer to you."

Abigail wrapped her arms around his neck. Through her tears she whispered. "From the day you rode into the *MC* with Patrick, you've been in my mind and my heart. Your love is all I want or need."

Sean held her close as their lips met, first lightly, then again and again as the passion raced through his being. Visions of his dream flashed through his mind. He pulled back so that he could look into her eyes.

"Where Patrick and I go from here, and what we will see, and what we will have to endure, only God knows. My selfish being would wish for you to be by my side, but where we are going, you cannot go. But I swear, if God is willing, I will come back to you."

***

The crowing of the rooster and Lisette found them still in each other's arms.

CHAPTER 33

Abigail adjusted the blanket over her father's lap. Even though the August sun shimmered on the bleached shingles of the stable and gleamed from the tops of the fence rails, he still complained of being cold. She had observed improvement in his strength over the past days and weeks, but he continued to have difficulty speaking and kept his cane near at hand.

She sat on the top step of the porch beside the pile of string beans that waited for her attention. Snapping beans was not her favorite pastime, but it was a simple chore that allowed her mind to wander.

Rather than immediately attack the job before her, Abigail reread Madison's letter. She wished he had been more succinct in his instructions. She had made one visit to Fairplay, but had no information to pass along. Rather, she had simply wanted to observe the two gentlemen referenced in the directive. She saw no need to force an encounter until the need arose.

Lisette called from the line where she was spreading sheets to dry. She pointed with a clothes pin at the lone rider cantering down the lane. Abigail recognized Edward by the way he rode, before she could actually see his face. She was annoyed by her quickened pulse, not sure if it was due to their last encounter, or if she might still have personal feelings for him. It was amazing how alike he and Sean were in stature, yet so different in temperament.

She slipped the letter in her apron pocket and pretended to concentrate on the beans in her lap.

Edward dismounted and flipped the reins over the porch rail. He nodded to Abigail. "It's good to see you back here..." His voice trailed off.

"Where I belong?" Abigail finished his sentence.

He ignored her comment. He brushed by her to speak to her father before returning to sit on the step beside her. He took a handful of beans into his lap.

She was amused by the sight of his big, rough hands twisting the ends from the bean pods and breaking them into the bowl between them. "You are quite handsome in your *Federal* uniform. It does seem a bit incongruous for you to be snapping beans instead of shooting at people."

He continued with several beans before he answered. "I'm not sure what 'in congress' means. But I do know a man will do strange things to be with the girl he loves."

Abigail bit her lip as she fought the blush she knew was creeping up her neck onto her face. She looked away. "A man should be careful how he uses the word love. It could come back to haunt him."

They both shuffled uncomfortably. Abigail broke the tension with a question that might prove useful. "Has your unit returned to Denver from Fort Union? Is the regiment intact?"

"Yes, we've been back for about a month now. Two companies have been sent to fight over in eastern Kansas territory. Things here have been quiet lately, since the rebels are back in Texas. Actually, it makes for a mighty boring time." He gave her a sidelong glance. "Is Paddy still with Madison?"

Abigail glanced back at her father. She finished the few beans left in her lap and said softly, "Let's take a walk down to the stable. I'll show you the new mare the boys brought down from the high country."

She slipped off the apron, folding it carefully so that

Madison's letter remained snugly inside the pocket. She couldn't help but wonder if Edward was here to gather information as much as he was to visit her and her father.

Edward untied his horse. Chickens scattered to make way for the three of them. Abigail contemplated her answer. She hoped a half-truth wasn't really a lie. "I'm not sure where Paddy is or what unit he's with now. Since their hard-fought victory at Glorietta Pass and then *your* destruction of their supply train, everything was thrown into confusion."

He toyed with a clod of dirt with the toe of his boot. "Should I apologize for that?"

"Of course not. War is war. We all must do what we must do." She touched his arm. "I thank you again for sparing me and Doc Bailey. You didn't have to do that."

He nodded. "I caught hell from Chivington for not destroying everything, but it was the humane thing to do. Besides, I couldn't let anything happen to you, you know that."

He picked up a clod and tossed it at a sparrow sitting on a fence post. "I hope Paddy's not still with Madison. His gang robbed a mail train headed for Fort Garland. Got a chest full of gold and payroll money. There's a bounty of $800.00 on their heads. We know they've set up camp again at Mace's Hole. Chivington's talkin' about putting together a posse to flush 'em out.

Abigail wasn't sure if he was telling her all of this to scare her, give her information, or just talking to have something to say.

They stopped to admire the new Appaloosa. Without looking at Abigail, Edward asked, "Did he kiss you?"

Shocked, Abigail turned to stare at him. Rather than answer, she unlatched the gate to the mare's stall. "I'll get a saddle and we can ride down to the slough."

***

They kept the horses at a canter. The ride gave Abigail time to collect her thoughts. At the same time, she was distracted by the blending of horse and rider beside her. They stopped at the water's edge to give the horses a rest and allow them time for a drink.

Abigail nodded toward the stallion. "Sabbath truly is a beautiful horse." She added, "And you ride him well."

Edward patted the neck of his steed. "He and I have been through a lot together. I'm still amazed I was able to stay on him last fall at the festival."

He traced the horn of his saddle with his gloved fingers. Without looking up, he asked, "May I visit again?"

Abigail replied incredulously, "Of course you can come to visit. You're family."

She bit the finger of her glove before she continued, knowing full well his true intentions. "No matter what side you or my brother are fighting on in this horrible war, Father has made it very clear that the *MC* is to remain neutral. As long as I am helping to run the ranch, I will honor his wishes." She took a deep breath, looked him in the eye, and with as much force as she could muster, added, "And until this war is over and all our boys come marching home again, I will remain neutral."

She looked into the western sky where the sun was sinking below the mountain peaks. "I must be getting back, as you should as well. Thank you for coming to visit Father. I'm sure he greatly appreciated it." Without giving him a chance to reply, she spurred the mare to a gallop.

***

Edward watched her go. He spat into the water between the cattails. *Neutral, indeed. She would not be neutral if it weren't for that black-haired Southerner. It's too bad that musket ball hadn't pierced his heart instead of his side. Maybe, before this war is over, I'll have a chance to rectify that.*

CHAPTER 34

Abigail toyed with her father's writing pen. She wanted to use as few words as possible to portray the message in case it fell into the wrong hands. At the same time, the warning needed to be clear. She dipped the point into the inkwell and carefully penned her cryptic message.

> *GM*
> *Your location is compromised.*
> *Posse is formed.*
> *Retreat is eminent.*
> *AM*

She looked it over again. She knew what she meant. She could only hope Madison would understand.

***

Abigail left William with the buckboard in front of Thompson's mercantile. She raised her skirt out of the dust of the main street of Fairplay, dodging a miner's string of mules and two drunken old-timers that reeked of booze and six months of sweat.

Saloons, poorly built log cabins and a dozen miners' tents

lined the thoroughfare. She reminisced of the days when the valley of South Park was inhabited by deer and antelope rather than gold-seeking men from all over the world. She could only hope no one would discover gold in her quiet, pristine valley over Weston Pass.

She checked in with Doc Adams and went next door to purchase her father's medications from the apothecary. Carefully, she picked her way back across the street to help William with their purchases. Admittedly, civilization made the acquisition of supplies easier, but she wasn't sure it was worth it.

She waited while Mr. Thompson checked over the list with William and two young Union soldiers finished their purchase of tobacco. She looked around to ensure no one else was present.

Her pulse raced to the reaction of her fears. She thought through the code Madison had given her. She cleared her throat. "Mr. Thompson, the snows on Eagle Mountain have come early this year."

Thompson jerked. He stared at her, wide-eyed. He looked around the store before he answered. "The sheep and goats have been brought down to the valley."

Abigail sighed with relief. "And they are safely in the fold."

She pulled an envelope from a concealed pocket in her bodice. "Here is the payment for our recent purchases. Should there be anything additional contained within, will you be certain to get it to the proper persons?"

He nodded and smiled. "You can be assured the matter will be handled discreetly.

CHAPTER 35

They had just finished decorating the Christmas tree when the package and letter arrived. With shaking hands, Abigail broke the seal on the envelope.

December, 1862
My Dearest Abigail,
Salutations from the great Republic of Texas.
Patrick is well. He sends his love and wishes for a Joyous Christmas to all there.
GM also sends his regards. He is grateful for your timely message. Our egress was uneventful. We rejoined our friends without incident.
Their retreat, however, was not without its difficulties. After our parting in SF, they traveled down the Rio Grande to Peralta which is south of Albuquerque. It was there they encountered Canby's forces. There was a hard-fought battle in the canals and trees of the town. It could have been disastrous for them, had not a sandstorm shielded their escape. It would seem that God gives us His protection, even though he withholds our victory.
In contrast, our endeavors were successful. We accomplished what we set out to do in the time that was

allotted.

Patrick was disappointed to receive word that your friend (and his) Florence has been taken by the fancy of a Union soldier. However, in typical Patrick fashion, it has not taken him long to recover. He has begun to woo a preacher's young daughter. Of course, this war has separated them as it has us. I suppose only time will tell the outcome of both.

That being said, I miss you more than mere words can express. Yet, I would wish on no one the experience of southern Texas. How I miss your snow-capped mountains and lush green valleys. Christmas on the Texas coast will not at all seem like a holiday. At least there should be a lull in the fighting during the season.

We have no idea where we will end up come spring. Texas seems safe from invasion, so Louisiana seems like a possibility.

As much as I long to be with you, I cannot, in all good conscience, ask you to wait for me until this war is over. The Lord only knows how long it may drag on or what the consequences may be. Therefore, I would hold you to no obligations. Only know that I have never before cared for anyone as I do you.

May you have a Blessed Christmas. I can only hope we may be together in the coming year.

With much affection,
Sean

Abigail wiped a tear from her cheek as she reread the last paragraph. *I long to be with you, but you don't have to wait for me.* She whispered to herself, "What is that supposed to mean? Sean McKay, if I didn't love you, I'd hate you."

She opened the package revealing a brooch of filigree silver surrounding a polished turquois stone. A note read, *The Indians here do fantastic work in silver. A beautiful piece of jewelry for a beautiful girl.* She shook her head and pinned it to the neck of her blouse.

The jingle of sleigh bells interrupted her thoughts. The

Andersons had arrived for Christmas dinner. Edward was at the door, knocking the snow from his boots. Abigail dried her eyes, folded Sean's letter, slipped it behind the clock on the mantle, and went to greet their guests.

***

Dinner and the exchange of gifts had been tense. Abigail wished they had cancelled this year. The war seemed to affect everything. Besides, Edward had pouted from the moment he came through the door. She wondered why he had come.

He stayed behind after the rest of the family had left. With the mood that he was in, she contemplated if she should have asked William or Lisette to stay with her, but it was too late.

She sat in one of the leather chairs in front of the hearth. He sat stiffly on the settee. He looked at her and then into the fire. He finally spoke. "What do I need to do? How can I ..." He glared at her with those steely blue eyes. "I need you. I want you. Don't you realize that?"

All Abigail could think was Sean's words of love and Edward's of want and need.

He stood as she did. He nodded toward her new brooch. He snarled, "Your new piece of jewelry looks like some of that cheap Indian junk down in New Mexico territory. I suppose your new southern beau sent that to you." He curled his lip. "Well, with any luck, our true American boys will take care of him and the rest like him." He turned and stomped from the room, the door swinging in the winter wind.

CHAPTER 36

The afternoon sun poured down its hot rays. Dust swirled up from the carriage wheels. "It seems quite hot and dry, even for the middle of the summer," Abigail commented. William nodded his agreement as he guided the team around two boys rolling a hoop down the center of the busy thoroughfare.

Abigail fanned herself, wishing for lighter clothes than all the petticoats and corset and hoops and yards of material of her dress. But this was a business trip, not a cattle drive.

Denver City had changed greatly since the last time Abigail had been there. Actual clapboard buildings had taken the place of lean-to shacks and canvas tents. In places, a board-walk lined the dusty street in front of some establishments.

A military wagon rumbled by, followed by a half a dozen soldiers. Abigail was grateful to have William by her side. He pointed to the only three-story building on the street. He dismounted, tied the horses to the hitching rail and helped her to the ground.

A robust gentleman in a top hat exited as they climbed the steps to the broad front porch. He held the door for Abigail, then rudely sniffed as William followed her into the crowded room. Abigail crossed the lobby to the wide mahogany desk. The room smelled of stale cigar smoke and musty wood. She had only been within the walls of the Denver House Hotel once before on the arm of her father for a July 4th gala. To be here without him was a bit intimidating, but Larimer had requested a meeting.

She was not sure if the stares of the men in the room were directed at her or William at her arm. She smiled inwardly at the thought if she had brought Running deer and Little Fox along. She was glad that William carried himself above any discriminating attitudes. She certainly felt safe with him at her side.

The man behind the desk looked down his nose over his wireframe spectacles. "How may I help you?" he asked coldly, looking first at Abigail and then at William.

"I'm Miss Abigail McFerrin. This is William McFerrin. I believe you have two adjoining rooms reserved for us."

The man sputtered. "Miss McFerrin, I did not recognize you. Certainly your room is ready." He hesitated. "However, I don't know that we have a room available for, uh, 'Mr. McFerrin'."

Abigail leaned across the counter. "Sir, our *father* owns half interest in this establishment. He sent word ahead for you to have two rooms ready for our arrival. I expect you to have two adjoining rooms ready by the time we reach the second floor. Is that understood?"

The man swallowed and nodded. "Yes, Ma'am. Rooms 2A and 2B at the top of the stairs on your right. I will have the boy bring your bags right up."

Abigail nodded and replied with forced politeness. "Thank you so very much."

She turned to William. "I'm so sorry for that little incident."

He shrugged. "I was prepared to rearrange his nose with my fist. However, you did a very nice job without me." She placed her arm on his and they ascended the stairs.

***

The paperwork on the table fluttered in the warm evening breeze from the open window. Abigail looked out onto the busy street below. It was difficult for her to believe it had been two years ago in a distant place south of here that there had been a battle in a narrow pass. It seemed such a distant place and time.

The balmy summer evening seemed to encourage pedestrians and riders to be out and about, long after the street lights had come to life. Tunes of dueling honky-tonk pianos from opposite ends of the street clashed their discordant melodies. Two drunken miners stumbled from the saloon across the street. A prostitute screamed at her patron who hurried down the side steps of the building, his pants in his hand.

William tapped the book in front of him. "Everything else seems in order for your meeting tomorrow with Mr. Larimer except for this one ledger. The numbers don't add up."

Abigail added them again. "You're absolutely correct. I will question him in the morning."

She poured them each a glass of water. "Thank you for coming with me. Father was as much relieved as was I when you agreed to accompany me. Besides, it is good to have another set of eyes going over all this paperwork."

He started to answer, but instead went to the window and pushed it open wide. "Do you smell that? It smells like smoke."

From down the street someone yelled, "Fire!" That was followed by more yells and the clanging of a fire wagon.

Quickly they gathered the papers together and placed them back into the leather pouch. William tucked it under his arm and they joined the crowd in the street. Flames engulfed two clapboard houses and smoke curled from the roof of a third. Even as the volunteer firemen pumped water over the flames, burning embers floated on the night breeze to the saloon across the street.

Abigail tugged at William's arm. She shouted over the roar of the fire and the yells of the crowd. He handed her the satchel of papers and his coat. She tried to stop him, but he had already run to aid the bucket brigade.

The dry shingles burst into flame like the kindling they were. The saloon glowed like a fiery inferno. An explosion, undoubtedly the kegs of liquor, sent burning debris in all directions.

Abigail wrapped the satchel of documents in William's coat. She ran to the end of the street to the bridge over Cherry Creek. She stumbled down the bank. Hastily she stuffed the coat under a slab of the bridge abutment and went back to join the losing battle of the bucket brigade.

***

The morning sun shone red through the smoke. The center of Denver City lay in smoldering piles of ashes. Only the banks of Cherry Creek had contained it.

Small knots of people shook their heads in disbelief. The owner of a mercantile sifted through the remains of his wares. A saloon keeper retrieved an unbroken bottle of whiskey. He shook his head and uncorked the bottle. In a tired, raspy voice he called out, "Drinks are on the house."

Exhausted, Abigail and William stepped around the debris in the street. The sign for the Denver House Hotel hung by one corner from a lone column. That and the stone steps were all that remained.

"Abigail. William."

Abigail turned. Larimer and his wife Rachel crossed the street from the direction of the burned out saloon. Rachel held out her arms. "You poor dears. We have a buckboard at the end of the street. Let us get you back to the house to get you cleaned up and get you some breakfast."

Abigail retrieved the satchel of documents and joined them. Over scrambled eggs and bacon, she asked, "Where do we go from here? Is everything lost?"

Larimer chuckled. "Ah, my dear, out of the ashes rise the Phoenix. In many ways, that fire last evening was a God-send. Now that Denver City has become established, it was time for some permanence. We will rebuild bigger and better than before. Your father and I can invest in a brick foundry. Then, as a founding father, I will insist that we rebuild with brick instead of wood. We will cobble stone the streets and provide board sidewalks. We will make this a city of which to be proud. The next time you come to Denver, there will be a fine, brick Denver House Hotel, with crystal chandeliers from the ceilings and velvet curtains at the windows."

Rachel patted Abigail's arm. "He is forever the dreamer, yet a visionary that makes things happen. Trust me, if anyone can do it, he will."

After a bath and a change of clothes, Abigail conducted the necessary business with Larimer. As they finished, he reached into his desk drawer. "I almost forgot this in all the excitement. This letter came for you back a few days. I wasn't quite sure why it came via my office, but I kept it for you."

Abigail waited to open it until she was alone in Mrs. Larimer's flower garden. She could not be sure, but it appeared that the seal had been broken and new wax added.

June, 1864

Dearest Abigail,

Your letters have been most appreciated. It is with true apologies that I have not written more often.

It is with great thankfulness to hear of your father's return to good health. I am sure it is of great relief to you.

As always, Patrick sends his love and best regards. By some grace of God, he and I have come through battle after battle relatively unscathed. That, sadly, is not the case with so many of our friends and comrades.

It has been my lot and privilege to see much of our divided country from north to south and east to west. I am constantly amazed by its diversity in both geography and people. It is no wonder we cannot get along.

My thoughts were that Texas could be a desolate place. Yet, it seems it was quite heavenly compared to Louisiana. The entire state is barely above sea level. Although there are places of great beauty, swamp land is prevalent everywhere, breeding mosquitos the size of hummingbirds with stings worse than that of the Yellow-jackets of southern Missouri.

Our men have fought bravely, often against horrendous odds. I have a tremendous respect for our Texas comrades. They fight with tireless abandon. Such was the case of our attack on Fort Butler just up the Mississippi from New Orleans.

You will appreciate the make-up of Fort Butler. It, like Fort Union, was an earthwork star fort. However, in this case, and unbeknownst to us, it was encircled by a brick-lined moat some sixteen feet wide and twelve feet deep. (Where are our good spies when we need them? Ha.)

Due to the nature of the situation, we attacked just after midnight. All went relatively well until we became trapped in the moat where we became sitting ducks for their artillery and marksmen on the walls. We were unable to advance or retreat. We acquired heavy loss of lives and many wounded including Colonel Madison, whom Patrick and I helped to escape during a truce negotiation. As has been so often the case, our men fought valiantly, but the victory was not ours.

From there, we were called up to the capital at Shreveport to join General Taylor with the intent to counter the Federal movement up the Red River. We first engaged the Union forces on the road south of Mansfield. They had allowed themselves to become strung out for some twenty miles. They were completely routed. It was the greatest victory of which Patrick and I have been a part. Over 1,500 Union soldiers were taken prisoner, twenty artillery pieces and two hundred wagons were captured and some 1000 horses and mules confiscated. I must say, this made up somewhat for the loss of our supply train at Glorietta.

We continued to harass the retreating Union forces. One afternoon, 200 of us while on patrol with Madison, encountered a force of (we were told later) 2000 Union soldiers near Pleasant Hill. We were initially pushed back to the trees and marshes of Bayou Fordoche. We held our ground and by nightfall had driven them back toward Morganza.

As so often, Colonel Madison proved once again his bravery, courage, and tremendous leadership abilities. We would follow him to the ends of the earth.

However, in my and Patrick's case, we will not be following him on up to Arkansas from here. We received our orders this morning. Due to the secrecy of the mission, I will be unable to write for an indeterminate amount of time. To be with you shortly would be my greatest desire.

As this war continues to drag on, my affections for you only grow stronger. I can only hope the same is true for you.

Yours,

Sean

Abigail folded the letter and returned it to its envelope. *A secret mission... see her shortly.* "Could he be back in Colorado?" She whispered to herself.

"A letter from Patrick, or is it from your southern friend?" Edward appeared from the shade of a sycamore tree.

Startled, Abigail tucked the letter into the folds of the satin sash at her waist. "A personal letter from a personal friend. Why? Are you spying on me?"

"Quite the contrary. We are stationed just outside the city. I only wanted to ensure your well-being after the disastrous fire last night. And to express my concern for your brother and his friend. There are rumors that some rebel spies have joined the Roberts gang down around Trinidad. I do hope Paddy's not one of them. You know what happens to spies and outlaws ."

Abigail bit her lip. "The last word I received was they were with Green's regiment when they drove the Federals down the Red River from Shreveport. But I do appreciate your concern."

To her relief, William appeared at the corner of the house. To Edward she nodded, "Now if you will excuse me, we must get on our way back to the *MC.*

***

Edward glowered as he watched her go. *Secret mission. His secret is not so secret after all.*

CHAPTER 37 (A)

Madison's words hung heavy on Sean's thoughts. *The Confederacy is broke. The blockades have stymied our income. The War Department is desperate for money.*

I'm sending you and Patrick back into Colorado. You are to meet up with Jameson and Henry Thompson. They've been with the Roberts Gang for the past year, robbing Union gold shipments and the like. It's not a lot, but it has been a steady stream of income for the Cause.

Dust from the horses' hooves threatened to choke them, in spite of the neckerchiefs covering their noses. The late summer's heat bore down with a vengeance. Sean could just make out Higgins' Station in the distance through the wavering heat-rays rising from the desert floor.

Patrick broke the silence. "This war has definitely given us some twists and turns. We joined up with Madison as spies, did a little outlawing with him, then some soldiering, and now we're back to being outlaws. Gotta wonder what will be next."

Sean coughed and took a swig from his canteen. "Not exactly what I was expecting. I hope you're not sorry I got you involved."

Patrick laughed. "Shoot no. Why, it's been one adventure after another. This will just be another chapter in the continuing saga." He slapped at a horsefly buzzing around his head. "What do you remember about the Thompson brothers?"

"Not much. They knew Madison down in Arizona. I think they were a part of his original spy ring. Decent men. Fought well at Glorietta."

Higgins' Station looked deserted. Any living being had been driven in by the heat. Sean and Patrick tied the horses in the shade of the scrub oaks behind the building. They dusted themselves off and looked for some sign of life.

Higgins met them at the door. "Paddy McFerrin. Good to see you, boy. And likewise, Mr. McKay. Been expecting you." He nodded toward the back corner of the room. "Couple friends of yours been waiting for you. I'll bring a bottle of whiskey to wash down the dust."

Jameson and Henry Thompson. Sean remembered them as soon as he saw them. Stocky fellows. Almost looked like twins. Good fighters.

After a few drinks and talk about the heat and the war, Patrick asked, "So what are we looking at? What's the situation here?"

Jameson took a drink, then stared into the distance as if to collect his thoughts. "Well, the Roberts boys are a little rough. Clyde's the oldest. Big bear of a man. He's the brains of the operation. We answer to him. He can be mean, but he's fair."

"He and his brother Samson fought with Jackson in both the Battles of First Manassas and Second Manassas. They lost two of their brothers in the latter battle. After that, they picked up their younger brother, Daniel from their farm in the bootheel of Missouri and headed out here."

Henry joined in. "They're not a bad sort. Just bitter. Daniel's the hot-tempered one. Keeps Clyde busy keeping him in line." He added. "Then there's an old prospector. Bart. He's a quiet one. Keeps to himself. Still not sure about him."

Patrick stroked the stubble on his chin. "How's the loot divided?"

"It's all divided evenly," Henry answered. "They keep

their share. Me and Jameson keep what we need to get by and send the rest by courier south for the Cause."

Jameson continued. "Clyde's expecting us. We're to meet him down in Maces Hole. He's got a half a dozen jobs lined up for us before winter sets in. Once the snow flies, we'll split up for the winter. Madison has made arrangements for the two of you to stay with a rancher and his wife, Constance and Charles Knowles, outside of Trinidad.

"If'n y'all are ready, let's head out."

CHAPTER 37 (B)

Sean watched the interaction between Constance and Charles Knowles, a silent harmony rarely seen, especially out here in the "wild west". Especially during war. His pulse jumped when he wondered what it would be like to have Abigail at his side like that. He quickly wiped that thought from his mind.

Constance placed the bowl of potatoes on the table. Young Joshua slid the platter of meat in front of his father, and younger Ruth carried the gravy. After they had taken their places at the table, Charles said grace.

He nodded to Sean and Patrick. "This delightful aroma of roasted venison is due to you boys. We are greatly appreciative."

Patrick smiled. "And we are greatly appreciative of your hospitality over these cold winter months."

Charles speared a slice of meat and handed the platter to Sean. "It's the least we could do for the cause. With my gimpy leg, I could hardly go fight."

Constance looked over her glasses at her husband. "You've done enough fightin' for whatever cause, gettin' wounded fightin' the Mexicans in '48." She nodded to Sean and Patrick as she passed the bowl of potatoes. "We do thank you boys for all the help you've been since ridin' in last fall."

Sean smashed a potato and covered it with gravy. "Will there be repercussions from the townspeople in Trinidad, if they find out you've been harboring Rebels and outlaws, do you think?"

Charles chuckled. "Not any more than if they find out young Patrick there has been courting the Reverend's daughter, Emily."

Patrick lowered his head and blushed as the children giggled.

Sean smirked. "From what I've seen of Miss Emily, she's a strong-willed young lady. If anyone can tame my good friend, I think it would be her."

Patrick kicked him in the shin under the table.

Mrs. Knowles became serious. "Now that the snows are melting, will you be returning to your..." she hesitated, "former occupation?"

Patrick used the tines of his fork to cut a groove in his potatoes, allowing the gravy to form a river over his venison. "At this point, it seems a bit useless, but those are our orders."

Sean shut his eyes. The feeling of despair and frustration waved over him, almost making him nauseous. "All of this has been such a waste of time. I would so much rather be on the battlefield, instead of..." He glanced at Constance and then at Charles. "Instead of relieving our Union Army friends of a bit of their gold for our own cause."

Charles sighed. "The news from back east isn't good. Richmond is under siege. Lee will most likely retreat south. Sherman has burned Atlanta and devastated a swath from the Mississippi River to the Atlantic. It's only a matter of time."

Patrick glanced at Sean then down at his plate. "We have placed our hand on the plow. We will continue to the end. There is nothing else we can do."

Constance looked over her glasses at them. "Doesn't sound to me like you boys are really taken with bein' outlaws. Why don't you just head out while you can?"

Sean looked at Patrick before he spoke. "We've talked

about that. We've been able to send a good bit of gold and currency down south, and harassed the Union boys a little along the way." He shook his head. "It just doesn't seem enough to really make our time worthwhile."

Patrick nodded his affirmation. "We've decided to do one more job, then take what we can and head down to find Madison."

Charles nodded. "Just be careful. We wish you God-speed."

Sean nodded to the older couple. "Thank you, sir. Again, we express our gratitude for your kindness. We will be leaving in the morning."

CHAPTER 37 (C)

The blackened shells of the buildings that had been Peterson's ranch were a ghostly reminder of the ravages of war. Sean sighed. It was here Abigail and his lives had begun to become entwined. He was not certain whether that had been a good thing or bad.

The click of four sets of horses' hooves on stone echoed off the canyon walls in the crisp morning air. Sean shivered and pulled his collar up a bit closer around his neck. It was unusually cold for this late in March.

The Thompson brothers had joined them the previous evening outside of Walsenburg. Sean liked Jamison and Henry. They made good outlaws just like they had been soldiers.

The smell of frying bacon welcomed them as they entered the back canyon beyond the burned-out buildings. The Roberts brothers were huddled around a fire. Clyde nodded. "Good to see ya, boys. I trust you wintered well."

Samson stirred the mixture in the skillet. "Get yourselves down here. Salt pork and gravy's about ready. Coffee's hot."

Daniel rubbed his eyes and growled. He looked like he was waking up from a two-day drunk.

Patrick poured each of them a cup of coffee while Samson

divided the contents of the skillet between them.

Daniel broke the silence. He nodded toward Patrick. "Hear-tell you's done took up with the Reverend's daughter down in Trinidad. How was she in bed?"

Sean grabbed Patrick's arm as each man's hand went instinctively to his sidearm. Patrick took a deep breath before he spoke. When he did, it was with a smile. "I did court the Reverend's daughter over the winter. I can assure you, she was a lady when I met her, and she is a lady yet today."

Daniel shrugged. "Too bad. I can assure you, none of the girls in Pueblo were ladies before we got there. And they sure as hell ain't ladies now."

Clyde snarled at his little brother. "That's enough. Shut your mouth and eat."

Jameson took a long drink of coffee. "Rumor has it y'all did a job on your own over Christmas. The stage between Fairplay and Canon City? Driver got shot?"

Clyde nodded. "We'd run out of gambling money. Besides." His eyes seemed to light up with excitement. "There's nothin' like the thrill of robbing a stage."

Daniel added. "Driver deserved to get shot. He called me a kid. I just shot him in the leg. He survived."

Sean considered the conversation he and Patrick had had the previous week. One more job and they were headed south. If this war was going to end in the Confederacy's defeat, he wanted it to end for him on the battlefield, not robbing stages.

A whistle drew their attention to the entrance of the canyon as Bart rode through. He swung down as Patrick poured him a cup of coffee. He nodded to Clyde, then looked around the circle of men. "Gentlemen. I have us some good news. As you know, I wintered over at Fort Bent. A few nights ago, I was playing cards with a Lieutenant. Got him liquored up until his tongue started flappin'."

He took a long drink of coffee, savoring the news. "Seems there's a big gold shipment coming down out of the mountains, plus the Army payroll, headed for Fort Union. Ought to be comin' through Pueblo day after tomorrow. The best part is – the Indians are restless out on the plains. A good part of the troops scheduled to guard the shipment are out hunting savages. It should be ripe fruit ready for easy picking."

Clyde looked around the circle of men. "What do you think? Y'all in?"

Sean looked at Patrick. They nodded to each other. They all voiced their agreement with the plan.

Clyde smiled and nodded. "Then let's go mine us some gold."

CHAPTER 37 (D)

The glow from the fire reflected from the walls of the canyon deep within Maces Hole. With each pass of the whiskey bottle, the laughter and story-telling became more raucous.

Clyde took a deep swig, then bellowed a deep guttural laugh. "That had to be the easiest robbery ever. Those Union boys looked like they had seen a ghost."

Samson joined in. "Paddy. That was one really great plan to meet up with them in that little wooded area instead of any of the other more logical narrow places along the trail. They didn't have a clue what hit them."

Patrick leaned into Sean. "What worries me. It was a little too easy."

Sean nodded. Quietly he replied. "Yes. I will be much relieved when we have our share of the loot and are headed south to meet Madison."

Henry joined his brother, running his fingers through the gold nuggets in one of the casks. "I've never seen so much gold in one place. This sure beats panning or digging for the stuff."

Bart growled. "Little do you know."

Clyde stood up. "Gentlemen. Get some sleep. We'll divide the spoils in the morning and then decide where we go from here."

Bart nodded. "I'll take the first guard duty, although there was no sign of our being followed."

Samson nodded. "Wake me up at midnight. I'll relieve you."

Even as Sean settled down, the whole scenario of the day nagged at him. As Patrick had said, it had all been too easy.

He had barely slipped into a dream-world when a pain stabbed the tender area from his earlier wound. As his vision cleared, the glint from the embers of the fire shown on a circle of rifles.

A voice growled. "Surprise, gentlemen. The Union law has arrived. Sorry to see you here Paddy. You really should find better friends." Another kick slammed into Sean's ribs. "Mr. McKay. Your worst nightmare has just arrived."

Edward!

CHAPTER 38

Abigail shed her leather jacket. She hung it over a post in the corral fence before returning to the young mare she was working to break. She looked up toward the Collegiate peaks. The snows were already receding rapidly, what little had come the past winter. She wiped the sweat from her eyes. It was unseasonably warm for April.

Alfred shouted and waved from the cook wagon. It was early to be taking the herds up to the high pastures, but the lack of snows and the early thaw had left the pastures short. She and Father had agreed with William of the need to move the cattle up earlier than usual.

She patted the neck of the young horse to calm her before walking around the perimeter of the enclosure. After several additional rounds, Abigail took the rope from the horse's neck to let her run. She would try to ride her tomorrow.

Abigail sat on the top rail of the fence. It seemed such a long time ago that she had sat here with Patrick and Sean. So much had happened in these four years. This war, which was supposed to be concluded in a matter of weeks, had dragged into months and years. She sighed. So many men had died. She breathed a prayer for Sean and Patrick and their safety, wherever they might be.

The warmth of the sun did little to brighten her thoughts. It had been over a year since Sean's last letter. Each trip to Fairplay and the one trip to Denver City to attend the gala of the opening of the newly rebuilt Denver House had only brought news and rumors of the escapades of the Roberts gang. Each report seemed to indicate they were becoming more emboldened as the Southern cause was slipping away with each defeat.

A call drew her attention to the lane. Dust curled up from the wheels of a fast approaching buggy. A distraught Florence hopped from the buggy almost before she got the equine stopped. "Oh, Abby, they've captured Patrick and Sean."

Abigail rushed to her. "Florence, calm down and tell me what's happened."

Florence explained the situation between sobs. "Peter, my soldier friend, just came to visit me. He was all excited. Edward had been given the approval by his superiors to form a posse with the intent of capturing the Roberts gang after their last confiscation of mail and Federal gold shipment."

Florence wiped her eyes with her sleeve, fighting to regain her composure. "According to Peter, they cornered five of the gang plus two rebels in a canyon outside Trinidad. The rebels were Patrick and Sean. They're bringing them to Denver City for a trial as spies."

Abigail consoled her friend. After sending her on her way, Abigail made hurried preparations for the trip to Denver City. She did not want to worry her father, so simply told him she needed to take care of some business with Larimer, which certainly wasn't a lie. Since William was on his way to the high pastures, she asked Running Deer and Little Fox to accompany her to the outskirts of the city. It was imperative that she talk with Larimer as quickly as possible.

***

Sean struggled to breathe. The pungent odor of moldy hay and horse dung filled his lungs. The ropes cut further into his wrists each time he attempted to move. He drifted in and out of consciousness from the beating earlier in the day.

The door swung open. Shadows danced in the flickering light of a torch. Sean could just make out his fellow captives tied together in a huddled mass across the manure covered floor of the dilapidated barn.

He cringed when his captor and assailant snarled, "Get him up. String him up by his wrists to that center rafter. I'm not through with him yet."

From across the gloom, Patrick uttered a plea. "Edward, let him be. You've done enough."

"Ah, Paddy, 'tis a pity you've chosen the wrong side of the war and the wrong friends along with it. Now a judge will seal your fate."

He kicked Sean in the side. "As for this piece of Rebel dung, I won't have had enough until he cannot even crawl back to your pretty sister."

Edward's cohorts jerked Sean to his feet. They untied his wrists, only to loop a rope around them once more. They tossed the end of the rope over the support of the center beam below the floor of the hay loft. Sean groaned as they stretched his arms above him until only the tips of his boots reached the ground.

Edward's fist against his jaw lifted Sean off his feet. The ropes cut into his wrists as the weight of his body strained against them. Blood filled his mouth and throat with each ensuing pummel. Sean's stretched gut served as a punching bag for Edward's pounding fists.

Finally, through the misty fog of half-consciousness, Sean heard Edward growl, "Let him down. Throw him over there on that manure pile where he belongs."

His assailants lowered Sean and threw him in a heap against the barn wall. Sean curled into the fetal position, every muscle screaming in agony, the acrid copper taste of blood on his tongue.

Even in his agony, Sean's attention was drawn to the voices outside the walls of his prison. He could just make out images in the pale moon light through the gaping cracks in the barn's siding. He fought the black clouds trying to overtake his mind, doing everything he could to keep his wits about him.

Sean could barely make out Edward's words of instruction to his men, but what he heard brought him back to reality. Edward growled, "Chivington sees a trial as a waste of time, as do I. Yet we cannot hang them here as they deserve." He hesitated, then continued. "We will do everyone a favor." He nodded back toward the barn. "Get your men in place, then bring the prisoners out, telling them they are to be moved to a different location. Then shoot them as they 'try to escape'. I want no survivors. I'm heading for Denver to break the news to the grieving sister and lover."

Sean willed his body to straighten. He gritted his teeth to keep from groaning. He tested the ropes at his wrists. His captors had not checked them after his beating. Using his teeth, he was able to loosen them enough to pull his hands free.

He attempted to stand, but nausea swept over him, so he crawled to Patrick and the others. Quickly he explained their situation, freeing Patrick's hands, who in turn did the same for the other five.

Holding the ropes around their wrists, they waited as the door swung open. The guards prodded them to their feet. Sean staggered toward the door, which gave him the opportunity to slam his body into the nearest guard. He shouted, "Now!"

The other six prisoners attacked the guards and then they scattered. Patrick helped Sean toward the tree line behind the barn. As they reached the shadows, a shot rang out. Patrick groaned and sagged to the ground.

He cried out in pain. "It's my leg. I think my knee is shattered." He pushed Sean away. "Go. The river is just beyond the trees. Leave me here. It's you he wants dead. He won't kill me."

Sean gritted his teeth against the pain from his beating. "There's no way in hell I'm leaving you behind, not after all we've been through together." He picked Patrick up and threw him over his shoulder.

Sean had no idea where he was going or what was ahead of him. He could hear the soldiers behind him. He dodged around a tree, stumbled on a root, and felt himself airborne just before they hit the icy waters of the Purgatoire. The melting snows had turned the usually small stream into a bank full expanse of churning icy waves.

They clung together, Sean doing his best to keep both their heads above the water. At least the cold water eased his pain – to the point he was quickly losing all feeling. At a curve in the stream, a tree branch snagged Patrick's shirt. At first, it dragged them under, but on the downward side of the limb, the water was somewhat protected. Together, they inched their way up the log and onto the bank.

Exhausted, they lay, trying to catch their breath. Suddenly, Patrick began to shake uncontrollably. Sean knew he was going into shock. He had to get his friend someplace warm.

In the distance, lights twinkled. The river had spit them out on the edge of Trinidad. Sean again hoisted Patrick on his shoulders and limped toward the town.

In the past year, they had been no strangers to Trinidad. Therefore, it was no problem for Sean to find his way through the back alleys in the blackness just before dawn. There was the slightest hint of pink in the eastern sky as Sean climbed the steps of the Methodist Church. He breathed a prayer of thanksgiving that pastor Graves never locked the door of the church.

He laid Patrick on the front pew and hurried next door to the manse. Patrick had been courting the Reverend's daughter the past several months. Sean's only hope was that Pastor Graves would show mercy in their time of need. He would need to leave Patrick in their care while he did his best to get to Denver City before Edward.

CHAPTER 39

Larimer rubbed his temples with his fingertips. He had assured Abigail that he would do everything in his power to help Patrick and Sean as well as the other member's of the Roberts gang. He, however, continued to drone on how difficult it might be. Their best hope would be for the war to end before it ever came to trial. He was sure they would be pardoned at that time.

Abigail trusted Larimer. She had faith in him, if for no other reason than her father respected him. Beyond that, she knew full well he was her best hope to make a case for her brother and Sean.

All those facts did nothing to keep her from the exasperation of listening to his incessant drivel that seemed to go along with every lawyer's admonitions. Her ears continued to listen, but her mind had long ago galloped elsewhere, with visions of Sean and Patrick bound and caged like animals.

Finally, he was running down like all good mantel clocks. "Now, my dear, I am of a certainty that you are quite drained due to your travel from your beautiful ranch to our fair city. I would encourage you to get a good night's rest at our lovely new hotel. We can discuss this at greater length in the morning.

Mrs. Larimer is expecting you about 9:00 for breakfast, if that suits you?"

Abigail nodded her affirmation and rose to leave. Without formality, an assistant burst through the door. "My greatest pardon, sir, but a message just arrived of a significant urgent nature."

Larimer snorted, "So, what is it, man? Don't just stand there."

The man stammered when he realized Abigail was present, but continued. "It would seem, sir, that the prisoners of former mention, attempted escape. They were all killed as a consequence of that attempt." He bowed to Abigail. "My sincerest condolences, Miss McFerrin." He backed his way out of the room.

Abigail fell back into her chair, stunned, with her hands to her mouth. Larimer slumped in his chair, his fingers again massaging his temples. Finally, he spoke as if from a distance. "My dear, we must not be too hasty in accepting the worst. Messages are often exaggerated by their carriers. Let's wait for confirmation of the news before we lose all hope."

Abigail heard his words, but his demeanor betrayed his true thoughts.

He went to her side before he continued. "Would it be better for you to stay with us this evening, rather than alone?"

Abigail shook her head. "I do appreciate your offer, but I need time to digest this news. I will stay at the hotel as planned and join you for breakfast. Hopefully, we will know more of the situation by then."

He put his arm around her as she stood to leave. "I will send one of my own messengers to reconfirm the information."

Abigail stepped from the stuffy confines of Larimer's office into the warm evening air. She steadied herself on the head of the stone lion at the top of the steps leading to the street below. The smell of blooming lilacs permeated the air. A flock of geese declared their passage through the sky. Horses, carriages, wagons and pedestrians vied for a place in the streets.

A boy called out, peddling the evening edition of the Denver Gazette.

How could the world proceed as normal? Did they not realize her world was crumbling at her feet?

She stumbled down the stone steps and made her way absentmindedly along the boardwalk toward the hotel. She stopped momentarily under a flickering streetlamp.

"I know you." A voice came from the shadows. "You was that lady at Fort Union, that Miss Dart something-or-other. The one who was really a confederate spy." Two Union soldiers came out of the dark alley, wreaking of whiskey.

Abigail's heart skipped a beat. "I assure you, I have no idea to what you are speaking."

"There's no mistakin' those red curls and pretty face. You's her alright."

Abigail feigned a stumble, giving her an opportunity to retrieve the derringer from its secret hiding place in the pocket of her skirt. However, it also gave her accusers time to tower over her, the vocal man grabbing her arm. In self-defense, she fired, grazing his leg. The other man came at her.

Abigail waved the gun in his direction. "This holds two shells. Would you like the second one in your gut?"

He helped his comrade to his feet. "You haven't seen the last of us. We'll be back with the constable and plenty more of our friends."

Abigail fought the impulse to faint. She staggered to the wall of the building at the corner of the alley for support. Suddenly an arm encircled her waist and a gloved hand covered her mouth. A familiar voice whispered, "Don't scream, and please don't shoot. We need to get you out of here."

She pushed his hand away. "Sean! How can it be? We were just told you were dead."

"I'll explain later. Right now, we need to get you away from here."

"I have a room at the Denver House. We can go there."

He guided her down the darkened alley. "No, they will

come for you there. We need a place they would never look."

Sean led her through a maze of alleys and streets she did not even know existed, bypassing the main thoroughfares. Soon, they were in a well-to-do residential area at the edge of the business district. They crossed through the back gardens of two large homes. Sean knocked on the rear door of a third, a large brick home with third floor dormers. A young girl peaked out through a sliding portal.

Sean asked, "Is Miss Lenore at home?"

Abigail clung to Sean's arm. She could hear the voices of men at the front of the house. A girl's laughter filtered from one of the upper rooms. After what seemed like an eternity, latches of the locks on the door were turned. The door swung open to reveal the form of Miss Lenore from Pueblo.

She smiled and nodded. "Mr. Donner and Miss Dartmouth, how good to see you again. What brings you to my humble house?"

Sean looked around to ensure no one was around. "It's Sean and Abigail, I'm afraid."

Miss Lenore laughed. "Mr. McKay and Miss McFerrin, I'm well aware who you are. There is little that Madam Lenore does not know that happens in Denver. Welcome, my dears. Come, let's get you in off the streets and out of harm's way.

CHAPTER 40

The familiar surroundings of the *MC* gave Abigail a sense of safety and security. She could not imagine that the soldier she had wounded or his friends knew who she really was or where she lived. It would, however, be comforting to have William and the ranch hands back after the cattle drive to the upper summer pastures.

Abigail shivered in spite of the warmth of the morning air. The nightmare of the past week was still vivid in her mind. Madam Lenore had been a God-send. She took them in, fed them and doctored Sean's wounds. Her stable boy retrieved their horses and helped them meet back up with Running Deer and Little Fox.

Sean had said little during their escape from Denver City or the journey back to the ranch. He had informed her that Patrick had been wounded, but assured her he was being well cared for. He wasn't forthcoming, however, regarding his black eye, cracked ribs, or the rope burns on his wrists.

Sean was stretched out on the floor of the porch, napping in the late morning sun. He arose when she appeared at the door and accepted the cup of coffee she had brought for him. Together, they sat on the top porch step, lost in thought, staring off into the distance.

She leaned against the porch post and studied his features. He was more handsome than she remembered from her first impression, in spite of his darkened right eye. His black curls hung to his shoulders, his beard neatly trimmed. She smiled as she remembered her first impression...*broad in the shoulders, narrow at the hips – with long strong legs like a good stallion.*

He returned her gaze. His eyes pierced through her as before. But now there was a sadness in place of the laughter. She raised her eyebrows as if to ask a question, but said nothing.

He looked back into the distance before he spoke. "I'm sorry," he said softly.

"Sorry for what?"

"For everything. For rooming with Patrick at the Point; for his becoming my best friend; for taking him to Great Oaks and getting him involved with my war." He took her hands in his big, rough hands. "For meeting you and getting you involved with this crazy war; for putting you in danger and in harm's way."

He looked away as he whispered, "For falling in love with you, when there is no chance of my fulfilling that love."

She squeezed his hands to force him to look at her. "You didn't force anyone to do anything. Remember what Madison said back in Santa Fe. Wars are started for a multitude of reasons. Certainly, there are some major ones, but many lie under the surface.

"In the same way, people fight in those wars for their own reasons. You were compelled for love of family, Patrick for his love for you, me for my love for both of you. Again, from Madison's words, even though we may not agree with everything that's going on around us, once we've put our hand to the plow, or our rifles to our shoulders in this case, there's no turning back."

She touched her hand to his cheek. "As for you and me, there's nothing to keep us from fulfilling our love."

He jerked his hands away. "Only the fact that I'm a

fugitive. Only the fact that I have nothing to offer you. I have no land. I have no money. I have no title. I don't even know if I still have a family."

A commotion down the lane interrupted her answer. A dozen Union soldiers galloped in their direction. Sean muttered a curse under his breath. "Edward. Does he never give up?"

Abigail started to rise. "Let me get the rifles."

Sean stopped her. "No. It would be two against twelve. I've caused enough problems. I will go and face whatever verdict that is handed down. My only hope is that I actually see a judge and a trial."

They stood together as Edward reined to a stop in front of them. Edward nodded to Abigail, then turned to Sean. "Well, Mr. McKay, we thought we might find you hiding here."

Sean shrugged. "Not hiding, just waiting for you and your henchmen to show up."

Edward motioned to two of his men. "Tie Mr. KcKay's hands, and make them secure this time. We don't want him slinking away again."

He turned back to Abigail. "Abby, I didn't want it to be like this. This is not at all the way I intended. But this Rebel scum has left me no choice."

Edward sneered as the men helped Sean onto the extra horse and tied his hands to the saddle. "It is my unpleasant duty to inform you that your friend is a thief, a murderer, a horse thief and a spy, any one of which is punishable by hanging from the end of a rope. It is our duty to take him over to Fairplay and put him in jail until a judge can get there for a trial."

He shook his head in mock sympathy. "I know you have some feelings for him now. But, you had feelings for me at one time, too. Now, I have a proposition for you, a proposal, if you will."

His voice softened. "Abby, we were meant for each other from the very beginning. I've always wanted you, needed you, cared for you. You know that. When you consider my proposition, you will see it is the best for everyone."

He swallowed. When he spoke, his voice had its former hard edge. "Mr. McKay deserves to hang for his crimes. However, I have the power to let him go free and be on his way. You hold the consequences in your hands. What I am offering is a proposal of marriage in exchange for Mr. McKay's freedom."

A scream welled up from the depths of Sean's being and echoed from the walls of the outbuildings. "No! Abigail, don't listen to him. Let them do what they will to me, but never, never marry him."

Edward turned to his men. "Get him out of here. Now!"

He turned back to Abigail. "What will your answer be?"

Abigail watched the men with Sean disappear over the horizon. As much as she felt her world crashing down around her, she resolved to never show that to Edward. With determination, she asked, "What guarantee do I have that you will not have Sean hanged as soon as we are married?"

"You have my word. The day after we are wed, he will be a free man."

Ice was in her glare. "I will never love you. I may become your wife. I may have your children, but I will never love you."

Edward stated matter-of-factly, "You will."

With resignation, she replied. "I will need a week to prepare. Also, I want the opportunity to see Mr. McKay in Fairplay, to ensure his wellbeing."

He nodded. "A week from today. Noon. I will have Reverend Shirley with me. I expect you to be ready."

As an afterthought, he added, "And if you must see the Rebel, so be it. Just make sure it's the last time." He wheeled his horse and was gone.

***

Raucous shouts and laughter of the returning ranch hands broke through Abigail's abyss of despair. She rubbed her backside and stretched her back as she stood to meet them. She had no idea how long she had sat on the porch step, but the sun was sinking over the mountain peaks.

William's smile immediately turned to a frown. "Abigail, what's wrong? You look as though someone has died. Oh, my heaven's, Father has not passed?"

Abigail shook her head. "No, Father is fine. Get washed up. Lisette should have supper about ready. I'll share the news with the three of you as we eat."

None of them did more than play with their food as Abigail recounted the saga of the past few days. She included her suspicions that Sean's beating and Patrick's wounds were of Edward's orders, if not attributed to him personally.

The reaction to Edward's proposal was mixed. Through gritted teeth, William uttered a curse. Lisette spewed a string of Creole words Abigail had no desire to translate.

Her father sat for the longest time staring at his plate, his trembling right fist firmly planted in the palm of his left. When he looked up, Abigail saw a look of anger as well as sadness in his eyes she had never witnessed before.

His voice trembled. His whole body shook. "I knew that boy had a mean streak in him, but I never thought he was capable of anything like this. You cannot go through with this. You cannot marry him."

Abigail looked at her upturned hands. "What other choice do I have?"

William spoke up. "We have enough ranch hands. We can ride over to Fairplay and bust Sean out of jail."

Abigail shook her head. "It's the law. If we break him out of jail, he'll always be on the run, always looking back over his shoulder."

Her father stood. His hands no longer shook. His voice rang with the authority Abigail remembered. "Then we will make the law work for us instead of against us."

He stroked his beard. Abigail was pleased with the gesture. Father was back in control of his senses as well as the situation.

He laid out his plan for them. "We have a week. William, take two of our best men. I will send a letter for you to take to

Larimer. I don't know the new governor, but he will. You were headed for Denver City anyway, were you not?"

Abigail gave William a puzzled look.

William grinned from ear to ear. "My bride has finally arrived from New Orleans. She is waiting for me at Denver House."

Abigail smiled for the first time since Edward had arrived with his men.

Her father continued. "Abigail, go to Fairplay and visit your friend. Don't give him any false hopes, but assure him we are doing everything we can. I will send some of our boys with Running Deer and Little Fox down to Trinidad to see if Patrick is well enough to ride."

He thought for a moment, then added. "If we are to have a wedding, the other ranchers should be invited. I will include a note for them to bring along a rifle, just in case. One thing is certain, my daughter is not marrying Edward Anderson."

He looked around the table. "We have work to do. Let's get at it.

CHAPTER 41

A rat, illuminated by the light from the moon through the one small, barred window, chewed on a morsel of dried crust. In the distance a dog barked, encouraging the other dogs in town to reply. The drunken laughter from the saloon down the street reminded him of the freedom he did not have. Odors from his own excrement and his unwashed body permeated the stale air of the tiny enclosure.

Sean had not wanted Abigail to see him like this, like an animal in a cage. She had been insistent, so the sheriff had allowed them a short visit. Sean wanted to hold her, to feel her lips on his, but that privilege was not his. She was able to slip him a note, and she was gone. Maybe gone forever. Who knew what tomorrow or the next day or the next week would bring. He despised the thought that her last remembrance of him might be of him behind the bars of a cell.

The note had simply said, "Don't lose hope." But that was three days ago. She could be married by now, even though she had said a week. Sean had no doubts that he was doomed, once Edward had what he wanted. From what Sean had seen of his arch enemy, it was that Edward left no loose ends when it came to him.

Sleep evaded him. The cramped space did not even allow

him to stretch his six-foot three-inch frame to its full extent. Shots rang through the street, bringing him to his feet. He pulled himself up, but could see nothing but the moon through the small portal to the outside.

More shots accompanied the first, followed by shouts and cheers. The sheriff burst through the door and announced with a shout, "The war is over. This bloody civil war is over. Lee has surrendered. The war is over." He raced out the door as quickly as he had appeared.

Sean slumped to the floor, his face buried in his hands. He had known it was inevitable after their victory/defeat at Glorietta, and the reports of the battle at Gettysburg and the siege of Richmond. Yet they had fought on. He had seen so many die, so many wounded. He thought of Patrick. Had he recovered? Was he still alive? Had he been captured, sitting now in some stinking cell?

He dozed, haunted by the visions of battle, the screams of the wounded, the stench of death. He cried out in horror as Abigail stood before the preacher beside the grotesque, ghoulish image of Edward.

And far off in the distance, Patrick's voice. "Sean. Sean, wake up. Come on, my good man. We've got to get you out of here and get you cleaned up. We've got a wedding to attend."

Sean shielded his eyes against the sun pouring through the open door of the jail. "Patrick, is that you? Wedding, what wedding?"

Patrick laughed. "You're a free man. We're free men. Larimer got us a pardon from the governor. Now, git your lazy butt off of that filthy floor. We've got a wedding to stop." He added with a slap on Sean's back, "And yours to celebrate, with any luck."

CHAPTER 42

Lisette hooked the last of the pearl buttons. "Girl, do you think you can go through with this?"

Abigail surveyed her image in the long mirror. Lisette had taken a plain white cotton dress, draped a lace shawl around the waist, and added pearl buttons to the back and pearls around the high lace collar. She kissed the older woman on the cheek. "You've done beautiful work on this dress. And yes, I'm ready as I'll ever be."

She met her father at the base of the steps and together they walked through the open door. She gasped at the scene before her. The corral had been raked clean. Family members from all seven ranches filled the benches and ranch hands lined the corral fence.

Edward and the preacher waited at the end of the aisle between the rows of benches under a canopy of horse blankets stretched between four poles, decorated with wild flowers. Abigail wanted to run, but instead walked with dignity, her head held high. She wanted to cry, but willed herself against it. She refused to look at Edward, but rather glared at the preacher.

Reverend Shirley droned on, finally coming to the point in the proceedings when he asked, "Is there anyone who would have cause to object to this marriage." Abigail wanted to scream, but held her tongue.

From behind them, a deep voice with a thick southern drawl pierced the air. "I do suh, I do."

Abigail and Edward turned in unison. He grabbed her arm to hold her in place.

Sean strode the length of the aisle. He was dressed all in black, save for the white silk ascot at his neck. His spurs jingled as he walked. His long dark locks hung to his shoulders, teased by the breeze. Abigail did not think she had ever seen anything or anyone more beautifully handsome.

Sean stopped before the trio. "As a southern gentleman, I could not allow a woman to be married under duress or against her will." He turned to Abigail. "Miss McFerrin, are you being forced to marry this – man?"

Edward squeezed her arm to the point she would certainly be bruised. However, she answered in a voice for all to hear, "I am most certainly being forced against my will into these proceedings."

Sean turned to address the gathering. "It is with mixed feelings that I would inform you that the war between the states has ended." A gasp of relief ran through the crowd.

Sean turned back to Edward. "And Mr. Anderson, because of that, you have been relieved of your duties and authority, and the governor has granted myself and my friend Patrick a full pardon for any crimes we may have committed as part of that conflict."

Sean leaned toward Abigail and whispered, "Please forgive me." He faced Edward with his feet set. "Now, Mr. Anderson, from myself and Patrick and all the others you have bullied and brutalized, here is a token of our appreciation." Sean's fist landed squarely on the side of Edward's nose. Blood flew as Edward fell in a heap. Mrs. Anderson and Florence screamed. The Anderson men jumped to their feet, but froze as rifles and pistols were cocked all along the fence.

Sean motioned to the ranch hands. "Get this pile of horse dung out of here." The Andersons followed while the remaining guests sat in stunned silence.

Sean faced Abigail. "Abigail McFerrin, you know that I love you. You also know that I have nothing to offer you but my love. I have no land. I have no title. Will you exchange a poor Southern Rebel for Edward Anderson, who came this day to make you his wife?"

Abigail smiled. She knew, for the first time in her life, where she belonged – in the arms of the man who stood before her. "Mr. McKay, I will gladly exchange any other man for a Rebel, as long as that Rebel is you."

Abigail hesitated, winked at Sean, and faced the gathering. "There is one indulgence I would request." She scanned the men standing across the back of the seated guests. One young lady stood in their midst, a tall, stately girl with long black curls and creamy-chocolate skin. She clung to William's arm, pride, yet apprehension in her dark eyes.

Abigail continued. "William, I understand your fiancée has joined us. I would like, if it is agreeable, for the two of you to join us here at this marriage altar."

William whispered to his companion. With tears in their eyes, they joined Abigail and Sean at the front of the congregation.

Abigail turned to the minister. "Now you can proceed."

The short, rotund man was visibly shaken. Beads of sweat dotted his forehead. His hands were shaking. He stammered, "I can't do this. I simply can't be a part of all this. I'm sorry, but this is just too much." Abigail watched in shock as he hurried down the aisle.

Patrick stepped forward, relying heavily on a crutch, his leg in a splint. "It would seem that there is more than one rebel exchange to be made this day. For you see, while I was recuperating from a gunshot wound in the home of a Methodist minister, I received confirmation of my application of license as a minister of the gospel. I was ordained in the church in Trinidad."

He stood before the two couples. "I would find it no

greater honor than to marry my best friend in this world, a friend whom I have fought beside, a friend who I carried from the field of battle and he me, Mr. Sean McKay to my beloved sister, Abigail. Along with them, I count it a great honor to join my brother William, to his espoused, Miss Marybeth Troubideaux, formerly of New Orleans, Louisiana, as husband and wife."

He raised his hand before the congregation. "Dearly beloved, we are gathered here in the sight of God…"

"To everything there is a season,
And a purpose under the heavens."

And they each thought, in their own way, "I belong."

APPENDIX

Fact and Fiction

As a Historical Fiction Writer, I feel it is my responsibility to keep the facts of history as true as possible. Although the main characters of *Rebel Exchange* are fictional, the people with which they came in contact and the major events of the story were real.

Fiction:

- The *MC* ranch is fictional. In fact, I needed to push the date of its existence a bit. I could find no record of ranches in Colorado as early as the 1840's, but it is possible that settlers could have made a deal with the Indians. There were trappers and traders there for centuries, and Fort Bent, a privately owned trading post on the Arkansas River, was built in 1833.
- The McFerrin's and the Anderson's are fictional characters.
- Miss Lenore and her brothel are fiction
- Peterson's ranch is fiction
- Corporal Wallace and Lieutenant Wilson are fictional characters.
- The Roberts Gang is fictional, but based on the Reynolds Gang of the same era.

Fact:

- The Arkansas River was the northern boundary of Mexico until the end of the Mexican-American War in 1848.
- William Larimer founded Denver City, CO in 1858.

- Colorado was made a territory in 1861.
- William Gilpin was the first governor of Colorado. He established the first regiment of Colorado volunteers which were not affectionately known as "Gilpin's Little Lambs".
- Mace's Hole was a hideout and training camp for Colorado Confederate volunteers.
- The names and descriptions of Fort Union in northern New Mexico, were factual.
- Chavez was a colonel at Fort Union, but he was not captured by Confederate forces.
- Sibley was commander at Fort Union prior to the Civil War. He did plan the Colorado Campaign. Although he was a poor leader, his invention of the Sibley tent and camp stove were used extensively by the Union forces and used by the US Army until the early 20th Century.
- George Madison led the San Elizario Spy Company, also known as the Santa Fe Gamblers and/or the Forty Thieves. After the Battle of Glorietta, it was reorganized as Madison's Spies and Guides. They harassed the Union forces around Fort Union and Fort Garland. There was a bounty put on their heads.
- Madison fought in all the related battles, and the incidences portrayed are factual. He was a brave soldier and an excellent leader, well respected by his men.
- Louisa Canby was known as "The Angel of Santa Fe" for her care of the wounded Confederate soldiers. She was to have said, "Whether friend or foe, the wounded must be cared for. They are the sons of some dear mother."
- The El Farol Cantina was a cantina in Santa Fe before the Civil War and is in existence yet today.

- The Battle of Glorietta was known as the "Gettysburg of the West."

The Colorado Campaign and the Battle of Glorietta are mostly relegated to the back pages of Civil War history, if reported at all. In all reality, the campaign was probably doomed from its inception. However, if it had been successful, it could have greatly changed the outcome of the war.

ACKNOWLEDGEMENTS

My sincere Thanks…

To my wife, Lynda, for her support and assistance in so many ways.

To Jen Johnson, for her fantastic photography and graphic skills.

To Serenity Orr, for her editing.

To Susie Holloway, for her encouragement and suggestions.

To Lucie Hirsch, for her expert advice.

To my readers along the way, for their valued opinions.

To the members of ACFW/KC West Writer's Group, for their continued encouragement.

And to Amazon CreateSpace, for giving those of us with a story to tell an avenue to tell our stories.

J Robert Johnson

About The Author

J. Robert Johnson has been a high school choral director, entrepreneur, business associate and is presently a freelance writer. He has a passion for history, especially those little known and oft forgotten nuggets from the archives of time. That is what brought him to the Battle of Glorietta and the ill-fated Confederate Western Campaign of the Civil War.

Robert is a native of Missouri and resides with his wife in the Kansas City area. When not writing, enjoying his children and grandchildren and/or traveling, he allows his BMW motorcycle to discover new roads for them to ride.

Contact: JRobertJohnson48@gmail.com

Website: JRobertJohnson.com

J Robert Johnson

Made in the USA
Lexington, KY
15 August 2017